Fletch slumped into the seat vacated by Betsy. "I don't know," he said to Freddie. "I don't think I'm gonna make it as a member of the establishment. It's all too new to me."

"You're in a position, all right," she agreed, nodding. "Between the fire and the bottom of the skillet. As a reporter, you're trained to find things out and report 'em. As a press representative, you've got to prevent other reporters from finding certain things out. Adversary of the press. Against your own instincts. Poor Fletch. You'll never make it."

"I know it."

"That's all right." She patted him on the arm. "I'll destroy you as painlessly as possible."

"Great. I'd appreciate that. Are you sure you're up to it?"

"Up to what?"

"Destroying me."

"It will be easy," she said.

Novels by
Gregory Mcdonald

Love Among The Mashed Potatoes (Dear M.E.)

Who Took Toby Rinaldi?

Flynn

The Buck Passes Flynn

Running Scared

Fletch

Confess, Fletch

Fletch's Fortune

*Fletch's Moxie

*Fletch and The Widow Bradley

*Fletch and The Man Who

*Published by
WARNER BOOKS

GREGORY MCDONALD

Fletch and the MAN WHO

WARNER BOOKS

A Warner Communications Company

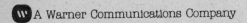 A Warner Communications Company

Printed in the United States of America

First Warner Printing: August, 1983

10 9 8 7 6 5 4 3 2 1

Fletch and the
MAN WHO

1

"Fletch, my man! Good! You got here!"

"Where?"

Shirtless and shoeless, Fletch was standing in a midtown motel room in a middle-sized town in a middle-sized state in Middle America. He had turned on the shower just before the phone rang.

"I want you to go to Dad's suite," Walsh Wheeler said. "Immediately. 748."

"Why don't you say 'Hello,' Walsh?"

"Hello." The sounds behind Walsh were of several people talking, men and women, the clink of glasses, and, at a distance, heavy beat music—bar noises.

"Why don't you ask me if I had a nice flight?"

"Stuff it. Isn't time for all that."

"Are we enjoying a crisis already?"

"There's always a crisis on a political campaign, Fletch. On a presidential campaign, all the crises are biggies. You've only got a few minutes to learn that." Despite the background noises, Walsh was speaking quietly into the phone. "Wait a minute,'' he said. At the other end of the phone someone was speaking to Walsh. Fletch could not make out what the other person was saying. His mouth away from the phone, Walsh said, ''Any idea who she is?'' There was more conversation wrapped in cotton. ''Is she dead?'' Walsh asked.

Steam was coming through the door of Fletch's bathroom.

''Who's dead?'' Fletch asked.

''That's what we're trying to find out,'' Walsh said. ''Your plane was late? You're late.''

''Landed unexpectedly in Little Rock. Guess the pilot had to drop off some laundry.''

''You were supposed to be here at six o'clock.''

''Your dad's very popular in Little Rock. Took a survey of an airport security cop. He said, 'If Wheeler doesn't become our next President, guess I'll have to run for office myself.' What a threat!''

Speaking away from the phone again, Walsh Wheeler said, ''Whoever she is, she has nothing to do with us. Nothing to do with the campaign.''

Fletch said, ''I wish I knew the topic of this conversation.''

''I'm downstairs in the lounge, Fletch,'' Walsh said. ''I'll handle things here, but you get yourself to Dad's suite *tout*.''

''It's ten-thirty at night, isn't it?''

''About that. So what?''

''I've never met the candidate. Your esteemed pa. The governor.''

''Just knock on the door. He doesn't bite.''

''And then what do I say to the next President of These United States? 'Wanna buy a new broom?' ''

''Never known you to be at a loss for words. Say, 'Hello, I'm your new genius press representative.' ''

''Barging in on The Man Who at ten-thirty at night without even a glass of warm milk—''

''He won't be in bed, yet. Doctor Thom's still down here in the bar.''

''Now, look, Lieutenant, a little clarification of orders would make the troops a little more lighthearted in their marching.''

"This could be damned serious, Fletch. Someone just said the girl is dead."

"Death is one of the more serious things that happen to people. Now, tell me, Walsh, what girl? Who's dead?"

Walsh coughed. "Don't know."

"Walsh—"

"A girl jumped off the motel's roof. Five minutes ago, ten minutes ago."

"And she's dead?"

"So they say."

"Terrible! But what's that got to do with your father? With you? With me?"

"Nothing," Walsh said firmly. "That's the point."

"Oh. Then why don't I take a nice shower, climb into my footy pajamas, and meet your dad at a respectable hour in the morning? Like between coffees number one and two?"

"Because," said Walsh.

"Oh, that's why! Walsh, a death in the motel where the candidate is staying shouldn't even be commented on by the candidate. People die in motels more often than they get warm soup from room service. I'm not saying one thing has to do with another—"

"I agree with you."

"I mean, you don't want to make a story by overreacting, by having me rush to your dad's suite in the middle of the night when I don't even know the man."

Walsh coughed again. His voice lowered. "Apparently she jumped, Fletch. They're saying from the roof right over Dad's suite. Over his balcony. Photographs have already been taken of the building. Arrows will be drawn."

"Oh."

"Arrows that swoop downward."

"Oh."

"The bored press, Fletch. Starving for any new story. Any new angle."

"Yeah. Implication being the young lady might have used the balcony of the candidate's room as a diving board to oblivion. Certain newspapers would make something of that. *Newsbill.*"

"I knew you had something other than pretzels between the ears."

"Potato chips."

"Go to Dad's suite. Answer the phone if it rings. Say you're new on the job and don't know what anybody's talking about."

"Easy enough. True, too."

"I'll try to have his phone turned off at the switchboard. But not all switchboards are incorruptible."

"I seem to remember having corrupted one or two myself. Suite number what?"

"748. I'll be right up. As soon as I ace the switchboard and do my casual act in the bar. Convince the press we're not reacting to the girl's death."

"Walsh? Give it to me straight. Does the girl have anything to do with us? I mean, the campaign? The presidential candidate?"

Walsh's voice dropped even lower. "It's your job, Fletch, to make damned sure she didn't."

2

She was alone in the elevator when the door opened.

In the corridor, Fletch was pulling on his jacket. For a moment, he thought his eyes were playing a joke on him: the girl with the honey-colored hair and the brown eyes.

"Freddie!" he exclaimed. "As I live and breathe! The one and only Freddie Arbuthnot."

"Fletch," she said. "It is true."

"Going my way?" he asked.

"No," she answered. "I'm on my way up."

He scooted through the closing doors. In the elevator, the button had been pushed for the eighth floor.

"I'm glad to see you," he said.

"You never have been before."

"Listen, Freddie, about that time in Virginia. What can I say? I was wrong. That journalism convention—you know, where we met?—was full of spooks, and I had every reason to think you were one of them."

"I'm an honest journalist, Mr. Fletcher." Freddie tightened her nostrils. "Unlike some people I don't care to know."

"Honest," he agreed. "As honest as fried chicken."

"Well known, too."

"Famous!" he said. "Everybody knows the superb work Fredericka Arbuthnot turns in."

"Then, why didn't you know who I was in Virginia?"

"Everybody knew except me. I was just stupid. I had been out of the country."

"You don't read *Newsworld*?"

"My dentist doesn't subscribe."

"You don't read the *Newsworld Syndicate*?"

"Not on crime. Gross stuff, crime. Reports on what the coroner found in the victim's lower intestine. I don't even want to know what's in my own lower intestine."

"I make my living writing crime for *Newsworld*."

"You're the best. Everyone says so. The scourge of defense attorneys everywhere."

"Is it true Governor Wheeler is making you his press representative?"

"Haven't met the old wheez yet."

The elevator door opened.

"One look at you," she said, "and he'll send you back to playschool."

He followed her off the elevator onto the eighth floor. "What are you doing in whatever town we're in, Freddie? Interesting trial going on?"

Walking down the corridor, she said, "I've joined the campaign."

"Oh? Given up journalism? Become a volunteer?"

"Not likely," she said. "I'm still a member of the honest, working press."

"I don't quite get that, Freddie," Fletch said a little louder than he meant to. "You're a crime reporter. This is a political campaign."

She took her room key from the pocket of her skirt. "Isn't a political campaign somewhat like a trial by jury?"

"Only somewhat. When you lose a political campaign in this country, you don't usually go to the slammer."

She turned the key in the lock. "Do I make you nervous, Fletcher?"

"You always have."

"You're going to tell me you don't know anything about the girl who was murdered in this motel tonight."

"*Murdered?*"

"You don't know anything about it?"

"No."

"She was naked and beaten. Brutally beaten. Don't need a coroner to tell me that. I saw that much with my own eyes. I would guess also raped. And further, I would guess she was either thrown off a balcony of this motel, or, virtually the same, driven to jump."

Fletch's eyes were round. "That only happened a half hour ago, Freddie. You couldn't have gotten here that fast from New York or Los Angeles or—or from wherever you hang your suspicions."

"Oh, you do know something about it."

"I know a girl fell to her death from the roof of this motel about a half hour ago."

"Dear Fletch. Always the last with the story."

"Not always. Just when there's Freddie Arbuthnot around."

"I'd invite you into my room," Freddie said, "but times I've tried that in the past I've been wickedly rebuffed."

"What else do you know about this girl?"

"Not as much as I will know."

"For sure."

"Good night, Fletcher darling."

Fletch stood foursquare to the door which was about to close in his face.

"Freddie! What is a crime reporter doing covering a presidential primary campaign?"

Door in hand, she stood on one tiptoed foot and kissed him on the nose.

"What's a newspaper delivery boy doing passing himself off as a presidential candidate's press secretary?"

3

"Who is it?" The voice through the door to Suite 748 was politely curious. Fletch was used to hearing that voice making somber pronouncements about supersonic bombers and the national budget.

"I. M. Fletcher. Walsh told me to come knock on your door."

The door opened.

Keeping his hand on the doorknob, his arm extended either to embrace or restrain, Governor Caxton Wheeler grinned at Fletch while his eyes worked Fletch over like a football coach measuring a player for the line. Fletch fingered his collar and regretted having put back on the shirt he had been wearing all day.

Governor Caxton Wheeler's face was huge, a map of all America, his forehead as wide as the plain states, his jaw as massive as all the South, his eyes as large and set apart as New York and Los Angeles, his nose as assertive as the skyscrapers of Chicago and Houston.

"Hello," Fletch said. "I'm your new genius press representative."

Smile growing stiff on his face, the presidential candidate stared at Fletch.

Fletch said: "Wanna buy a broom?"

"Well," the governor said, "I want a clean sweep."

"And I'll bet you want to sweep clean," Fletch said.

"Were you ever one of them?" the governor asked.

Fletch looked around him in the motel corridor. "One of who?"

"The Press."

"The Press is The People, sir."

"Funny," said The Man Who. "I thought the government is. Come in."

The governor took his hand off the doorknob and wandered in stockinged feet into the living room of the suite.

Fletch closed the door behind him.

The living room was decorated in Super Motel. There was a bad painting on the wall, oil on canvas, of a schooner under full sail. (In Fletch's room there was a cardboard print of the same ship under full sail.) The four corners of the coffee table surface and the hands of the chair arms had chipped gold paint on them.

There were several liquor bottles on a side table.

The governor nodded to them. "Want a drink?"

"No, thanks."

"I was afraid you'd say that."

"May I get you one?"

"No." The governor sat on the divan. "My wife doesn't approve. She says I have to get all my energy and all my relaxation from The People. I doubt if the sweet thing knows it, but what she is describing is a megalomaniac."

The Man Who wore an open, washed-out, worn, sagging brown bathrobe. Over the breast pocket, in green, was CW. The robe draped his big, bare, white belly.

Fletch's eyes moved back and forth from the deep tan of the governor's face and the lily whiteness of the governor's belly.

"You look like you just got home from summer camp,"

the governor said. "Will the press accept you?" Fletch said nothing. The governor had not asked him to sit down. "A campaign is tough, and it's exciting, and it's boring. Not to worry." On the coffee table in front of the governor, papers had spilled out of a brief case. "By the end of this campaign— if we win this primary, that is—you'll look as dissipated as a schoolchild in March."

The other side of the room, beyond the governor, was a sliding glass door onto the balcony. The drapes were open.

Slowly, as if wandering aimlessly, Fletch crossed the room to the balcony doors. Trying to make the question sound conversational, he asked, "If you lose this primary, is the campaign over?"

"You win votes in a primary; you win contributions. You lose, and the contributions dry up. Motels and gas stations expect even presidential candidates to pay their bills. It's the American way."

Fletch snapped on the balcony light outside the glass doors. "Does the press know you're short of funds?"

The governor did not turn around in the sofa to look at Fletch. "We don't issue a financial report every day. But we have to get the message out through the press that we need money. If they ever thought our campaign was broke, they'd desert us faster than kittens leave a gully in the January thaw."

On the balcony, the snow and ice, the slush, had been stirred up, walked on. A section of the railing had been scraped clean of snow.

"Have you been out on the balcony tonight?" Fletch asked.

Finally the governor turned around in his seat. "No. Why? At least, I don't think so."

"Somebody has been."

"Some of the press were in earlier. For drinks. Some of the staff. Lots of cigarette smoke. I might have stepped out for some fresh air. I do things like that. Or a quiet word with someone. Must be slushy out there."

Fletch turned off the balcony light and pulled the drapes

closed. "Would there be people in your suite if you weren't here? I mean, other than hotel staff?"

"Sure." The governor turned around to face the coffee table again. "For traffic, my suite is second only to O'Hare International Airport. In fact, where is everyone now? Why isn't the phone ringing?"

"Walsh had it turned off at the switchboard." Fletch went through the living room and down the little corridor to the front door of the suite.

"Why did he do that?"

Fletch opened the door and tried the outside knob. "Your door is unlocked."

"Sure. People come in and out all the time. What are you, a press agent or a security man?"

Fletch closed the door and came back into the living room. "Looks like you need a good security agent."

"Flash is all I need for now. He doesn't bother anybody. So," the governor said, "you and Walsh knew each other in the service. I remember hearing about you."

"Yes, sir. He was my lieutenant."

"Was he any good that way?"

"You mean your son? As a lieutenant?"

"Yeah. What kind of a lieutenant was he?"

"Pretty good. He'd show up once in a while."

The governor chuckled. "But not too much, eh?"

"He was okay. Let us do our jobs. Didn't care about much else."

"That's my boy. Run a hands-off administration. Walsh thinks you'd be just right for this job." The governor wrinkled his eyebrows. "Insisted you be flown in immediately. Wants me to announce first thing in the morning that you're my new press secretary."

Fletch shrugged. "I was available."

"Which means you were unemployed."

"Working on a book," Fletch said.

"On politics?"

"On an American western artist. You know: Edgar Arthur Tharp, Junior."

"Oh, yeah. Great stuff. But what's that got to do with politics?"

"Not much."

"You used to work for newspapers?"

"A lot of them." Fletch grinned. "One after another."

"Are you saying you weren't successful as a journalist?"

"Sometimes too successful. Depends on how you look at it."

The governor sat back and sighed. "A kid who looks like he belongs on a tennis court with an interest in cowboy art: as a politician's press agent, you're not a dream."

"Isn't American politics a crusade of amateurs?"

"Who said that?"

"I did. I think."

"You're wrong. But it has a nice ring to it." Leaning over, the governor made a note on one of the papers on the coffee table. "See? You're working already. Displaying talent as a phrasemaker." He sat back and smiled. "That line might be worth thousands of dollars in contributions. You sure no one said it?"

"No."

"I'll say it. Then it will have been said."

"I thought you said the statement is wrong."

"I don't qualify as an amateur. Elected to Congress twice, the governorship three times. But every new campaign is a starting over." The governor flipped the pen onto the table. "Anyway, Walsh says you're smart, resourceful, and willing to work cheap. Workin' cheap doesn't sound so smart to me."

"Then make me smarter," Fletch said. "Pay me more. If it would make you happier. I don't mind."

The governor chuckled. "Guess it's time Walsh had a real pal somewhere in this campaign. All the pressure has been comin' down on him. Hasn't had a day off, an hour off, since I don't know when. He's got a much harder job than the one I've got. He does all the logistics: who goes where, when, why, says what to whom. My firing James last night didn't make it any easier for him. Or me. You heard about all that, I suppose?"

"Walsh told me something about it last night when he phoned. Read the press reports at the airport."

The governor's face looked truly sad. "I knew James for twenty years. No: twenty-two, to be exact. Political reporter for the down-home newspaper. The newspaper that endorsed me for both Congress and the governorship. James was a personal advisor, a good one, totally honest. Even had Washington experience. I thought if I ever ran for President, he sure would be with me. To the end. Then he screwed up. Brother, did he ever screw up."

"The newspapers said he resigned over a policy dispute with you. Something about South Africa."

"The press was kind to us on that one. The policy dispute was not about South Africa. It was about Mrs. Wheeler." The governor took a deep breath. "The first incident wasn't so important. I was able to get people to laugh it off. He mentioned to some reporters in the bar that Mrs. Wheeler spends two and a half hours each and every morning getting up and putting on her face."

"Does she?"

"No. She spends time making herself beautiful, of course. Every woman does. It's damned hard on a woman, living out of suitcases, going from motel to motel, making public appearances all day, damned near all night. She always looks nice. Anyway, the newspapers reported it."

"It was reported with a vengeance."

"Made her look like a very superficial, self-indulgent woman. I turned it into a joke, saying that's why we had to have two bathrooms on the second floor of the governor's mansion. I said that on the road I'm apt to spend two hours every morning just trying to find my razor."

"Yeah, that was good."

"It was just this week that James really screwed up. It was in the newspapers yesterday. He told the press Mrs. Wheeler canceled—at the last minute, mind you—a visit to the Children's Burn Center so she could play indoor tennis with three rich old lady friends."

"True?"

"Look—what does Walsh call you, Fletch?—she made time

to play tennis with some friends she hadn't seen in years, wives of some influential fat cats around this state, who would never have forgiven her if she didn't make time for them. She raised some badly needed money for this campaign.''

"Schedule conflicts must happen all the time."

"You bet. And it's the press representative's job to shag a foul ball like that, not pitch it to the press. I'm convinced James went out of his way to make sure the press got the wrong slant on that story.''

"Yeah, but why would he do that?"

"God knows. He's not the world's greatest admirer of my wife. They've had a few disagreements over the years. But liking people has nothing to do with politics. In this life, if you stay with only people you *like,* the normal person would have to move every ten days. Politics is advantageous loyalty, son. Loyalty is what you buy, with every word out of your mouth; loyalty is what you sell, with every choice you make. And when you sell loyalty, you'd better make sure your choice is to your own advantage. James sold out twenty-two years of loyalty to me for the dubious twelve-hour pleasure of embarrassing my wife in public.''

Listening, Fletch had wandered to every part of the living room. The governor's shoes were not anywhere in the room.

"If Mrs. Wheeler had to cancel an appointment, she had to cancel an appointment, and that's all there is to it. If you don't know what our daily schedule looks like, feels like yet, you will within a few days." The governor lowered his voice. "If you stay with us, that is."

"I understand."

"What do you understand?"

"I understand the job of press secretary is to keep paintin' the picket fence around the main house. Just keep paintin' it. Whatever's goin' on inside, the outside is to look pretty."

The governor smiled. "The question is, Mr. I. M. Fletcher . . .'' The governor took a cigar stub from the pocket of his robe and lit it. "By the way, what does I.M. stand for?"

"Irwin Maurice."

"No wonder you choose to be called Fletch. The question

is, Mr. Irwin Maurice 'Fletch' Fletcher—have I got it all right?''

"Tough on the tongue, isn't it?''

"The question is''—the governor brushed tobacco off a lower tooth—"what do you believe in?''

"You,'' Fletch said with alacrity. "And your wife. And your campaign. Is that the answer you want?''

"Not bad.'' The governor squinted at him over the cigar smoke. "For a start. Why do you want to work on this campaign?''

"Because Walsh asked me. He said you need me.''

"And you were between jobs . . .''

"Working on a book.''

"You got the money to take time off and work on a book?''

"Enough.''

"Where'd you get the money?''

"You can save a lot of money by not smoking.''

"What do you think of my domestic policy?''

"Needs refining.''

"What do you think of my foreign policy?''

"Needs a few good ideas.''

The governor's grin was like seeing a chasm open in the earth. "I'll be damned,'' he said. "You're an idealist. You mean to be a good influence on me.''

"Maybe.''

The governor looked at him sharply and seemed to be serious when he asked: "And do you have any good ideas?''

"Just one, for now.''

"And what would that be?''

"To be loyal to you.'' Fletch grinned. "Until I get a better offer. Isn't that what you just said politics is all about?''

Scraping the ash off his cigar onto a tray, the governor said, "You learn fast enough. . . .''

4

"Where's Dr. Thom?"

"Coming right up."

"I want to go to sleep."

Walsh Wheeler had entered his father's suite without knocking. Fletch saw that Walsh knew the door was unlocked.

In the living room, Walsh handed his father a piece of paper from the top of the sheaf he was carrying. "Here's your schedule for tomorrow."

The governor dropped the paper on the table without looking at it.

Walsh handed Fletch two sheets of paper, one from the top of the pile, one from the bottom. "Here's Dad's schedule for tomorrow . . . and Mother's schedule for tomorrow. Have these copied and under the door of every member of the press by six in the morning. All the press are on the eighth floor of this motel."

"Is there no one on the eighth floor but members of the press?"

"I don't know. I guess so. No reason why you shouldn't

deliver to every door on the eighth floor. We're not trying to keep Dad's whereabouts a secret. Leave some downstairs on the reception desk, too. And have some on you to hand out to the local press." Walsh poured out two Scotches with soda and handed one to Fletch. "Oh, yeah. At the back of the campaign bus there's a copying machine. For your use and your use alone." Walsh smiled at his father. "James's first major press announcement was that if any member of the press touched his copying machine, James would disarm him or her—literally." Walsh sipped his drink. "Maybe you should make the same announcement."

"Don't tell Fletch to do anything the way ol' James did it. One thing might lead to another."

"A copying machine and a quick wit," Walsh said. "That's all you need to be a press representative, right?"

"He's got a quick wit," the governor said. "He makes me laugh."

"Oh, yeah." Walsh sat next to the best reading lamp. He made himself look comfortable, legs crossed, drink in hand, papers in lap. "How do you guys like each other so far?"

The governor looked at Fletch and Fletch looked at the governor.

"Don't know how the press will accept him," the governor said. "Fletch looks like breakfast to someone with a hangover."

Smiling, Walsh looked up at Fletch. "What do you think, Fletch?"

"Well," Fletch drawled, "I think Governor Caxton Wheeler can get this country moving again."

"I believe it!" Walsh laughed.

"I'll say one thing," the governor chuckled. "There's been so much cow dung on the floor since he came into the room, I had to take off my store-bought shoes!"

Fletch looked from one to the other. "Where *are* your shoes?" he asked.

Father and son continued their moment of easy, genuine admiration, love for each other, enjoyment in each other.

Fletch sat down.

"Okay, Dad, let's go over your schedule for tomorrow, just quickly. We've only got a few days before the primary in this state. We've got a real chance to win, but we haven't won yet. Without killing you, we've got to make the best use of your time."

Slowly, the governor sat up and took the schedule in his hands. He yawned. His cigar stub was burned out in the ashtray.

"Seven forty-five," Walsh said, "you'll be at the main gate at the tire factory. These guys are worried about two things: foreign import of tires, of course; and they're afraid their union bosses will call a strike sometime in April."

"Union boss name?" the governor asked.

"Wohlman. By the way, Wohlman's wife has just left him, and some of the membership say this is making him act meaner and tougher toward management than they want."

Dully, the governor said: "Oh."

"At eight-thirty, you're having coffee with Wohlman, first name Bruce, and . . ."

Only glancing at the items on the governor's schedule for next day, Fletch listened. Walsh seemed the perfect aide. He had the answers to most questions the governor asked. *"Where's breakfast?" "There will be a breakfast box on the bus."* He made notes to get the answers he did not know. *"How far does a farm family have to go to get to a medical facility 'round there?" "I'll find out."* Walsh did not balk at taking anything on himself. And he was not insistent, but gently urging when the governor began to balk. *"Why am I at Conroy School at ten o'clock? I keep telling you, Walsh, ten-year-olds don't vote. Isn't there some better use of my time this close to the primary?" "Their parents do, Dad, and so do the teachers, and all their relatives. And they're all more interested in the future generation and education than they are in bank failures in Zaire. That's what they're living and working for." "I'll be late for the downtown rally in Winslow. Then I'll have to do more I-couldn't-find-my-toothbrush jokes." "We'll have a band playing until you get there."* Sitting on the divan, the governor seemed to get more old, fat, and tired as the session went on.

Walsh, on the other hand, seemed to have attained some level of nirvana. His tone of voice did not alter. His speech pace, even with the governor's interruptions, was consistent. His concentration was as steady as an athlete's in midgame.

Walsh had changed since his days in uniform, of course. He was heavier by twenty pounds; his hair was thinner. His skin was gray. There was something in Walsh's eyes that had not been there before. Instead of being just ordinary human eyes, looking around casually, seeing and not seeing things, Walsh's eyes now seemed overfocused, too bright, rather as if whatever he was looking at was getting his full concentration. Fletch wondered whether in fact Walsh was seeing anything.

"If all goes well," Walsh concluded, "we'll have you at the hotel in Farmingdale by six. The mayor of Farmingdale is throwing a dinner for you. Well, he's throwing a dinner for himself, a fund-raiser, but you're the main attraction."

"What do I have to do the next morning?"

"Thought you might like to catch up with the newspapers. Bed rest."

"Put a hospital visit in there," the governor said. "Farmingdale must have a hospital. Special attention on any kids with burns."

"Yes, sir." Walsh made a note.

The governor rubbed his eyes. "Okay, Walsh. Anything else I'm supposed to know?"

Walsh glanced at Fletch. "There's something you're not supposed to know."

The governor looked at each of them. "What am I not supposed to know?"

"A girl jumped off the roof of this motel about an hour and a half ago."

"Dead?"

"Yeah."

"How old?"

"Twenties. They say."

"Damned shame."

"Apparently she jumped from the roof right over your windows."

The governor looked at Fletch. "So that's why you showed up at my door tonight? Checked the balcony. The door." He looked at Walsh. "Turned off the phone. You guys are working together already."

"People had been on your balcony," Fletch said quietly. "Your front door was unlocked."

"You don't know anything about it," Walsh said.

"In fact, I do," the governor said. "I heard the sirens. Saw the ambulance lights flashing. How can I pretend it didn't happen?"

"I guess she actually jumped just as you were coming into the hotel."

"No one said she jumped," Fletch said. "Someone told me the girl was naked and had been beaten before she hit the sidewalk."

"Anyone we know?" the governor asked.

Walsh shrugged. "A political groupie, best I can find out."

"No."

"A political *groupie*?" asked Fletch.

"Yeah," Walsh said. "There are people who think political campaigns are fun. They follow the campaign—literally. They travel from town to town with the candidate's party, try to get into the same hotels—generally just hang around. Women mostly, girls; but men too. Sometimes they turn into useful volunteers."

"Was this girl a volunteer?" the governor asked.

"No. Dr. Thom saw the body. Said he thinks she's been with us less than a week. Never saw her doing anything for the campaign."

"Name?"

"Don't want you to know her name, Dad. When reporters ask you about her, I don't want the expression on your face that you'd ever heard her name before."

"Okay. Can we do something nice? Send flowers—?"

"Nothing, please. She was just someone who happened to be in the motel. Fletch has the job, as of right now, of denying this girl had anything to do with the campaign. And without making an issue of it."

Fletch said, "You said the woman had been trailing this campaign for almost a week."

Walsh said: "That's the problem."

• • •

A thin man in an oversized sport coat, carrying a little black bag, entered the suite. He too did not knock.

The governor said to him, "Want to go to sleep, Dr. Thom."

"Go to sleep you will," said the doctor. "You're not getting eight hours every night."

"I will tomorrow night," the governor said. "If all goes well."

"Come on," Walsh said to Fletch. "We've got one or more things to do."

As Walsh and Fletch were leaving the suite, Dr. Thom was saying, "You've got to get eight hours every night, Governor. Every night. If Walsh can't work it out for you, we'll have to get someone else to run your campaign."

"Listen, Bob. I got real tired around four o'clock today. Couldn't think. Started repeating myself."

"Okay," Dr. Thom said. "Okay. I'll give you something after lunch tomorrow. . . ."

5

"Got to leave Mother's schedule in her suite for her," Walsh said as they walked down the corridor. His jaw was particularly tight.

"Does this Dr. Thom travel with the campaign?" Fletch asked.

"Shut up."

The door to Suite 758 was unlocked. Walsh seemed to know it would be.

They entered a suite identical to the one they had just left. The chips on the gold paint seemed identical. The painting of the ship was oil on canvas. Even the bottles on the bar seemed identical, with identical quantities missing.

The lights in the room were low.

Walsh dropped a schedule on the coffee table. "Close the door," he said to Fletch. "Let's sit down a minute."

Fletch closed the door.

Walsh did not brighten the lights. He sat in an armchair identical to the one he had just left in his father's suite, at the side of the room next to a reading lamp turned low. "Mother isn't due in on the plane from Cleveland until after one. We can talk a little.''

"Didn't know your parents were separated," joked Fletch. He sat in the same chair he had just been in. At least it looked and felt the same.

Carrying on at his regular pace, Walsh said: "Yes. Dr. Thom travels with the campaign. He is available to the candidate and his wife, the staff, members of the press, volunteers, bus drivers, pilots, whoever else. Have ringing in the ears? See Dr. Thom. Intestinal problems? Line forms at the rear.''

"That's not what the question meant, Walsh.''

"No. That wasn't what your question meant." Walsh took a deep breath. "My parents are not separated. On the campaign trail mostly they stay in separate suites because their schedules are different. Their sleep is important. They have different staffs, for the most part.''

"Have you lost your sense of humor?" Fletch asked.

"I don't like stupid questions in the corridor of a public hotel.''

"There was no one in the corridor, Walsh. It's past midnight.''

"Don't care. Someone could have heard you.''

Fletch noticed that across the dark living room, the door to the bedroom was closed.

"You either understand what I'm saying, Fletch, or you can go back to Ocala, Florida, and play the horses, or whatever you were doing.''

"So what are you saying, Lieutenant? Give it to me in small words, simple sentences.''

"Loyalty, Fletch. Absolute loyalty. We're on a campaign to get my father, Governor Caxton Wheeler, elected President of the United States. I want you to be the campaign's main press representative. As such, you will see things and know things you will question. When this happens, you are to ask me, but you are to ask me in private. You just saw Dr. Thom carry his little black bag into Dad's room after midnight. And you were going to ask me about it in the corridor of a public hotel.''

"That's a no-no," Fletch said.

"That's a no-no. Maybe you're going to see and hear things that surprise you, things you don't like. You don't have to be very old in this world to lose your idealism. Nothing and no one is perfect. When that happens, you shut up about it."

"You mean like when your mother cancels a visit to a children's burn center to play indoor tennis with some old cronies—"

"You sure don't point it out to the press. And if the press happens to pick it up, you put the best face on it possible."

"Walsh, I hate to break your cadence, but I think I know all this. I even accept most of it."

"And you watch the jokes you make. America wants to go to bed at night thinking of the candidate and his wife doing the same things they're doing: vying with each other for the bathroom sink to brush their teeth, sharing a reading lamp in bed, saying little good-night words to each other. Their actually staying in separate suites is logistically necessary, but the public doesn't want to know that. It disturbs the image. It gives certain sick minds the thought that having separate suites gives Dad the opportunity to have other ladies in his room, and therefore they leap to the conclusion that he does."

"I made that joke to you. Privately."

"You see, Fletch, there's always the difference between the image and the reality."

"Really?"

"We put out this image that the governor and his wife are campaigning for the presidency, and that they can take everything in stride, be everywhere at once, make speeches, give interviews, pat children on the head, travel constantly, stand up for hours at a time—yet live, eat, and sleep like normal people. Of course they don't. Of course they can't."

"Dr. Thom is controlling your dad with pills. Or shots. Or something."

"Dr. Thom puts my father to sleep at night, wakes him up in the morning, gives him one or two energy boosters during the day. This is a fact of a modern campaign. It's being done with medical knowledge and medical control."

"And it doesn't affect him?"

"Sure it does. It keeps him going. It permits him to get more out of himself, over longer periods of time, than is humanly possible."

"The world's on a chemical binge."

"Take your eighteenth-century man. Fly him through the air at nearly the speed of sound. Walk him through crowds of screaming, grabbing people, any one of whom might have a gun and the intent to use it. Have sirens going constantly in the ears. Put him in front of a television camera and have him talk to a quarter of a million people at the same time, his every word, his every facial expression being weighed, judged, criticized. Do this for weeks, months at a time. See what happens to him. The basic constitution of the human being hasn't changed that much, you know."

"What about you, Walsh?"

"What do you mean?"

"Your dad indicates to me you're under even more stress than he is."

"I'm a little younger than he is."

"Is Dr. Thom helping you out, too?"

"No." Walsh looked into his lap. "I just keep going. What else can't you accept?"

"That young woman, Walsh."

"What about her?"

"It's entirely possible she was thrown from the balcony of your dad's suite. The snow on the balcony had been messed up. Including on the railing. Apparently these principal suites—your parents'—are not locked."

"What of it?"

"A death? A murder?"

"Do you know how many people in this world die every day because of bad governments?"

"I would say hundreds."

"A conservative guess. Let's not keep a potentially great president out of office because some insignificant woman hits a sidewalk too hard."

"What about the local police? Aren't they going to investigate?"

"I've already handled that. The mayor found me down-

stairs in the bar. He said he hoped this unfortunate incident
was not disturbing to the candidate or his party. Asked me to
let him know if any of his police pestered us about it."

"You're serious?"

"Told him if anybody had any questions, they should be
referred to Barry Hines."

Fletch rolled his eyes. "Things sure are different on a
presidential campaign."

"Frankly, I think His Honor, the Mayor, was chiefly
worried," Walsh said with mock solemnity, "that with all the
national press crawling around, a murder in his fair city might
get national attention. Spoil his image of Homeland, America,
if the once-his-city gets national attention it's for murder."

"These political reporters wouldn't know how to report a
murder anyway," Fletch said. "They're specialists. They
have no more interest in murder than they do a boxing match.
Beneath them."

"I suppose so."

"Even if there were a murder on the press bus, they'd have
to call in police reporters. They have no more ability to report
a murder than your average citizen on the street. Which is
why I'm so curious as to why we do, in fact, have one crime
writer with us."

"Do we?" Walsh asked absently.

"Fredericka Arbuthnot. *Newsworld*."

Walsh said, "Tomorrow at dawn, this campaign rolls out of
this town, probably never to come back. Good luck to the
local police. I hope they solve their problems. But I don't
want any investigation of this death to touch the campaign.
It's just a public relations problem—one you've got to man-
age." Walsh relaxed more in his chair. "Enough of this. Not
important. In general, all I'm saying is, if you're going to be
with us, you're going to be with us all the way."

"Why do you want me with you?"

"You've had a lot of experience with the press, Fletch."

"I've worked for a lot of newspapers."

"You ought to know how the press works."

"Very hard."

"How they think."

"Slowly but tenaciously."

"Hill 1918, Fletch."

"Nineteen when?"

Walsh's eyes focused on the dark carpet. Despite the slight smile on his lips, his hairline seemed to pull back and his face turned even more white. "Twelve of us left. Surrounded by the enemy. Who knew we'd had it and were coming in to wipe us out."

"Are you about to tell me a war story?"

"Hundreds of 'em. Either we dug in and got killed. Or tried to blast our way out and got killed."

"War stories . . ."

"You, dogface Fletcher, didn't let your lieutenant choose either obvious alternative. You argued with me. Until I got the point."

"Never could handle authority very well."

"You had us move out of the obvious position, climb the trees, and tie ourselves to the branches. We disappeared. Three days we hung in those goddamned trees."

"Must've gotten hungry."

"It was better than being dead with our parts in our mouths."

"You were big enough to take the suggestion, Walsh."

"I was scared shitless. I couldn't think. The enemy rummaged around below us. They even shot each other. Carried off their dead. They never thought Americans would do such a thing."

"I was saving my own life, *hombre*."

"Your buddy—what's his name? Chambers? You ever see him anymore?"

"Alston Chambers. Yeah. We talk frequently. He's a prosecutor in California."

"You know how to make the best of a bad situation, Fletch. And a presidential campaign is one bad situation after another."

Fletch glanced at his watch. "It's getting late."

"I've got lots of files to give you tonight. Anyway, what would you be doing if you were home now?"

"Listening to Sergio Juevos, probably."

"Oh, yeah. The Cuban drummer."

"A harpist, actually. From Paraguay."

"A Paraguayan harpist?"

"You've never heard him?"

"You mean, he plays the harmonica?"

"He plays the harp."

"I don't think I've ever heard anyone play the harp."

Across the dark living room, the door to the bedroom opened.

"You haven't lived," Fletch said.

Walsh sighed. "Just like the old days, Fletch."

"What old days? I thought all days are twenty-four hours. Do some get to be older?"

"Bending my brain," Walsh said.

She came across the room like a specter. She was in a long, gray robe. Her blond hair hung to her shoulders.

Doris Wheeler was much bigger than Fletch expected. Her true size had not come across to him on television or still pictures, maybe because she was usually seen standing next to the governor, who was also a big person. She was tall with extraordinarily big shoulders for a woman.

Fletch stood up.

"Walsh? What are you doing at this hour of the night?"

"Dropping off your schedule for tomorrow." Walsh shot his thumb toward the piece of paper on the coffee table. "Why are you back from Cleveland so early?"

"Had Sully make me an earlier plane reservation. Left the symphony benefit at intermission. I've heard Schönberg." Walsh had not stood up. Doris Wheeler's eyes fastened on Fletch's shirt collar. "Who's this?"

"Fletcher," Walsh said. "Here to help handle the press. Just making sure he's housebroken."

"Why are you up talking so late?"

"War stories," Walsh answered. "Haven't seen each other since the Texas-Oklahoma game. That right, Fletch?"

Doris leaned over her son. She kissed him on the mouth.

"Walsh, you've been drinking." She stood up only partway.

"Had to spend some time in the bar, Mother. Something happened. This girl—"

Doris Wheeler slapped her son, hard. Her hand going down to his face looked as big and as solid as a shovel.

"I don't care about any girl, Walsh. I care about you walking around with liquor on your breath." Walsh did not move. He did not look up at her. "I care about getting your father elected President of the United States."

Fully, stiffly erect, she walked back across the living room. "Now, go to bed," she said.

The door to the bedroom closed.

Fletch stood there quietly.

Walsh's face was two kinds of red. It was dark red where his mother had hit him. It was bright red everywhere else.

Walsh kept his eyes on the papers in his lap.

"Well," Walsh finally said, "I'm glad I gave you my lecture on loyalty, before you saw that."

6

"Good morning, ladies and gentlemen of the press," Governor Caxton Wheeler said heartily.

From the back of the bus, a man's voice snarled: "*Men* and *women* of the press."

"Women and men," corrected the woman sitting next to Freddie Arbuthnot.

"Persons of the press . . . ?" offered the governor.

Fletch was standing next to the governor at the front of the bus. At six-thirty in the morning the governor apparently was slim, tanned, bright-eyed, and fully rested. He did not use, or need to use, the tour bus's microphone. Also, he did not leave much room for the person standing beside him at the front of the bus.

As a politician will, he filled whatever space was available to him.

"Don't forget the photographers," wire service reporter Roy Filby said. "They don't quite make it as persons."

"Dearly beloved," said the governor.

"Now you're leaving out Arbuthnot!" said Joe Hall.

"All creatures great and small?" asked the governor.

"Why's that man up there calling us a bunch of animals?" Stella Kirchner asked Bill Dieckmann loudly. "Trying to get elected game warden or something?"

"It gives me great pleasure," the governor said, "to introduce one of your own colleagues to you—"

"Hardly," said Freddie Arbuthnot.

"—I. M. Fletcher—"

"Politicians will say anything," said Ira Lapin.

"—whom we've employed to hand out press releases to you—"

"He spelled Spiersville wrong already this morning!" shouted Fenella Baker. "It's *ie*, everybody, not *ee*!"

"—do your research for you, free of charge, dig out an answer to your every question, however obtuse and trivial, and generally, to say things about me I'd blush to have to say myself."

"He's a complete crook," said the man wearing the *Daily Gospel* badge.

"Now, I know some of you miss ol' James," continued the governor. "I do too . . . more than you'll ever know." The governor pulled his touch-of-sentiment face. To Fletch, seeing the expression in profile, it seemed the governor was too obviously clocking the seconds he held the expression. "But, as you know, ol' James decided he wanted to go somewhere more agreeable."

"Yeah," Lansing Sayer said. "When anyone goes to play tennis, James wants to go play tennis."

"So," said the governor, coloring slightly behind the ear, "I'll leave ol' Fletch in your hands." Walsh had told Fletch to ride the press bus that morning. "Try not to chew him up and spit him out this morning. Can't promise you that lunch is going to be that good."

"Hey, Governor," shouted Joe Hall. "Any response yet to the President's statement on South Africa last night?"

Waving, the governor left the bus.

Fletch picked up the microphone. The bus driver turned on the speaker system for him.

"Good morning," Fletch said. "As the governor's press

representative, I make you the solemn promise that I will never lie to you. Today, on this bus, we will be passing through Miami, New Orleans, Dallas, New York, and Keokuk, Iowa. Per usual, at midday you will be flown to San Francisco for lunch. Today's menu is clam chowder, pheasant under glass, roast Chilean lamb, and a strawberry mousse from Maine. Everything the governor says today will be significant, relevant, wise, to the point, and as fresh as the lilies in the field."

"In fact," Fenella Baker said, trying to look through the steamy window, "it's snowing out."

The other side of the motel's front door, Doris Wheeler was climbing into the back of a small, black sedan. Today the campaign would head southwest in the state; the candidate's wife would go north. The governor would ride the campaign bus, in front of the press bus.

"Any questions you have for me," Fletch continued, "write backwards and offer to your editors as think-pieces. Just ask your editors to label such fanciful essays as 'Analysis.' "

"Fletch, is it true you're a crook?" Roy Filby asked.

"No," said Fletch, "but if any of you run short of cash, just ask me and I'll put you in contact with people who will supply you with all you want at a modest charge of twenty-percent interest daily."

"Oh, you work for a credit card company, too?"

"Is it true you saved Walsh Wheeler's life overseas?" Fenella Baker asked.

"That's another thing," Fletch said. "I will never evade any of your questions."

He turned the microphone off and hung it up.

7

"How does it feel to be an adversary of the press?" From her seat on the bus, Freddie Arbuthnot grinned up at Fletch.

"Some people," announced Fletch, "think I always have been."

"This is Betsy Ginsberg," Freddie said about her seat-mate, a slightly overweight, bright-eyed, nice-looking young woman.

"Terrific stuff you write," Fletch said to her. "I've never read a word of it, but I've decided to say things like that on this trip."

Betsy laughed. The diesel engine straining to move the bus out of the motel's horseshoe driveway was making as much noise as a jet airplane taking off.

Freddie pressed her elbow into Betsy's ribs. "Move," she said. "Let me be the first to sink teeth into this new press representative."

"You're just saying that," Betsy said, moving out of her seat, "because he's good-lookin'."

"Is he?" said Freddie. "I never noticed."

Fletch slumped into the seat vacated by Betsy. "I don't know," he said to Freddie. "I don't think I'm gonna make it as a member of the establishment. It's all too new to me."

After doing his copying and delivering chores the night before, Fletch finally had taken his shower and climbed into bed with all the folders Walsh Wheeler had given him. There was a folder stating the candidate's position on each campaign issue, as well as on issues that had not arisen and probably would not arise. Some of the positions were crisp, concise, to the point. Others were longer, not as well focused, and had to be read two or three times before Fletch could discover exactly where the candidate was hedging his position. There were personnel folders, with pictures and full biographies, of each member of the candidate's staff. And there were other folders, not as well organized, on most of the members of the press traveling with the campaign. Some of these too had photographs, personal items regarding their families, political leanings, a few significant clippings. Fletch may have been asleep when the phone rang to wake him up. He wasn't sure.

"So far," he said to Freddie, as the press bus rolled along the highway, "I've received two lectures on absolute loyalty."

"What do you expect?" she asked.

Fletch thought a moment. "I don't believe in absolutes."

"You're in a position, all right," she agreed, nodding. "Between the fire and the bottom of the skillet. As a reporter, you're trained to find things out and report 'em. As a press representative, you've got to prevent other reporters from finding certain things out. Adversary of the press. Against your own instincts. Poor Fletch."

"You're a help."

"You'll never make it."

"I know it."

"That's all right." She patted him on the arm. "I'll destroy you as painlessly as possible."

"Great. I'd appreciate that. Are you sure you're up to it?"

"Up to what?"

"Destroying me."

"It will be easy," she said. "Because of all those conflicts in yourself. You've never tried to be a member of the establishment before, Fletch. I mean, let's face it: you're a born-and-bred rebel.''

"I bought a necktie for this job."

She studied his solid red tie. "Nice one, too. Looks like you're already bleeding from the neck."

"Got it in the airport in Little Rock."

"Limited selection?"

"No. They had five or six to choose from."

"That was the best?"

"I thought so."

"You only bought one, though, right?"

"Didn't know how long this job would last."

"Glad you didn't make too big an investment in your future as a member of the establishment. Are you going to tell me about last night?"

"What about last night? I saw you to your room and got the door closed in my face."

"Last night a woman landed dead on the pavement outside your candidate's seventh-floor motel room window. Don't you read the papers?"

"I read the papers. Today's big story is about a hockey riot—"

"To hell with today's big story," Freddie said. "I'm interested in tomorrow's big story."

"Tomorrow's big story will be about how badly the police behaved at the hockey riot."

Freddie talked to herself in the bus window. "This here press representative thinks he can get away with not talking about the young woman who got thrown to her death through the governor's bedroom window last night."

"Come off it. I don't know anything."

"You ought to."

"I noticed none of you hotshots asked the governor about it this morning."

"Questions at this point would be ridiculous."

"Of course."

"At least, questions directed at him."

"But I'm fair game?"

"The definition of a press representative. You are game as fair as any seasoned, roasted, carved, and chewed."

"Freddie, I only know what I heard on television this morning. Her name was Alice Elizabeth Fields—"

"Shields."

"In her late twenties."

"Twenty-eight."

"From Chicago."

"You got that part right."

"She was naked when she landed on the sidewalk. Apparently, she had been brutally beaten beforehand."

"She wasn't raped," Freddie said. "Don't you find that odd?"

"I find the whole thing terrible. Sickening."

The two big buses hurried down the highway through the swirling snow. Behind them were a few cars filled with more staff, volunteer workers, one or two television vans.

"And, Fletch, it is possible her point of departure was the balcony outside the governor's suite."

Slowly, he said, "Yes. The governor had had press and other people in for drinks earlier in the evening. I happen to know the front door to the suite was left unlocked."

"I see. Thanks for being frank with me."

"I know you don't print speculation."

"And"—Freddie sighed—"she had been traveling with the campaign all week."

"Not traveling with the campaign. Just following it. She was some sort of a political groupie. She had no position with the campaign."

"As far as we know. I recognized her when I saw her picture in this morning's *Courier*."

"Had you ever spoken to her?"

"Two or three days ago. In whatever town we were in. I was using the motel's indoor pool. So was she. I said, 'Hi'; she said, 'Hi'; I dove in, did my laps, when I got out, she was gone, I think."

"How would you characterize her?"

"A wallflower. I think she wanted to be with the campaign,

but didn't know how to be assertive enough to become a volunteer or something.''

"Any chance of her being a real camp follower? A prostitute?''

"Definitely not. But you'd have to ask the men.''

"I will.'' Suddenly Fletch wanted a cup of coffee. "A local matter,'' Fletch said. "To be investigated by local police. Someone said she hit the pavement just after the governor came into the hotel. While he was still in the lobby, or in the elevator or something.''

"May I quote that?''

"No.''

"Why not?''

"Because I don't know what I'm talking about.''

"Truer words you never spoke.''

"Seeing I'm being so frank with you, how about telling me why Fredericka Arbuthnot, investigative reporter for *Newsworld*, specialist in crime, especially murder and other forms of mayhem, is assigned to the presidential campaign of Governor Caxton Wheeler?''

"Having any luck in finding out?''

"I'm asking the only person I know. You.''

"You've gone to the source.''

"The horse's mouth, as it were.''

"Going to wear me down with relentless questioning?''

"Going to give it a try.''

"The answer's simple: there's been a murder.''

"That was after you arrived, Ms. Arbuthnot. Not even you, I think, awesome reporter that you are, can predict where and when a murder is going to happen a week before the event.''

"Oh, dear,'' she said. "You don't know.'' She leaned over and began rummaging in the yellow and blue sports bag at her feet. "I didn't think you did.'' She sat up with a damaged notebook in her hand. And out of it she took a newspaper clipping. She handed it to him. "Almost a week ago,'' she said. "Another murder. Very similar.''

He read the item from *The Chicago Sun-Times:*

Chicago—The body of a woman was found by hotel employees this morning in a service closet off a reception room at the Hotel Harris. Police say the woman was brutally beaten about the face and upper body before being strangled to death.

The night before discovery of the body, the reception room had been used by the press covering the presidential campaign of Governor Caxton Wheeler.

Chicago police report the woman, about thirty, wearing a green cocktail dress and high-heeled shoes, was carrying no identification.

Fletch's desire for a cup of coffee was becoming acute.

He handed the clipping back to her. "The press," he said. "How did you pick up an item like that?"

"You don't know about *Newsworld*'s fancy new electronic systems." She was putting the clipping back into the falling-apart notebook, and the notebook back into the sports bag.

Fletch was having the sensation of thinking without thought. "Up-to-date?"

"So fantastic they take out each other's plugs and then say good night to each other."

"That's up-to-date."

Still leaning over, Freddie appeared to be reorganizing her sports bag. "Be kind to your office computer," Freddie said. "It may be related to someone high up in the National Federation of Labor."

"We're being overcome by machines."

Freddie sat up again. "They'll have their day. Or so they predict. And they're always right. Right?"

"No. Freddie, how far have the Chicago police got with this other murder?"

"Talked with my friend Sam Buck this morning. They still haven't identified the woman."

"Fingerprints on the neck?"

"She was strangled with a cord."

"Oh. Have the Chicago police assigned anyone to this campaign?"

"They can't. Different jurisdictions. They have to treat it

as strictly a local matter. They're concentrating on hotel staff.''

Fletch looked at what he could see of the other people on the press bus, their heads tipped to read, a man's leg extended into the aisle. "It's a pretty safe bet the murderer isn't a member of the Hotel Harris staff.''

"I'd take that bet," Freddie said. "I reported the details of the murder last night to Detective Buck in Chicago this morning.''

"Will they assign someone to the campaign now?''

"He said the ways in which the women were murdered are not similar enough.''

"Two women beaten and then murdered? I see a similarity.''

"One was fully clad, the other naked. One was strangled, the other pushed to her death. Stranglers seldom use any other method of doing people in.''

"Was the woman in Chicago raped?''

"No.''

Across the aisle, one row ahead of them, sat a heavy man in a bulky overcoat. He was staring straight ahead, expressionless. His eyes bulged. He looked like a frog on a pod.

"Freddie, most likely we have a murderer traveling with us.''

"It's that possibility, old man, that has me here. Any reporting I do on the campaign itself, I will consider just routine.''

Fletch nodded toward the frog-on-the-pod across the aisle. "Is that the Russian?''

"Solov," said Freddie. "Correspondent from *Pravda*. Here to report on the campaign, get a line on The Man Who for the Kremlin. Wonderful free country, we have here.''

"Does he always stare that way?''

"I don't know if he always has," Freddie laughed. "He does now. He's fixated.''

"On what?''

"He discovered certain channels on American cable television. The pornographic ones. He's up all night, every night, watching it. Don't ever get the hotel room next to him.

Electronic slap-and-tickle all night long. They say he's been catatonic since he arrived.''

"I wonder if he builds up enough of a head of steam to beat women to death.''

"Oh, not Boris. I understand he's written several articles on the moral degeneracy of America. He thinks we all look at that stuff.''

"Would you say he's sexually aberrant?''

"Yes, he's sexually abhorrent.''

"I said aberrant.''

"Who cares?''

Roy Filby came down the aisle and stopped by Fletch's chair. "Hey, Fletcher. Going to give us the real lowdown on the Mooney murder?''

A huge factory was looming on the flat, snowy horizon.

Fletch said, "Great stuff you're writing these days, Roy.''

Roy laughed and banged Fletch on the shoulder. "Great house parties you give, Fletch. Someday invite me to one.''

"I've given my last house party in Key West,'' Fletch said.

Roy continued down the aisle. There was a rest room in the back of the bus.

"I suppose these murders could be coincidences,'' Fletch said.

"Could be,'' said Freddie. "Not likely.''

"I hope so,'' said Fletch.

Studying his face whimsically, Freddie asked, "So how do you like your new job now?''

"Not much. Freddie, let's you and I agree not to be adversaries on this matter. Tell me what you know as you find out.''

"Okay,'' she said. "If you tell me what you know.''

"I will. At least I think I will.''

"And you know downright well, Fletch, that the moment's going to come when I have to print what I know.''

"Sure. But I know you won't go off half-cocked. I'm not too keen on people who beat up women.''

The bus was beginning to slow. There was an enormous metal tire standing on the roof of the factory.

"What are you thinking now?'' she asked.

"It's your job to report. It's my job to protect the candidate and his campaign as much as I can. If the murderer is a member of the press, then it's no problem for the candidate. The press is assigned to the campaign. If the murderer is a volunteer"—Fletch waggled his hands just above his lap—"then it's not so bad. The candidate didn't necessarily have anything to do with his selection. If the murderer is a member of his immediate staff, then it's very, very bad. It would mean his judgment of people isn't too reliable. People would say, 'If he put such a person on his staff, think whom he might name Secretary of Defense.'"

Still studying him, Freddie asked, "And if the murderer is the candidate himself?"

Fletch was looking at his still hands in his lap. "Then you'd have one helluva story," he said quietly.

8

By the time he got off the bus, Fletch could see the governor's nose was already red with cold. Snow was blowing from the northwest and there was a fresh inch or two on the ground. Lights were on in the old red-brick factory. Not a bit dwarfed by the big factory, the governor stood in the main gate, shaking hands with most of the factory workers as they arrived. He was wearing a red-and-black checked, wool hunting jacket over his suit vest, and thick-soled black workers' boots. To the workers who shook his hand as they passed by, the governor said such things as *"Mornin', everything okay with you? Gimme a chance to be your President, will ya?"* and the workers answered such things as *"Mornin', Governor, like your stand on the waterway." "Got to make more jobs, you know? My brother hasn't found a job in over two years." "With ya all the way; my aunt's runnin' your campaign over in Shreve, ya know?" "Hey, tell Wohlman we don't want a strike, okay?"* Some of those who did not shake hands waved as they passed by and said such things as *"How're doin', Caxton? Good luck! You'll never make it!"* Others were too shy to shake the governor's hand, or say anything. And others scowled at him or at their boots as they went through the gate.

Ten meters away, close enough to see everything and hear almost everything, the press stood shivering in a herd, their noses aimed into the wind like sheep hunkered in a stormy pasture, in case The Man Who got shot, or seized by his heart, or overtaken by some indiscretion.

Standing in the factory gate, the governor looked peculiarly alone. No one was standing near him—not his wife, not Walsh, not his speechwriters, volunteers. . . .

The campaign staff were all on the warm, well-lit bus.

"Where do we pick up the congressman?" Lee Allen Parke yelled. He was standing in the front of the bus with two women volunteers, one about thirty, the other about sixty.

"At the school," Walsh said. In his shirt sleeves, he stood in the middle of the bus, revolving slowly, like a teacher during students' workbook time.

From the folders he had studied, Fletch could match names to faces.

At a little table, speechwriters Phil Nolting and Paul Dobson were in heavy, quiet discussion. They were both drawing lines on a single piece of paper on the table. They looked like architects roughly designing the structure of a building.

Barry Hines, the campaign's communication chief, sat in a reclining chair talking on the telephone.

Along the side of the bus, three women sat at pull-out tables, typing.

That morning's newspapers littered the bus's floor.

Dr. Thom was not in the forward section of the bus.

As Fletch moved down through the noise and confusion of the bus, Walsh shouted, "You all know Fletch!"

None of them did. In response to the shout, they all looked at Fletch and returned to what they were doing. Now they knew him.

"Hey, Walsh!" Barry Hines yelled from the telephone. "Vic Robbins! Upton's advance man?"

"What about him?" Walsh asked.

"His car just went off a bridge in Pennsylvania. Into the Susquehanna River."

"Dead?"

"Unless he was wearing a scuba tank."

"Confirm that, please," Fletch said to Barry. "Pennsylvania State Police."

Barry Hines pushed a button on the telephone in his lap and dialed O.

Walsh pointed to the last typist in the row. Instantly she pulled the paper she was working on out of her typewriter and inserted a fresh piece.

Walsh dictated: "Upon hearing of the tragic death of Victor Robbins, Governor Caxton Wheeler said, 'There was no one who had better technical understanding of American politics than Victor Robbins. The heartfelt sympathy of Mrs. Wheeler and myself go out to Vic's family, and to his friends, who were legion. I and my staff will do anything to help Senator Upton and his staff in response to their great loss.' "

"Yeah," Barry Hines said, pushing another phone button. "He's dead."

Walsh took the typed statement from the woman and handed it to Fletch. "Why am I doing your work for you?" He smiled. "Immediate release to the press, please."

Paul Dobson asked, "Should Caxton mention Robbins's death in the Winslow speech, Walsh?"

"Naw." Hand rubbing the back of his neck, Walsh turned in a small circle in the middle of the bus. "Just wish Upton weren't going to get all that free press in Pennsylvania, of all places. Why the hell couldn't Robbins have driven himself off a bridge in a smaller state? South Dakota?"

Phil Nolting said, "Some advance men will do anything to make a headline."

"Yeah," said Dobson. "Let's send a suggestion to Willy in California. California's a big state, too. Must have some bridges."

"More active press, too," Nolting said. "The weather's nicer."

Fletch was standing at the copying machine, running off the Victor Robbins press release.

The factory whistle blew. Through the steamy window, Fletch saw the governor turn and go through the factory gates by himself.

"Where's he going?"

The press herd had turned their noses from the wind and were looking toward the campaign bus.

"In to have coffee with the union leader," Walsh answered, not even looking. "What's his name—Wohlman. He'll also have coffee with management."

"Coffee, coffee," said a huge-chested man in a black suit who had stepped through the stateroom door at the back of the bus. "Coffee is bad for him."

"You know Flash Grasselli?" Walsh asked. "This is Fletcher, Flash." Fletch got his hand crushed in the big man's fist. "Flash is Dad's driver, etc."

"And friend," Flash said.

"Couldn't do without Flash," Walsh said, and the big-chested man nodded as if to say, *Damn right.*

"Glad to meet you," Fletch said.

At the front of the bus, while Fletch was trying to get by, Lee Allen Parke was saying quietly to the two volunteers, "Now, you make sure the congressman is made right comfortable, you hear? No matter what time of the morning he comes aboard, you have an eye-opener mixed and ready for him. If he doesn't want it, he won't drink it. . . ."

The press was gathered around the foot of the steps of the campaign bus.

"Where's the statement?" Fenella Baker demanded. Her lips were blue with cold.

"What statement?" Fletch asked.

"The governor's statement regarding Vic Robbins's death." Fenella was staring at the papers in Fletch's hands. "Idiot."

"How do you know about Robbins's death?" Fletch asked. "We got the news only three minutes ago."

"Give us the damned statement!" Bill Dieckmann shouted. "I've got the first phone!"

"You know the governor couldn't possibly have made a statement," Fletch said. "He's in the factory!"

"Are you playing with us?" Ira Lapin yelled.

"No," Fletch said. "Here are the statements." He tried to hand them out, but they were grabbed from him.

Bill Dieckmann said to Betsy Ginsberg, "You I can outrun."

"With a strong tail wind," Betsy said.

"You must have wires screwed into your heads," Fletch muttered.

Andrew Esty scanned the statement, then looked up at Fletch. There was rage in his face. "There's no religious consolation in it! In the statement!" Esty wore a *Daily Gospel* button even in the lapel of his overcoat.

"God," Fletch said.

At varying speeds, the members of the press slid through the snow and wind to the telephones inside the factory's main gates.

Except Freddie Arbuthnot. She stood in the snow, grinning up at Fletch.

"Not interested?" Fletch asked.

"Already phoned it in," Freddie said. "Such a statement has three parts. Compliment the deceased's professional expertise. Consolation for family and friends. Offer of help to opposing campaign. Did I miss anything?"

Fletch watched as a dirty, old taxi pulled up at the factory's main gate. The factory was an expensive taxi ride from anywhere.

"Amazing bunch of savages. Screaming for the governor's statement on a matter they knew the governor couldn't even know about yet."

"Ah, Fletch," Freddie said. "You're turning establishment already."

A man had lifted a battered suitcase out of the taxi. Money in hand, he was arguing with the driver.

"Who's that?" Fletch asked.

Freddie turned around. "That," she said definitely, "is bad news. Mr. Bad News, himself." Turning back to Fletch, she said, "Mr. Michael J. Hanrahan, scourge of respectable journalists everywhere, lead dirt-writer for that chain of daily lies and mischief, the scandal sheet going under the generic name *Newsbill*."

Carrying his suitcase in one hand, a portable typewriter in

the other, overcoat hems flapping in the wind, the man was lumbering toward the campaign bus. The taxi driver was shouting something at him, which could not be heard in the wind.

"That's Hanrahan? I hoped never to meet him."

Hanrahan turned his head and spat toward the taxi driver.

"I thought Mary Rice was covering us for *Newsbill*."

"Mary's a mouse," Freddie said. "Hanrahan's a rat."

"'lo, Arbuthnot." With either a smile or a grimace, Michael J. Hanrahan tipped his profile toward her, looking at her out of the corner of his eye. "Made it with any goats lately?"

"Always a pleasure to witness your physical and mental degeneracy, Hanrahan," Freddie answered. "How many more hours to live do the doctors give you?"

Hanrahan didn't put down either his suitcase or his typewriter case. He shivered in his overcoat.

The skin of his face was puffy, flushed, and scabrous. Between the gaps in his mouth were black and yellow teeth. His clothes looked as stale as last month's bread.

"Never, never use a toilet seat," Freddie advised Fletch, "after Hanrahan has used it."

Hanrahan laughed. "Where's this jackass Fletcher?" he asked her.

"I'm the jackass," Fletch said.

Hanrahan closed his mouth, tried unsuccessfully to breathe through his nose, then opened his mouth again. "Oh, joy," he muttered. "This kid doesn't even go to the bathroom, I bet. Probably been taught not to. It isn't nice." He put his chin up at Fletch, who was still on the stairs of the campaign bus, and tried to give Fletch a penetrating look with blood-shot eyes, each in its own pool of poison. "Boy, are you in trouble."

"Why's that?" Fletch asked.

"'Cause you've never dealt with Hanrahan before."

"Dreadful stuff you write," Fletch said.

"All you've had to deal with so far are these milksop pussycats mewing for your handouts."

"Meow," said Freddie.

"You're gonna work for me," Hanrahan said. "You're gonna work your shavvy-tailed ass off."

"What do you want, Hanrahan?"

"I want to sit down with your candidate. And I mean now."

"Not now."

"Today. Within a few hours. I need to ask him some questions."

"About what?"

"About dead broads," Hanrahan snapped. "That broad in Chicago. That broad last night. The brutally slain debutante your candidate leaves behind him everywhere he goes."

"*Newsbill*'s electronics must be as good as *Newsworld*'s," Fletch said to Freddie.

"*Newsworld*'s doesn't use such colorful words," Freddie said. "Archaic though they may be."

"Hell, Hanrahan," Fletch said, "that matter's already wrapped up."

Hanrahan squinted. "It is?"

"Yeah. They took Mary Rice into custody an hour ago. Your own reporter. From *Newsbill*."

"Bullshit."

"He's right, Hanrahan. We all know how far you *Newsbill* writers will go to make a story. Mary just got caught this time."

"The police knew the murderer was Mary because she left someone else's notes at the scene of crime," Fletch added.

Even Hanrahan's neck was turning red. "You know how many readers I got?" he shouted.

"Yeah," Freddie said. "Everyone in the country who can't read, reads *Newsbill*. Big deal."

"They all vote," Hanrahan insisted to her.

"More's the pity," Freddie said to the ground.

"I want to get together with your candidate now," Hanrahan said. "And no more juvenile crap from you!"

"Doubt the candidate will have all that much time for you, Hanrahan."

"What's the matter?" Hanrahan took a step forward.

"Doesn't little boyums like the smell of big bad man's breath?"

"Highly indicative, I'm sure," Fletch said.

"You put me together with your candidate, let me work him over with my bare knuckles, or tomorrow *Newsbill*'s readers are going to be told Governor Caxton Wheeler refuses to answer questions about two recent murders on his campaign trail."

"You just do that, Hanrahan." Fletch turned to climb the bus steps. "It will be the first time you've ever written the truth."

9

"Listen to this." Dr. Thom was stretched out on the bed in the candidate's stateroom at the back of the bus. He was reading a book entitled *The Darwinian Theory as Fossil*. " 'For thousands of years, we have been told perfection is not attainable, but a worthy aspiration. In this post-Freudian era, we are told normalcy is not possible, but a worthy aspiration. In one scheme, we might achieve excellence; in the other, mediocrity. In one scheme, we fear despair; in the other, depression.' " The doctor put down the open book on his chest. "What can I do for you?"

"Need to ask you a couple of questions." Fletch had knocked, entered the stateroom at Dr. Thom's drawled "Enter if you must," and sat in one of the two comfortable swivel chairs at the stateroom's desk.

Dr. Thom spoke with extraordinary slowness. "Anyone trying to handle the press can have anything he wants from me: poisoned gas, flamethrowers, machine guns, hand grenades. If I don't have such medical and surgical tools on hand, I shall secure them for you at greatly reduced rates."

"At the moment, I'm inclined to place an order," Fletch said. "I just met Michael J. Hanrahan, of *Newsbill*."

"The press ought to be an extinct species," Dr. Thom drawled. "They never evolved to a very high level. You can tell by the way they go along the ground, sniffing it. I might suggest to the candidate that the press be handed over to the Department of the Interior. That way their extinction will be guaranteed."

"Got to have the free press," said Fletch.

"Do you really think so? Neither the substance of America's favorite sport, politics, nor the substance of America's favorite food, the hot dog, can bear too much analysis. If the innards of either American politics or the American hot dog were too fully revealed, the American would have to disavow and disgorge himself."

"You against motherhood too?"

Dr. Thom clicked the nail of his index finger against the cover of the book on his chest. "On the evolutionary scale, Woman and The Bird, of course, are superior." He cleared his throat. "Which is why, of course, Man invented the telephone wire."

"I understand you were one of the first people to get to the body of Alice Elizabeth Shields last night."

"I was."

"Will you tell me about it?"

"Have you a morbid curiosity?"

"Fredericka Arbuthnot and Michael J. Hanrahan are not on the press bus to count the votes in congressional districts. They're crime writers."

"You mean the death of Ms. Shields might affect the campaign in some way?"

"They tell me two young women have been murdered on the fringes of this campaign just this last week."

"Oh, dear. And the perpetrator might be one of us?"

"There's a good possibility of it."

"And you'd like to get the facts before they do, so you can put the right spin on them."

"And do so very quietly. Without appearing to do so."

Dr. Thom studied the roof a moment. "Don't the police

have anything to do with this? Or have they read their own statistical success-rates at solving murders and given up on them? Plan to limit their activities henceforth to placing parking tickets on stationary, nonargumentative cars, at which function they are very good?''

"The murders are too spread out. Different jurisdictions. We are blessed in this country by not having a national police force.''

"Ah, yes. Guaranteeing that only the smaller, narrower-visioned criminal gets caught.''

"Tell me what happened last night.''

"I was in the bar. A bellman came in—or the doorman, whatever he was. I'm not sure whether he was looking for a responsible person, a motel manager, a doctor, or for a drink. He said, sort of choking, so that his voice stood out in the tired, somber crowd anyway, 'Someone jumped off the roof. She's naked.' ''

"Exact words?''

"I may not remember everything said in the bar last night, about Senator Upton, Senator Graves, the Middle East, and *The Washington Post*, but I do remember those words exactly. It took a moment for them to sink in.''

"Who was with you in the bar at that point?''

"I had been talking with Fenella Baker and Betsy Ginsberg. I had been talking with Bill Dieckmann earlier, but I think he'd left some time before. The usual faces in a motel bar. A few morose businessmen drinking themselves to sleep. A few long-haul, tongue-tied drivers desperate to talk with anybody about anything.''

"That all?''

"All I can remember. After the event, of course, after the ambulance had come and gone, the press were in the bar in force. Some had just thrown on coats over their pajamas.''

"Tell me about going out to the girl. Examining her.''

"Due to the high incidence of malpractice suits these days, you know doctors do not rush in where even fools fear to tread. Of course, if I ever come across a lawyer lying on the sidewalk, I'll tread on his face.''

"You don't like lawyers either?''

"Even lawyers' mothers don't like lawyers. If you do a survey, I think you'll find that lawyers' mothers are the strongest advocates of legal abortions in the land."

Fletch fought the mesmerizing quality of the doctor's manner of speech. "Going through the lobby, did you see Governor Wheeler coming in?"

"No. No, I did not. I didn't see the governor at all last night until I went to his suite."

"To put him to sleep."

"To put him to sleep. A middle-aged couple, nicely dressed, was standing over the girl. The man was just taking off his overcoat to cover the body. I asked him not to do that. I wanted to examine her."

"Was she still alive at that point?"

"No. I would say death was nearly instantaneous the moment she hit the pavement."

"Not before?"

"I don't think so. My guess is that she landed on the back of her head, breaking her neck, then crashed on her back."

"What evidence did you see that the girl had been beaten before she fell or was pushed?"

"Her face was badly bruised. Banged eye—her left, I think—blood from her nose, blood from lips, two broken front teeth, two or three badly fractured ribs on her left side. Compound fractures, I mean."

"The coroner announced this morning she had not been raped."

"So what motive? Robbery? Who'd want to steal her clothes? Certainly a beaten, naked female suggests rape."

"Would you say she was a good-looking woman?"

Again Dr. Thom studied the ceiling. "Not beautiful, in any way. Not much makeup, if any. A slim build, well-proportioned body, good muscle tone. A plain woman, I'd say."

"While you were examining the girl, a crowd collected?"

"A small crowd. Mostly the press."

"Do you remember who was in the crowd?"

"I did glance through the crowd, to make sure no small children were there. That Arbuthnot woman was there. Now, there's a handsome woman. Fenella Baker had followed me out from the bar. I will not comment on her beauty, or lack thereof. One or two others, I'm not sure who. A truck driver from the bar was the only one who really tried to be helpful."

"I understand you had seen the Shields woman before."

"Yes. I had noticed her the last few days—in the hotel elevators, lobbies."

"Why did you notice her?"

"I noticed her because she was one place one day and the next place the next day. She didn't appear to have anything to do with the campaign. Although I did see her breakfasting with Betsy Ginsberg one morning."

"Did you ever see her with any men?"

"Not that I remember. I think she drove herself in a little two-door Volkswagen."

"Why do you think a woman like that would traipse after a political campaign the way she did?"

"It's a candidate's job to be attractive, isn't it? That's why they wear those glue-on tans. Power attracts. They attract all sorts of creatures. Even you and me."

The engine of the bus roared. Immediately the bus began to move.

"Hey!" Fletch stood up. "I'm supposed to be on the other bus."

With his finger holding his reading place, Dr. Thom closed his book. "Guess I should let the patient use the bed." He sat up on the bunk, swinging his legs over the side.

Fletch was rubbing the steam off the window.

Taking off his red-and-black checked hunting jacket, Governor Wheeler opened the stateroom door.

"How do," he said to the two men using his stateroom.

"How many cups of coffee did you have, Caxton?" Dr. Thom asked.

"Just two. But they were black." The candidate smiled as if he had gotten away with something.

"Don't blame me if you jitter."

"What am I supposed to do, ask for skim milk everywhere I go? Caffeine's important to these guys."

In the door behind the governor, Walsh said, "Vic Robbins

drove himself off a bridge this morning in Pennsylvania. Dead.''

"Yeah?" The governor was putting his hunting jacket on a hanger, and the hanger back in the closet. "He was a real weasel. Have I made a statement?''

"Yup.''

"Sent a wreath?''

"Will as soon as we know where to send it. You'd better hit something big and hard in Winslow, or you'll get zilch on the nightly news. The accident will make good, easy television film.''

"Yeah. Like what?''

"Phil and Paul are trying to come up with something.''

"What have they got so far?''

"Pentagon spending.''

"Hell, anything anybody says about that has smelled of hypocrisy since Eisenhower. And he saved his complaints for his farewell address. Get something with a little pizzazz.''

Dr. Thom said, "You want anything, Caxton?''

"Yeah. A brain transplant. Go away. Don't come back until you can do one.''

Fletch tried to follow Dr. Thom through the stateroom door.

"Hang on, Fletch,'' The Man Who said. "I think it's time you and I got to know each other a little better.''

10

"Sounds like gangland, doesn't it?" chuckled Governor Wheeler after the door was closed. "A member of the opposition gets knocked off and we've got a wreath ordered before we know where to send it." He sat in the chair Fletch had just vacated and indicated Fletch should sit on the bed. "American politics is a bit of everything: sports, showmanship, camp meeting, and business negotiation." He bent over and began taking off his boots. "Ask me some questions."

"Ask anything?"

"Anything your heart desires. You know a man more from his questions than from his answers. Who said that?"

"You just did."

"Let's not make a note of it."

"I've got a simple question."

"Shoot."

"Why do you want to be President of the United States?"

"I don't, particularly." The Man Who was changing his socks. "Mrs. Wheeler wants to be Mrs. President of the United States." Smiling, he looked up at Fletch. "Why do you look so surprised? Most men try to do what their wives want them to, don't they? I mean, after ten, fifteen years in the same business, most men would quit and go fishin' if it weren't for their wives driving them to the top. Don't you think so?''

"I don't know."

"Never married?"

"Once or twice."

"I see." The governor, socks changed, shoes on, laces tied, sat back in the swivel chair. "Well, Mrs. Wheeler worked hard during the two congressional campaigns, and the three campaigns for the statehouse, and she worked hard in Washington and in the state capital. It's her career, you see, as much as mine. For my part, I began to see, five or six years ago, that I might have a crack at the presidency, so I deliberately started sidling toward it, positioning myself for it. I'm a politician, and the top job in my career is the presidency. Why not go for it?''

"You mean, you have no deep convictions..."

The governor was smiling. "The American people don't want anyone with deep convictions as President of the United States. People with deep convictions are dangerous. They're incapable of the art of governing a democracy because they're incapable of compromise. People with deep convictions put everyone who disagrees with them in prison. Then they blow the world up. You don't want that, do you?''

"Maybe I don't mean convictions that deep."

"How deep?"

"Ideas..."

"Listen, Fletch, at best government is a well-run bureaucracy. The presidency is just a doorknob. The bureaucracy is the door. The doorknob is used to open or close the door, to position the door this way or that. But the door is still a door."

"All this stuff about 'highest office in the land'..."

"Hell, the highest office in the land is behind a schoolteacher's desk. Schoolteachers are the only people who get to make any real difference."

"So why aren't you a schoolteacher?"

"Didactic but not dogmatic is the rule for a good politician. Who said that?"

"No one yet. I'm still thinking about it."

"The President of the United States should be a good administrator. I'm a good administrator. So are the other gentlemen running for the office, I expect."

"And you don't care who wins?"

"Not really. Mrs. Wheeler cares." The Man Who laughed. "Your eyes keep popping when I say that."

"I'm a little surprised."

"You really wouldn't want an ambitious person to be President, would you?"

"Depends on what one is ambitious for."

"Naw. I'm just one of the boys. Got a job people expect me to do, and I'm doin' it."

"I think you're pulling my leg."

Again The Man Who laughed. "Maybe. Now is it my turn?"

"Sure. For what?"

"For asking a question."

"Do I have any answers?"

"We established last night you've taken this job on the campaign to feed some ideas into it. Last night, going to sleep, I was wondering what ideas you have."

"Really sticking it to me, aren't you?"

"Sometimes you know a man by his answers."

"Governor, I don't think you want to hear Political Theory According to Irwin Maurice Fletcher, scribbler and poltroon."

"I sure do. I want to hear everybody's political theory. Sooner or later we might come across one that works."

"Okay. Here goes." Fletch took a deep breath.

Then said nothing.

The governor laughed. "Called your bluff, did I?"

"No, sir."

"Talk to me. Don't be so impressed. I'm just the one who happens to be running for office."

"Okay." Fletch hesitated.

"Okay?"

"Okay." Then Fletch said in a rush, "Ideology will never equalize the world. Technology is doing so."

"Jeez."

Fletch said nothing.

In the small stateroom in the back of the presidential campaign bus, The Man Who looked at Fletch as if from far away. "Technology is equalizing the world?"

Still Fletch said nothing.

"You believe in technology?" the governor asked.

"I believe in what is."

"Well, well." The governor gazed at the steamy window. "Always nice to hear from the younger generation."

"It's not a political theory," Fletch said. "Just an observation."

Gazing at the window, the governor said, "There are many parts to that observation."

"It's a report," Fletch said. "I'm a reporter."

Only dim light came through the steamed-over, dirt-streaked bus window. No scenery was visible through it. After a moment, the governor brushed his knuckles against the window. Still no scenery was visible.

"Run for the presidency," The Man Who mused, "and see America."

The stateroom door opened. Flash Grasselli stuck his head around the door. "Anything you want, Governor?"

"Yeah. Coffee. Black."

"No more coffee today," Flash said. "Fresh out."

He withdrew his head and closed the door.

The Man Who and Fletch smiled at each other.

"Someday . . ." the candidate said.

"Why is he called Flash?"

"Because he's so slow. He walks slow. He talks slow. He drives slow. Best of all, he's very slow to jump on people." The governor frowned. "He's very loyal." He then swiveled his chair to face Fletch more fully. "How are things on the press bus?"

"Could be better. You've got a couple of double threats there, that I know of."

"Oh?"

"Fredericka Arbuthnot and Michael J. Hanrahan. Freddie's a crime writer for *Newsworld* and Hanrahan for *Newsbill*."

"Crime writers?"

"Freddie is very sharp, very professional, probably the best in the business. Hanrahan is utterly sleazy. I would deny him credentials, if I thought I could get away with it."

"Try it."

"*Newsbill* has a bigger readership than the *New York Times* and the *Los Angeles Times* put together."

"Yeah, but *Newsbill*'s readers are too ashamed to identify themselves to each other."

"So has the *Daily Gospel* a huge readership, for that matter."

"How did we attract a couple of crime writers? Did somebody pinch Fenella Baker's uppers?"

"The murder last night, of Alice Elizabeth Shields, was the second murder in a week that happened on the fringes of this campaign."

" 'On the fringes,' " the governor repeated.

"They may not be connected. Apparently, Chicago police don't think so. There's a strong possibility they are connected. Strong enough, at least, to attract the attention of Freddie Arbuthnot and Michael J."

" 'Connected.' To the campaign?"

"Don't know."

"Who was murdered in Chicago?"

"A young woman, unidentified, strangled and found in a closet next to the press reception area at the Hotel Harris."

"And the woman at the motel last night was murdered?"

"Clearly."

"You're saying I should get myself ready to answer some questions about all this."

"At least."

"So get me ready."

"All right. Tell me about your arriving back at the hotel last night."

The governor swiveled his chair forward again. "Okay. Willy drove me back to the hotel after the Chamber of Commerce speech."

"Willy Finn, your advance man?"

"Yeah. He flew in as soon as he heard James was out on his ear. We had a chance to talk in the car. After he left me last night, he flew on to California."

"Any idea what time you got to the hotel?"

"None at all. I think Willy was to be on an eleven-o'clock flight."

"You entered the hotel alone?"

"Sure. Presidential candidates aren't so special. There are a lot of us around. At this point."

"Go straight to the elevator?"

"Of course. Shook a few hands on the way. When I got to the suite and opened the door, I saw flashing blue lights in the air outside. Through the living room window. I turned on the lights and changed into my robe. I looked through things people had stuffed into that briefcase."

"You weren't interested in what caused the flashing blue lights, the sirens?"

"My life is full of flashing blue lights and sirens. I'm a walking police emergency."

"Are you sure?"

"What do you mean?"

"You didn't go out onto the balcony, lean over the rail and look down?"

"No."

"Why weren't you wearing your shoes when I got there?"

The governor grinned puckishly. "I always take my shoes off before I go to bed. Don't you?"

"It wasn't because they were wet from your being out on the balcony?"

"I wasn't out on the balcony."

"Someone was. The snow out there was all messed up."

"As I said, a great many people were in that room earlier. I might have even gone out on the balcony myself earlier. That I don't remember."

"You didn't stop at any point on your way to your suite? On another floor, to see someone? Anything?"

"Nope. What's the problem?"

"It doesn't work out, Governor."

"Why not?"

"Time-wise. Either you passed a mob on the sidewalk gathered around a dead girl . . ."

"Possible, I suppose."

"But not likely."

"No. Not likely."

"Or, while you were in the lobby, people—including Dr. Thom—rushed out of the bar to the sidewalk to see what had happened."

"I didn't see either thing."

"One thing or the other had to be true, for you to see the flashing police and ambulance lights from your suite when you got there."

The governor shrugged. "I bored the Chamber of Commerce people to death, but I don't think I killed anybody after that."

"How come Flash wasn't with you last night? Isn't he sort of your valet-bodyguard?"

"I don't like having Flash around all the time. Sometimes I like to sneak a cigar. Also, he doesn't get along too well with Bob."

"Dr. Thom."

"Yes. Bob calls Flash a cretin."

Fletch sat more forward on the edge of the bed. "Hate to sound like a prosecutor, Governor, but did you have personal knowledge of Alice Elizabeth Shields?"

The governor looked Fletch in the eye. "No."

"Do you know anything at all about her murder?"

Again the steady look. "No." In an easier tone, he said, "You seem awfully worried. What should I do? Do you think I should make a statement?"

"Not if it looks like this."

"What should I do? You say we've got these two crime writers attached to us. They're going to write something, sometime . . ."

Fletch said, "I think it would look politically good for you to make a special request; ask the Federal Bureau of Investigation to come in and investigate."

"God, no." The governor pressed back in his chair and then forward. He bounced. "F.B.I. crawling all around us with tape recorders and magnifying glasses? No way! Nothing else would get reported. Nothing I say or do. The story of this campaign would become the story of a crime investigation. It would overwhelm everything I'm doing.''

''I'm sure a discreet enquiry—''

''Discreet, my eye. Just one of those gumshoes comes near this campaign . . . The press would sniff him out before he got off the plane.''

''At some point in the campaign, you get to have Secret Service protection—''

''I'm not going to call for it before anybody else does. I'm in no more danger than any of the other candidates. What would be my excuse? I saw a man at the Chamber of Commerce dinner last night carrying a gun?''

''Did you?''

''Yes.''

''There's a man named Flynn, used to this upper-level sort of thing, I think—''

''No, no, no. Aren't my reasons for not doing so clear?''

''Two women have been murdered—''

'' 'On the fringes of the campaign'—your own words.''

''It might happen again.''

''You run a big campaign like this through the country, and everything happens. Advance men fall off bridges into icy rivers—''

Flash stuck his head around the stateroom's door again. ''Coming up to that school, Governor.''

''Okay.''

Flash came in, closing the door behind him.

''You straight-arm this, Fletch. I'm sorry about the whole thing. I do not take it lightly. But we cannot let this campaign get sidetracked by something that is utterly irrelevant to it. Is that understood?''

''Yes, sir.''

The governor stood up. Flash had taken the governor's suitcoat off a hanger on the back of the door, brushed it, and was holding it out for him. ''Interesting talking to you,'' the governor muttered.

''My privilege,'' Fletch said quietly.

The governor had his hands in the pockets of his suit coat. "Got any money?" he asked.

"Sir?"

"I mean coins. Quarters. Nickels. Dimes. Thought I'd try something out at the school. Got any coins, Flash?"

"Sure." Fletch gave the governor all the coins he had, except for one quarter. Flash gave the governor all his coins.

"And, Fletch, keep those two crime writers away from me."

"Yes, sir."

"Arbuthnot and Hanrahan." The governor was smoothing his jacket. "Sounds like a manufacturer of pneumatic drills."

11

"Yeah, that made pictures," Walsh was to say to his father at the end of the Conroy School visit. "Good for local consumption. Nothing compared to Robbins's dumping himself in the Susquehanna River, though. That will lead the national news. In Winslow you've got to come up with something new, Dad. Say something new. You've got to."

Clearly, The Man Who enjoyed his stop at Conroy Regional Primary School.

All the little kids were agog, but not, at first, at The Man Who might be the next President of the United States.

At first they were dazzled by the big buses with fancy antennas and cars and station wagons in the campaign caravan, *all these people from Washington.*

About Stella Kirchner: *Look at that lady's boots! They got red lines in them! That lady's boots got veins all on their own!*

About Fenella Baker: *Ever see so much face powder? Why don't she itch? 'Spose she's dead?*

About Bill Dieckmann, Roy Philby, etc.: *Bet not one of those dudes could dribble a basketball a half a whole minute.*

About the photographers, wearing more than one camera around their necks: *What they need so many cameras for? They only got two eyes!*

In the school auditorium, while Walsh kept glancing at his watch, the school band played "America" six times, the last no better than the first. The school principal made a speech of introduction, asking the students if they all knew where Washington is. "On the news programs!" The little girl with the gold star on her collar, officially called upon, answered, "There's one in the upper left by Seattle, and one in the middle right by the District of Columbia."

And the principal asked how long one can be President of the United States.

"Forever!"

"Six years!"

"No, four years!"

"Until you get shot!"

Governor Caxton Wheeler made a little speech, goal-orienting the children. He said the country needs good people who believe they can make a difference for the good of the world.

The Man Who was slow to leave the school. He stood among the children. He played magic with coins he took from his pocket. First he made a coin disappear somewhere between his hands. Then he found the coin in a child's shirt pocket, her ear, his mouth. He leaned down and found a vanished coin in the sneaker of a brightly beaming black boy. Instantly the boy searched his other sneaker. To each child he fooled he gave the coin that mysteriously had disappeared from his hands and just as mysteriously reappeared in some unlikely place, such as up the child's own sleeve.

The children quickly forgot about the cameras and the lights and the "city dudes." They stood on chairs and piled on top of each other, tumbled over each other, begged to be the next fooled by the presidential candidate. The governor laughed as hard as the children. His eyes were as bright as theirs.

They pressed against him. "Don't go, sir. You're better than gym!" He hugged them to him.

The members of the press straggled every which way.

"Hey, Fletch," Roy Filby stage-whispered. "Want to go to the boys' room and pull on a joint?"

Fenella Baker was debating the abortion issue in a loud voice with the dry-mouthed school principal.

Andrew Esty was insisting to someone who could have been a math teacher that *Deuteronomy* be tried as a teaching method.

Mary Rice told Fletch that Michael J. Hanrahan was asleep on the press bus.

A photographer terrified little girls by bringing his camera close to their faces and setting off flash bulbs rapidly. "Look at that skin! Awesome! What kind of crèmes do you use, honey?"

Outside the school's main office, some of the reporters bent over the low wall phones, jabbering rapidly in low voices. Other reporters waited.

What's the story? Fletch wondered. Today presidential candidate Caxton Wheeler urged children to continue growing up?

Outside it had stopped snowing. But the sky was still gray and heavy.

"That was nice," Fletch said to Walsh on the driveway in front of the school.

"Yeah. Dad used to play those tricks on me. It was how he gave me my allowance every week."

"Does he still?"

Walsh grinned. "I still think money should come out of my own nose." As his father approached, he said, "Yeah, that made pictures. . . ."

Two of the television station wagons already were leaving the school's parking lot. The rear end of one wagon slid sideways entering the road.

In the driveway, the governor was waving good-bye to the children through the school windows. "I've got an idea for the Winslow speech, Walsh," he said. "Let me work on it."

"The congressman is supposed to be here." Walsh turned around to face the campaign bus. Then he said, "My God."

At the steps of the campaign bus, between the two women volunteers who were to be the reception committee for the congressman, stood a petite, grandmotherly woman.

The governor turned around.

On the steps of the bus, volunteer coordinator Lee Allen Parke raised his hands in futility.

"The congressman," observed the governor, "appears to be a congressperson. You gave me the name Congressman Jack Snive."

"That isn't Jack Snive," admitted Walsh. "Somebody goofed."

"What is her name?" the governor asked.

"No idea. What district are we in?" Walsh's eyes scanned the face of the school building. "Are we at the right school?"

"Oh, yes," the governor said. "They couldn't have played 'America' that badly without practicing it." He sighed. "Guess I'll have to call her 'Member.' Strikes me as slightly indecent, but that's politics."

Putting his hand out to the congressperson, the candidate trudged through the slush. "Hi ya," he said happily. "I was looking for you. How are you feeling? Great job you're doing for your district."

He helped her aboard the bus. Smiling at his son, he said to her, "I want to hear what your plans are for the next four years."

12

"Oooooo," said Betsy Ginsberg when Fletch stopped at her aisle seat on the bus. "Is it now I get your attention?"

The bus went over a speed bump in the school driveway. Fletch grabbed on to the backs of the seats on either side of the aisle.

"Just wanted to ask you if you want a typewritten copy of the candidate's profound remarks at Conroy Regional School."

"Sure." She smiled puckishly. "You got 'em?"

"No."

"Pity. Deathless remarks gone with the wind."

"What kind of a story did some of you find to phone in? I saw you at the phone."

"You don't know?"

"No idea."

"Some press rep. you are. You ever been on a campaign before?"

"No."

"You're cute, Fletcher. But I don't think you should be on this one, either."

"What happened?"

"Tell me what happened between you and Freddie in Virginia."

"Nothing. That's the trouble."

"Something must have happened. She's mentioned it."

"Just a case of mistaken identity. At the American Journalism Alliance Convention a year or two ago."

"That the one where Walter March got killed?"

"Yeah."

"So what happened, besides the old bastard's getting killed?"

"I told you. Mistaken identity. Freddie thought she was Fredericka Arbuthnot, and I didn't."

"But she is Fredericka Arbuthnot."

"So I was mistaken."

Andrew Esty rose from his seat at the back of the bus and came forward in a procession of one. He stood next to Fletch. "Mr. Fletcher, that stop at the school raises several issues I'd like to talk to the candidate about."

"Nice stuff you're writing these days, Mr. Esty," Fletch said. "Circulation of the *Daily Gospel* testifies to it."

"Thank you," Andrew Esty said sincerely. "About praying in the public schools."

"I used to pray in school," Roy Filby said from the seat behind Betsy. "Before every exam. Swear like hell afterward."

"What about it?" Fletch asked Esty.

"Is the candidate against children being allowed to pray in school?"

"The candidate isn't against anyone praying anytime anywhere."

"You know what I mean: the teacher setting the example."

"My teacher was a Satanist," Filby said. "She corrected our papers with blood."

Esty glared at him. "The issue of people praying together on federal property—"

"The governor has a position paper on this issue." Standing on the bus swaying down the highway, Fletch's legs and back muscles were beginning to remind him he hadn't really slept in thirty hours.

"I'd like to point out to you, and to the candidate," Esty said unctuously, "that prayer is led in federal prisons."

"Jesus!" exclaimed Filby. "Esty's got a whole new issue. Go for it, Esty! Go, man, go!"

"Officially sanctioned prayer," Esty said precisely.

"Right," said Betsy. "What have prisoners got to pray for?"

"Obviously," Esty continued, "that's a similar so-called violation of the principle of the separation of Church and State."

"Right on," said Betsy. " 'The last person seen by the condemned man was the Sanitation Department's Joe Schmo. Looking at the sanitation worker's green uniform, the condemned man's final words were, "Please wrap my mortal remains in the *Daily Gospel*. Sunday edition, if possible." ' "

"It's a matter of public prayer on government property," Esty said. "Either you can or you can't."

"Would you like an exclusive interview with the candidate?" Fletch asked.

"Yes. There are one or two things of this nature I'd like to ask him about."

"Me too," chirped Filby. "I want to ask him if he'll permit Shubert's 'Ave Maria' to be sung at the White House!"

"I'll see what I can do," Fletch said to Esty.

Down a few seats, seated at a window, Solov stared bug-eyed, blankly. Behind him, Fenella Baker was beckoning at Fletch.

To Betsy, Fletch said, "I have a question for you, okay?"

"The answer is yes," she said. "Anytime. You don't even have to bring a bottle of wine."

Andrew Esty, fingering his *Daily Gospel* button, was glaring at Betsy Ginsberg. He had given up glaring at Roy Filby.

"Later," Fletch said to Betsy.

Roy Filby said to Fletch, "Marvelous, the issues the press dreams up for itself, isn't it?"

Fletch stepped around Esty and went down the aisle to Fenella Baker.

"Two or three questions," she said busily. "First is, did

you save the life of Walsh Wheeler while you were in the service together?"

"No, ma'am."

"What is your relationship with Walsh Wheeler?"

"We were in the service together. He was my lieutenant."

"People do make up stories," she said.

"Don't they just?"

"Have you been close friends ever since?"

"No, ma'am. Last time I saw Walsh was at a football game more than a year ago."

"Were you surprised when you were asked to take on the job of press rep. on this campaign?"

"It's only temporary," Fletch decided. "Until they can find someone with more experience. I'm not worth writing about."

"I agree," she said. "I do hope they find someone who can spell."

Fletch too wondered why Fenella Baker's face didn't itch. Surely some of that powder had been on it since the days of Jimmy Carter.

"Now about this Shields woman—"

"Who?"

"The girl who was murdered last night."

"Was her name Shields?"

"You know perfectly well what I mean."

"I saw your report on it in the newspaper this morning. Great piece."

"I didn't write on it this morning, mister."

"Oh yeah. You did a think-piece on the hockey riot."

"Are you crazy?"

"I must be. I'm here."

"I wouldn't have written on the Shields murder this morning. It isn't a story yet."

"It isn't?"

"It's not a national story until some connection is made between the girl and the campaign."

"Oh. I see."

"What is the connection between the girl and the campaign?"

On a seat at the rear of the bus, Michael J. Hanrahan

appeared to be asleep. His head lolled back on a cushion. His jaw was slack. While Fletch watched, Hanrahan lifted a whiskey pint to his lips and poured down two swallows. He did so without opening his eyes or changing the position of his head.

"What girl?" Fletch asked.

"Next you're going to ask me, 'What campaign?' Are you stupid as well as crazy?"

"I'm trying to follow you, Miss Baker, Apples and bananas—"

"Add up to fruit."

"—make mush."

"Someone said she had been traveling with someone on the campaign. Now, who was it?"

"News to me."

Lansing Sayer, standing in the aisle, touched Fletch on the waist.

Fletch stood straight and turned around. "Are you rescuing me?"

Sayer too turned his back to Fenella Baker. "Fenella," he said, working his mustache histrionically, "is the original eighty-pound bully."

"Great stuff you're writing, Mr. Sayer," Fletch said.

"Want to warn you, ol' boy. Your man is going to be attacked on the so-called welfare shambles in his state. Incidents of people committing welfare fraud."

"When?"

"As soon as he gets back up over thirty percent in the national polls."

"Thank you."

In his seat forward in the bus, Bill Dieckmann was doubled over in pain. Eyes squeezed closed, he held his head in both hands. His white skin glistened with sweat.

Going forward in the aisle, Fletch leaned over and whispered to Freddie, "Do you know what's wrong with Bill Dieckmann?"

Freddie craned her neck to see him. "He does that."

"Does what?"

"Suffers terrible pain. He even whimpers. I think he blacks

out sometimes. I mean, I think there are times he doesn't know what he's doing.''

Fletch watched him from where he stood. "Isn't there anything we can do for him?''

"Guess not.''

Fletch looked forward and aft. "This bus is full of loonies.''

"Pressures of the campaign," Freddie said. She continued reading Jay Daly's *Walls*.

Fletch put his hand on Dieckmann's shoulder. "You going to be all right, Bill?'' Dieckmann looked up at him with wet eyes. "Want me to stop the bus? Get Dr. Thom?''

With both hands, Dieckmann squeezed his head tighter. "No.''

"I will, if you want. What's the matter?''

Eyes squeezed closed again, rocking forward and back in his seat, Dieckmann said in a hoarse whisper, "Leave me alone.''

"You sure?''

Dieckmann didn't answer. He suffered.

"Okay," Fletch said. "If you say so.''

He went back up the aisle to where Betsy was sitting. She was reading Justin Kaplan's *Walt Whitman*.

He bent over her and spoke quietly. "Someone said he saw you having breakfast a few days ago with the girl who was murdered last night.''

"That's right. I did. The breakfast room was filled. People were waiting. The hostess seated us together. Two single women.''

"Did you talk?''

"Sure. Civilities over toast.''

"You're a reporter, Betsy. I suspect you found out one or two things about her.''

"Not really.''

"Like not-really what?''

"She was an ordinary, nice person. She'd been working as a sales clerk in a store in Chicago. Mason's, I think, mostly in the bookshop.''

"Is that all?''

"She liked to read; said she read three or four books a

week. Asked me if I'd read certain people, such as Antonia White, William Maxwell, Jean Rhys, Juan Alonzo. She said Saul Bellow once came up to her counter and asked her for something, some book they didn't have, and he was very courteous about it. She recommended Antonia White's *Frost in May* in particular because, she said, she had gone through parochial schools in Chicago. A Catholic high school; I think she said Saint Mary Margaret's.''

"That was the extent of your conversation?"

"No." Betsy was dredging her memory. "Her father had been killed in an accident when she was nine years old. He worked for the Chicago Waterworks or something. When he was in a ditch, a pipe landed on his head. So she could never think of going to college, you see."

"Oh. Anything else?"

"Her mother never recovered from her father's death, got stranger and stranger, and finally five years ago committed herself to a state home."

"Nothing else?"

"Well, she lived alone in a studio apartment. Married sister, living in Toronto, four children. Her husband owns a gun shop. Sally—that is, Alice Elizabeth Shields; she called herself Sally—had been engaged a couple of times, once to a Chicago policeman who got another girl pregnant and decided he'd better go marry her. Sally never married."

"Is that all you've got?"

"She had something like thirty-seven hundred dollars in a savings account. So she quit her job, sublet her apartment, packed up her Volkswagen, and came a-wandering."

"You didn't get much out of her."

"Just civilities over toast."

"What was her Social Security number?"

"You think I'm nosy?"

"You are a reporter, after all."

"I wasn't interviewing her."

"Why was she following the campaign?"

"Didn't know she was, at that point."

"While you were having breakfast with her, did she mention anyone who is traveling with the campaign by name?"

Betsy thought. "No. But she did seem to know I'm a reporter."

"I wonder if it was something you said."

The bus, at high speed, was climbing a left-curved hill. Fletch had to push off the seat backs not to land on Betsy.

"I mean, she didn't ask me anything about myself."

"You think she had a chance?"

"We were just talking."

"While you were at breakfast with her, did anyone from the campaign say hello to her, nod to her as he went by, wave from across the breakfast room?"

"Not that I remember. She seemed a lonely person."

"Eager to talk."

"As long as she didn't have to be assertive about it."

"You were in the motel bar last night."

"Yes. Drinking rum toffs."

"What's a rum toff?"

"Yummy."

"At any time did you see this girl—Sally, you called her—in the bar with anybody, or leave the bar with anybody, anything?"

"I'm not aware of ever having seen her again since I had breakfast with her in Springfield."

"But you saw her Volkswagen trailing the caravan."

"No. I don't know a Volkswagen from an aircraft carrier."

"They're different."

"I expect so."

"Sea gulls seldom follow a Volkswagen."

"Oh. Well, at least I know the connection between the Shields woman and the campaign."

"What?"

"There isn't one. At least, as far as you can find out. So I won't worry about it. As a story. Yet. Will you tell me if you discover there is a connection?"

"Probably not."

"After all I just told you?"

"Not much. You said so yourself."

"Now I have a question for you."

"You just asked one."

"Walsh has never married, has he?"

"Yes, he likes girls."

"Oh, I can see that. Why don't you introduce me to him? You're his friend."

"You don't know him?"

"Not really. I mean, I've never been introduced as a woman to a man. As a reporter I know him."

"I see."

"He looks like he might go for the homebody type."

"You're a homebody?"

"I could be. If the home had a nice address on Pennsylvania Avenue."

"Sixteen-hundred block."

"Right."

"Lots of rooms to clean."

"You've never seen me with a mop."

"No, I haven't."

"Pink lightning. Flushed with excitement. Ecstasy. You ought to introduce us."

"I will."

"Somebody in a presidential family ought to marry a Ginsberg. We do nice table settings."

"Agreed."

"Tell him you and I worked together in Atlanta."

The bus slowed. The bus driver was looking through the rearview mirror at Fletch.

"I never worked in Atlanta."

"I did."

"Oh. Okay."

"Irwin!" the bus driver shouted.

"Irwin!" Roy Filby echoed. "I'd rather see one than be one!"

"Telephone!" the bus driver shouted. In fact, a black wire led from the dashboard onto his lap.

Fletch said, "We have a telephone?"

"Not for the use of reporters," Betsy said. "Staff only. Want to hear what James said about the duplicating machine?"

"I've heard."

Fletch went forward. The bus driver handed him the phone from his lap.

"Hello?" Fletch said. "Nice of you to call."

Barry Hines said, "You'd better come forward, Fletcher."

"I've always been forward."

"I mean into this bus. Watch the noon news with us."

"Sure. Why?"

"Just heard from a friendly at U.B.C. New York that something unsavory is coming across the airwaves at us."

"What?"

The phone went dead.

Brake lights went on at the rear of the campaign bus. It headed for the soft shoulder of the highway.

Fletch looked for a place to hang up the phone.

"Guess we're stopping for a second. Got to go to the other bus."

The press bus was following the campaign bus onto the soft shoulder.

"Just put the phone back in my lap," the driver said. "I'm not expecting any calls at the moment."

Fletch put the phone in the bus driver's lap.

"How did you know my name is Irwin?" Fletch asked.

The bus driver said: "Just guessed."

13

"We're almost late for the rally in Winslow," The Man Who commented.

"A band will be playing, Dad."

Again the governor tried to see the world through the steamy bus window. "But it's cold out there."

The buses pulled back onto the highway and were gathering speed.

On the campaign bus a small-screened television set had been swung out behind the driver, high up. It faced the back of the bus. A commercial was running for feminine sanitary devices.

"My apologies, ma'am," the presidential candidate said to the congressperson, "for the bad taste displayed by my television set. Not a thing I can do about it." They were sitting next to each other on an upholstered bench at the side of the bus. "Not a damned thing."

Fletch stepped over the governor's feet. He stood near Walsh. "What is it?" He hung on to a luggage rack.

The television newsperson came on and mentioned the

news leads: "Coming up: Senator Upton's advance man killed in automobile accident in Pennsylvania; aftermath of a hockey riot, numbers injured and arrested; presidential candidate Caxton Wheeler hands out money to schoolchildren on the campaign trail."

"Jeez!" Fletch turned toward the back of the bus. Arms akimbo, Flash Grasselli stood against the stateroom's closed door. "Would you believe this?"

"Sure," Walsh said. "It's true."

"At least I'm not the number-one news lead," the governor said. "Guess they don't think too badly of bribing school-children."

" 'Bribing schoolchildren,' " echoed Fletch.

Phil Nolting said, "That's what they're gonna make out of it."

A commercial was running for "Sweet Wheat, the break-fast cereal that makes kiddies yell for more."

"Yell with the toothache," Paul Dobson said. "They're yelling because it makes their teeth hurt!"

"Make 'em hypertensive with sugar at breakfast," Phil Nolting intoned, as if quoting, "then slap 'em down at school."

Except for Barry Hines, who was talking quietly on the telephone, those aboard the campaign bus suffered silently as a few more details were given of Victor Robbins's death, film was run; of the hockey riot, film was run. Then: "This morning at Conroy Regional School Governor Caxton Wheeler, while on his campaign for the presidency, handed out coins to the primary school students." Film was run. The Man Who, surrounded by excited children, was doing some trickery with his hands. Then the camera zoomed in to show in close-up the governor's hand press-ing a coin into the hand of a child. "Some received dimes, others quarters, others half dollars. And some got none at all. . . ."

"Did one run all the way home?" Phil Nolting asked.

"Must have," Paul Dobson said. "Somebody must have told on us."

On screen the newsperson was sitting with an extremely

thin, hawk-nosed, nervous-looking woman. "Here in our studio with us is the distinguished pediatric psychiatrist, Dr. Dorothea Dolkart, author of *Stop Resenting Your Child* and *Face Up to Bed-wetting*."

"Jeez," said Paul Dobson. "How can these experts get to the television studios so fast? It's only been an hour. Don't they have other jobs?"

"Doctor Dolkart, you've just seen here on our studio monitor presidential candidate Caxton Wheeler handing out coins to some of the pupils at Conroy School. Can you assess for us the effect this would have upon the pupils?"

"Extremely damaging. Traumatic. First, there is the point that here we have an adult who is making himself popular, or trying to, by the device of handing out money."

"Setting somewhat the wrong standard, you think?"

"An absolutely materialistic standard."

"In fact, he's teaching the children you can buy friendships."

"And this happened in a school setting, where children are used to learning things. With authority, if you understand me."

"Yes. The effect upon the children who didn't receive any money . . . ?"

"Disastrous. Very few people in this country have greater prestige in the eyes of children—in the eyes of any of us—than a presidential candidate. Maybe the President himself, a few football players, what have you. Meeting, even seeing, a man who might become the most powerful leader on earth, is one of the most memorable experiences of our lives. For those who did not receive any coin at all from Governor Wheeler, the implied rejection is severe. These children this morning were scarred for life and, I might add, totally unnecessarily."

On the campaign bus The Man Who said, "Oh, my God."

"And the children who did receive the coins? Do they feel better about things?"

"No. If anything, they feel worse. Because completely arbitrarily they were singled out for this special attention, this gift, from a grown-up of the greatest prestige. It would have been one thing if the candidate had handed out coins to children who had won the honor through some sort of an academic or athletic contest. As it is, the children who actually got the coins from the governor have been burdened with terrible guilt feelings because they received something which they know they didn't deserve, while their schoolmates got nothing at all. . . ."

"I guess James would have stopped me from doing that." The Man Who hung his head in his hands. "He would have known how it would look to the press. What they could make of it. Handing out money to kids. Gee. I guess ol' James is laughing up his sleeve at this moment, wherever he is."

Fletch said to Walsh, "I'm beginning to suspect I have a short career as a press representative."

"It's an impossible job," Walsh said.

The television was offering the usual variety of weather reports.

"Well." The governor put his hand on the hand of the grandmotherly congressperson. "Guess I just wrecked the life of every schoolchild in your district." He smiled at her. "Do you agree?"

She lifted her hand from under his on the divan. "Yes, Caxton. It was totally irresponsible of you. Damned insensitive."

He looked at her a moment to see if she was serious. She was. He stood up and wandered to the back of the bus where Walsh and Fletch were standing.

"Sorry," Fletch said to him. "I thought it looked nice. Was nice."

"Got to be aware of how things look to the press," Walsh said. "Every damned little thing. What they can make of it."

"How do we pick up from here?" Fletch asked the governor. "Make a statement . . . ?"

The governor smiled. "Naw. Let them hang themselves on their own silliness. Psychiatrists be damned. I don't think the American people are apt to consider an older man handing out coins to little kids as Beelzebub." He beckoned Flash forward with his finger and called Barry Hines. When they came, he said, "Listen, guys. In Winslow I don't want that old bitch on the platform with me."

"The congressperson?" Barry asked in surprise.

They were speaking softly.

"Body-block her. Trip her. Hide her purse. Slow her down. I don't care what you do. Just keep her off the platform."

"This is her district, Dad."

"I don't care. She's lookin' to speak against me, anyway. Let's not give what she has to say against me the prestige of pictures of her standin' with me."

"Okay," Flash said.

"We'll show the old bitch exactly how sensitive I am."

The governor opened the door to the stateroom. "Come here, Fletch."

"Yes, sir?"

"Close the door."

Fletch did so. "Again, I'm sorry about that. I never dreamed the press—"

"I'm not about to chew you out."

"You're not?"

"'Course not. Who was the first one to say 'If you can't stand the heat get out of the kitchen'?"

"Uh—Fred Fenton?"

"Who was he?"

"Cooked for Henry the Eighth." The governor gave him a weird look. "Buried under the chapel at the Tower of London. Forgot to take the poultry lacers out of roast falcons."

The governor chuckled. "You're making that up."

"Sure I am."

"Got anything for me?"

"Anything . . . ?"

"You've been on the press bus most of the morning."

"Oh. Yeah. Lansing Sayer says Upton's team is going to hit you with some evidence of welfare fraud in your state. As soon as you climb back over thirty percent in the popularity polls."

"That so? Good for them. That's smart. There's welfare fraud in every state. Also housebreaking and vandalism. I'll get Barry on that. Have his people put together my record on stopping welfare abuse. Also, let's see: the amount of welfare fraud in other states. I'll make an issue of it myself as soon as I get near thirty percent in the polls.''

"Amazing how things become campaign issues."

"Anything else?"

"Andrew Esty wants an exclusive interview with you."

"The *Daily Gospel* guy?"

"Yeah. He's trying to develop something. If people are allowed to pray together in federal prisons, why not in public schools?"

"Wow. 'Take Prayers out of Prisons.' "

"I think he means 'Put Prayer back in Schools.' "

"No foolin'."

The bus was going slowly, obviously in traffic. It was stopping and starting, probably at red lights.

"What do we do for him?" Fletch asked.

"Pray for him," the governor said. "Anything else?"

"Found out more about the woman murdered last night. An intelligent, apparently unattached, lonely woman."

"How do you know she was intelligent?"

"She was a reader. From her reading."

"Political reading?"

"No."

The bus was inching forward. A band could be heard playing.

"Very quickly I'm going to get tired of that topic." The governor leaned over and looked through the steamy window. Instinctively he waved at the crowd outside with the flat of his hand. Fletch was sure no one outside could see the candidate through the windows. "Someday I'd love to have a Klezmer band playing for me," the governor said. "I love Klezmer bands."

The bus stopped.

"Walk out with me." The governor took Fletch's arm in his fist. "Stay between me and that congressbitch. Paddle her backward. Got me? Give it to her in the ribs, if you have to."

"Gotcha."

"And tell Lansing Sayer he can have an exclusive interview with me anytime he wants it."

"Yes, sir."

When Fletch opened the stateroom door, their ears were assaulted by the band's playing "Camptown Races."

" 'Jacob, make the horse go faster and faster,' " the candidate said. " 'If it ever stops, we won't be able to sell it.' "

14

"It's nice of you all to come out and give me a chance to talk to you, on such a cold, raw day," The Man Who said. The noontime crowd was crammed into the smallest intersection in Winslow. Advance man Willy Finn had planned the rally for the smallest outdoor space in Winslow deliberately. A small crowd looks bigger in a small space; a larger crowd looks huge. The presidential candidate had attracted a good-sized crowd. "You know, a presidential campaign is just a crusade of amateurs. I can tell you, my friends in Winslow, this campaign to let me serve you the next four years in the White House needs your help."

Standing in slush at the edge of the crowd, Fletch said to himself, "Wow."

At his elbow, Freddie Arbuthnot said, "He said something new."

The mayor, the city council, the chief of police, the superintendent of schools, a judge, the city's oldest citizen (standing up at ninety-eight, bundled well against the cold), probably two dogcatchers and the fence-viewer were the reception committee awaiting the candidate as he got off the bus. A band was playing "The Battle Hymn of the Republic." Not moving from the bottom of the bus steps, Governor Wheeler shook hands with each member of the committee, said a few words to each. The mayor then led him through the crowd to the platform set up on the corner of Corn Street and Wicklow Lane, gestured to the band for quiet, and did his Man-Who speech, peppered with many references to his own efforts to gain control of the city budget.

Fletch watched Barry Hines and Flash Grasselli escort the short congressperson in entirely the wrong direction, right into the middle of the crowd, where she got bogged down shaking hands and listening to her constituents' griefs.

Fletch introduced himself to the local press. He handed out position papers on the crop subsidy programs. He and the local press and only some of the national press stood in a roped-off area to the right of the platform.

Some members of the national press, Roy Filby, Stella Kirchner, Betsy Ginsberg, Bill Dieckmann—who seemed completely recovered—had spotted a bar-café half a block up and decided to go there for drinks during The Speech. "Tell us if he gets shot, or hands out money to the crowd or something, Fletch."

Three television cameras were atop vans and station wagons. News photographers stood near the platform.

Hanging from the second-floor windows of the First National Bank of Winslow at the corner of Corn and Wicklow was a huge American flag. It had forty-eight stars.

Now The Man Who was saying, "The world has changed, my friends. You know it and I know it, but the present incumbent in the White House doesn't seem to know it. His brilliant advisors don't seem to know it. None of the other candidates, Republican or Democrat, who want to see themselves in the White House the next four years seem to know it. . . ."

"This isn't his usual speech," Freddie said. "This isn't The Speech."

" . . . It used to be that what happened in New York and Washington was important in Paramaribo, in Durban, in

Kampuchea. Nothing was more important. Well, things have changed. Now we know that what happens in Santiago, in Tehrän, in Peking is terribly important in New York and Washington. Nothing is more important.''

Fletch said: "Wow."

" . . . The Third World, as it's called, is no longer something out there—separate from us, inconsequential to us. Whether we like it or not, the world is becoming more sensitive. The world is becoming covered with a network of fine nerves—an electronic nervous system not unlike that which integrates our own bodies. Our finger hurts, our toe hurts and we feel it as much as if our head aches or our heart aches. Instantly now do we feel the pain in Montevideo, in Juddah, in Bandung. And yes, my friends in Winslow, we feel the pain from our own, internal third world—from Harlem, from Watts, from our reservations of Native Americans . . ."

Fletch said: "Wow."

Freddie was giving him sideways looks.

" . . . There is no First World, or Second World, or Third World. This planet earth is becoming integrated before our very eyes!"

"He's not going to . . ."

"He's not going to what?" she asked.

" . . . You and I know there is no theology, no ideology causing this new, sudden, total integration of the world. Christianity has had two thousand years to tie this world together . . . and it has not done so. Islam has had six hundred years to tie this world together . . . and it has not done so. American democracy has had two hundred years to tie this world together . . . and it has not done so. Communism has had nearly one hundred years to tie this world together . . . and it has not done so."

"He's doing it."

"He's doing something all right," she said.

Fletch's eyes studied the faces in the crowd. He was seeing faces blue with cold, noses red. He was seeing eyes fixated on The Man Who might become the most powerful person on earth, have some control over their taxes and their spending, their health care, their education, how they spent their days and their nights, their youths, working years, and old age, their lives and their deaths. For the most part, in the cold, their ears were covered with scarves and mufflers.

The congressperson was working with as much speed as possible through the thick crowd to the platform. She was still allowing her hand to be shook, still mouthing a responsive sentence here and there, but her face was stony. With all apparent graciousness, Barry Hines and Flash Grasselli were still turning her around to face the bulk of her constituency.

" . . . You and I know what is tying this world together, better than any band of missionaries, however large, ever have or ever could; better than any marching armies ever have or ever could . . ."

"What is he saying?" Freddie demanded. She checked the sound level of the tape recorder on her hip.

Fletch said, "Gee, I dunno."

"Today," The Man Who continued, "satellites permit us to see every stalk of wheat as it grows in Russia, every grain of rice as it grows in China. We can see every soldier as he is trained in Lesotho or Karachi. We can fly to Riyadh or Luzon between one meal and another. Every economic fact regarding Algeria can be assimilated and interpreted within hours. It is possible to poll the entire population of India regarding their deepest political and other convictions within seconds. . . ."

Freddie said: "Wow. Is he saying what I think he's saying?"

Walsh Wheeler, who had been walking slowly, unobtrusively through the crowd, began to move much more quickly toward the campaign bus. The congressperson had struggled her way through the crowd and was almost at the steps to the platform.

"I dunno."

" . . . You and I, my friends, know that technology is tying this world together, is integrating this world in a way no theology, no ideology ever could. Technology is forming a nervous system beneath the skin of Mother Earth. And you and I know that to avoid the pain, the body politic had better start responding to this nervous system immediately! If we ignore that which hurts in any part of this body earth, we shall suffer years more, generations more of the pain and misery of spreading disease. If we knowingly allow wounds to fester in any particular place, the strength, the energies of the whole world will be sapped!''

The crowd of photographers on the steps to the platform was blocking the congressperson's ascent. She could not get their attention, to let her up.

''... American politics must grow up to the new realities of life on this planet! Technology brings us closer together than any Biblical brothers! Technology makes us more interdependent than any scheme of capital and labor! Technology is integrating the people of this earth where love and legislation have failed! This is the new reality! We must seize this understanding! Seize it for peace! For the health of planet earth! For the health of every citizen of this planet! For prosperity! My friends, for the very continuation of life on earth!''

There was a long moment before anyone realized The Man Who was done speaking. Then there was applause muffled by gloved and mittened hands, a few yells: ''Go to it, Caxton! We're with you all the way!'' The band began to play ''Hot Time in the Old Town Tonight.''

At the edge of the platform, The Man Who shook hands with the congressperson as if he had never seen her before, keeping his arm long, making it seem, for the public, for the photographers, he was greeting just another well-wisher. He waved at the crowd and passed the congressperson in the mob on the steps.

At the front of the bus, Walsh Wheeler, Paul Dobson, and Phil Nolting were in heavy consultation.

''Wow,'' said Fletch, still in the press area. ''I never knew it was so easy to be a wizard.''

Freddie said, ''You know something about all this I don't know. You going to tell me?''

''No.''

Freddie Arbuthnot frowned.

She turned back toward the platform. The grandmotherly congressperson was shouting into a ringing amplification system. She was not at all heard over the band.

''But what does it mean?'' Freddie asked.

''It means,'' Fletch answered, ''he's made the nightly national news.''

15

Approaching him, Governor Caxton Wheeler grinned at Fletch. "How do you feel?"

"Like Adam's grandfather."

At the foot of the campaign bus's steps, the governor was still grinning when he turned to his son. Walsh and Phil Nolting and Paul Dobson looked like a wall that had come tumbling down at the blast of a single trumpet. Each face had the same expression of stressed shock.

"How'd I do?" the governor asked.

Walsh's eyes darted around, seeing if any of the press were within earshot. Outside their little circle was a group of thirty to forty retarded adults who had been brought from their institution to meet the presidential candidate.

"'You've got to tell us when you're going to do something like that, Dad."

"I told you I had an idea."

"Yeah, but you didn't mention you were going to drop a bomb—a whole new departure."

"A new speech." Phil Nolting's eyes were slits.

"Sorry," the governor said. "Guess I was really thinking about it while that congressperson was babbling on about the waterway."

"The question always is—" Paul Dobson said in the manner of a bright teacher. "You see, we've got to be prepared to defend everything you say before you say it."

"You can't defend the truth, anyway?" the governor asked simply. "I can."

"Hi, Governor," one of the retarded persons, a man about thirty-five, said. "My name is John."

"Hi, John," the governor said.

"It might have been a great speech, Dad, I don't know. We all just feel sort of punched out by your not telling us you were going to do it."

"I wasn't sure I was going to do it." The governor smiled. "It just came out."

"We'll get a transcript as fast as we can," Dobson said. "See what we can do about it."

The governor shrugged. "It felt right." He put out his hand to one of the retarded persons, a woman about thirty. "Hi," he said. "Are you a friend of John's?"

Aboard the campaign bus, coordinator of volunteers Lee Allen Parke was connecting a small tape recorder to a headset. A typist was at her little desk, ready to work.

"Lee Allen," Fletch said. Parke didn't answer. "Just a simple question."

"Not now," Lee Allen said. "No questions now, please." He said to the typist, "We've got to have an exact transcript of whatever the governor just said, sooner than soonest." He placed the headset over the typist's ears. She settled the earphones more comfortably on herself.

All the buttons on the telephone in Barry Hines's chair were flashing. The phone was not ringing. Barry Hines was nowhere in sight.

"Ah, Lee Allen—" Fletch began.

Lee Allen pressed the *play* button and listened through a third earphone. "Loud and clear?" he asked the typist. She nodded in the affirmative. "My God," he said, listening. "What is the man saying?"

"Lee Allen, I need to know about Sally Shields, Alice Elizabeth Shields—"

"Not now, Fletcher! All hell has broken loose! The governor just went off half-cocked, in case you didn't know."

"No. I didn't know."

"First he's caught bribing schoolkids. Then the hard-drinkin', sexpot congressman we were told to expect turns out to be somebody's great-grandmother. By the way, there's a pitcher of Bloody Marys in the galley, if you want it. Then he makes like Lincoln at Gettysburg at Winslow in a snowstorm. And the day's barely begun!"

"Well begun," Fletch consoled, "is half done."

"Not by my watch." To the typist, who was listening and typing, Lee Allen Parke shouted, "Can you hear?" She nodded yes with annoyance. "We need every word," he said. "Every word."

"You could have answered me by now," Fletch said firmly.

Lee Allen Parke still held the earphone to his head. "What? What, what, what?"

"Did Alice Elizabeth Shields apply to you for a job as a volunteer, paid or otherwise?"

"How do you spell Riyadh?" the typist asked.

"No," Lee Allen said impatiently.

"She didn't?"

"Some of the volunteers reported the caravan was being followed by a Volkswagen. That's all I know about her."

"He said something new?" Bill Dieckmann shouted. His face looked like someone had knocked his hat off with a snowball.

He was one of the group returning to the press bus from the bar–café.

"I guess he did," Fletch admitted.

"New-new?"

Betsy Ginsberg said, "*Nu?*"

Bill Dieckmann's face looked truly alarmed.

"New," said Fletch. "I'm not sure how germaine...."

"Ow," Stella Kirchner said. "Who's got a tape?" She looked sick.

"All those people presently usurping telephones in downtown Winslow," Fletch said. "I expect."

Betsy said, "Have you a tape? Honest, Fletch, I promise we won't spring a story like presidential-candidate-bribes-schoolchildren on you again if you let us hear your tape."

"Ain't got one," Fletch said. "Transcripts will be ready in a minute."

"'Transcripts,'" Dieckmann scoffed. "My editors should read it on the wires while I'm airmailing them a transcript—right?"

"Not on my wire," moaned Filby.

"What did the governor say?" Kirchner asked.

"Well," Fletch said, "roughly he said the world is getting it together despite man's best ideas."

They all looked at him as if he had spoken in a language foreign to them.

"Nothing about the waterway?" Filby looked about to faint.

"Nothing about the waterway," Fletch said.

"Shit," said Filby. "I already reported what he said about the waterway—what he didn't say about the waterway."

Fletch led her onto the campaign bus.

"Oooo," said Betsy in fake cockney. "Don't they live well, though? Telly and everything."

Walsh was chatting with Lee Allen Parke.

"Walsh," Fletch said, "this is Betsy Ginsberg."

"I know Betsy." Walsh gave Fletch an odd, questioning look.

"Not as a person," Betsy said.

"Yeah," said Fletch. "She does nice table settings."

The governor got on the bus while Fletch was collecting copies of the transcripts from the volunteers.

"Come on back here, clean-and-lean," the governor said.

They went into the stateroom together. The governor closed the door. "Sit a minute."

"I'm supposed to be handing these out." Fletch indicated the transcripts in his hand. "Sir."

"They can wait." The governor took off his overcoat and dropped it on the bed. "Tell me what you think."

"I think you're damned eloquent. Sir."

The governor dropped himself into the swivel chair. Fletch did not sit.

"Thank you."

"Take a germ of an idea like that—"

"More than a germ, I think."

"You're brilliant," Fletch blurted.

"Thank you. Now tell me what you think."

Fletch felt himself turning warm. "Frankly, I, ah—"

"You—ah?" The governor was looking at him with patient interest.

"I—ah—didn't know a presidential campaign is so impoverished for ideas. Sir." The governor laughed. "I mean, I thought everything was sort of worked out from the beginning; you knew what you were saying, had to say, from the start."

"You were wrong. Does that surprise you?"

"I'm never surprised when I'm wrong."

"Part of the process of a political campaign is to go around the country listening to people. At least, a good politician listens. You said something this morning that struck me as eminently sensible. Something probably everybody knows is true, but no one has yet said. Probably only the young have grown up with this new reality in their guts, really knowing it to be true."

"Yes, sir. Maybe."

"I think people vote for the man who tells them the truth. What do you think?"

"I hope so. Sir."

"I do too. Politicians aren't philosophers, Fletch. They're not supposed to be. No one wants Tom Paine in the White House. Or Marx. Or Eric Hoffer. Or Marcuse. But they don't want anyone in the White House who doesn't pursue general truths, or know a general truth when he trips over one, either." Rocking gently in his swivel chair the governor

watched Fletch standing stiffly at the stateroom door, and
chuckled. "I think I enjoy shakin' you up. I bet everybody
who has ever met you before has thought you real cool, boy."
Fletch swallowed hard. "That right?"

"I . . . may . . . I . . . ah—"

The governor laughed and held out his hand for a transcript. "Let me have one of those."

Fletch handed him one from the top. He nearly dropped the
pile.

The governor began reading it. "Better see what I said."

16

"Get your damned ass up here." It was clear from Walsh's voice that he meant to be taken seriously.

"Yes, sir, Lieutenant, sir," Fletch said into the hotel room phone. "Please tell me where I'm to get my damned ass up to, sir."

"Room 1220."

Instantly the phone went dead.

Fletch tripped over his unopened suitcase in his scramble for the door.

Fletch had spent the afternoon popping back and forth between the press bus and the campaign bus.

Using the phone on the press bus, he had spent a long time talking with the governor's advance man, Willy Finn, in California, about the arrangements made for that day in Spiersville, that night in Farmingdale, the next day in Kimberly and Melville. Finn had nothing to say about the governor's Winslow speech, although he had already heard of it. He seemed sincerely upset by the death of Victor Robbins.

With the others Fletch visited Spiersville. He grabbed a bag

of stale donuts from a drugstore, ate four of them, spent time
with the local press, provided them with whatever material
they requested. On the wall of a warehouse was scrawled:
LIFE IS NO FUN. Fletch had first seen that message, in English,
on walls and sidewalks in northern Europe in the early 1980s.
After the Spiersville visit, it was discovered that someone had
broken a window of the press bus with a rock.

During the hour-long ride to Farmingdale, Fletch played
poker with Bill Dieckmann, Roy Filby, and Tony Rice. He
won twenty-seven dollars.

In the corridor of the Farmingdale hotel, the doors to an
elevator were open.

Hanrahan was in the elevator. He either smiled or grimaced
at Fletch.

"Up?" Fletch asked.

Hanrahan didn't answer, just kept whatever that facial
expression of his was.

A lady on the elevator finally said, "No, we're going
down." She was wearing a purple cocktail dress and brown
shoes.

Fletch pushed the button for the next elevator.

Walsh flung open the door of Room 1220 immediately
Fletch knocked on it. "What's going on?" he asked.

Door closed, they stood in the short, dark corridor outside
the bathroom. "Okay," Fletch answered. "I'll give the twenty-
seven dollars back."

"Some foul-smelling, crude, filthy-looking reporter was in
my room before I ever got here. He was in here when I
arrived."

"A foul-smelling, crude, filthy-looking reporter?"

"Said he was from *Newsbill*, for Chrissake."

"Oh, *that* foul-smelling, crude, filthy-looking reporter.
Hanrahan, by name. Michael J."

"He was waiting for me when the bellhop let me in.
Sitting in that chair." Walsh stepped into the bedroom and
pointed at one of the chairs near the window. "Smoking a
cigar." The ashtray on the side table had a little cigar ash in
it. "Bastard. Wanted to show me how very, very resourceful

he is, I suppose. Privacy, locked doors don't mean a thing to
Mr. *Newsbill*."

"He was trying to intimidate you."

"He doesn't intimidate me. He makes me damned mad."

Walsh was saying he was mad, but his eyes were not
particularly angry. They appeared more restless, as if he
would have preferred thinking about something else. His
voice was not hot with anger, but more cold with annoyance.

Fletch was hearing a complaint being lodged more as a
matter of form rather than from emotion.

"Michael J. Hanrahan is a foul-smelling, crude, filthy-
looking bastard," Fletch agreed. "He writes for *Newsbill*. I
wouldn't dignify him by calling him a reporter."

"I thought we had someone else from *Newsbill*—that
thoroughly stupid woman, what's her name?"

"Mary Rice."

"Is she any relation to Tony?"

"No. Mary is writing for *Newsbill*. On the campaign
supposedly, but I see her reports seldom get above the
blatantly sensational. I mean, one report she did reported that
one of Lee Allen Parke's great-great-great-grandfathers was a
slave owner."

"Jeez."

"Meaningless stuff."

"Does *Newsbill* ever report from anywhere but the bedroom?"

"Bedrooms, bars, police courts. Runs pages of horoscopes.
Stars on the stars. As news."

"Not only that," Walsh said, "but while I was downstairs
I was attacked by some gorgeous broad who said she was a
reporter for *Newsworld*."

"Oh? What did she want?"

"A complete list of the names of everyone who was in my
father's suite last night. Plus a complete list of names of all
the people who might have had access to his suite last night.
What's she looking for?"

"That's Fredericka Arbuthnot."

"Yeah. Arbuthnot. Since when is *Newsworld* raking smut?"

"You gotta understand, Walsh. Hanrahan and Arbuthnot

are crime writers. That's about all they have in common, but that's what they are. That's their job. They report on crime.''

"So what are they doing on our campaign bus?''

"A woman was murdered last night at the motel we were in.''

"Aw, come on.''

"Another woman was murdered at the Hotel Harris in Chicago while the campaign was there. She was found in a closet off a room being used by the press covering this campaign.''

Walsh sighed. "Can't we deny campaign credentials to crime writers?''

"I've thought of it. Frankly, I think it would get their wind up. Make them more persistent. You can't deny there is something here, Walsh.''

"Not much.'' Walsh glanced at his watch. "Dad wants us in his suite to watch the national news with him.''

"What were Hanrahan's questions?''

"Didn't give him a chance to ask many. I yelled at him, yelled at the bellman, started to phone hotel security, yelled at him some more, called you.''

"So what did he ask you?''

"Said he wanted to ask me about my military record.''

"Your military record? What's that got to do with the price of beans?''

"I told him he could ask the Department of Defense and get my whole record in black and white.'' Walsh had straightened his greenish necktie and was putting on his greenish suit jacket. "Bastard. I didn't shove him through the door, but I had my fingers firmly on his back.''

"Not a whole lot I can do about this, Walsh.'' Fletch opened the door. "The press has the right to inquire.''

When they were in the corridor, Fletch tried the knob of the door to Walsh's room. The door was locked.

"Tell that bastard,'' Walsh said, heading for the elevator, "that if I ever find him in my room again, or the rooms of either of my parents, or of any staff member, I'll have him thrown in jail.''

"Walsh,'' Fletch said, "he'd love that.''

17

"Referring to what he termed the New Reality, Governor Caxton Wheeler, campaigning in Winslow today, seems to have brought a whole new topic and tone to the presidential race. . . ."

Such was the lead on the national nightly news on all three commercial networks. The words differed slightly, but the melody was the same.

Barry Hines sat cross-legged on the floor in front of the three television sets he had set up in the governor's bedroom.

The governor sat in a side chair, watching all three sets. He was in his shirt sleeves, his tie around his collar not yet tied, his shoes off. Flash Grasselli was hanging the governor's clothes in the closet. Fletch was sitting on the edge of the bed. Walsh was standing.

"Victor Robbins died in vain," Walsh quipped. "Upton didn't get the news lead."

"No," the governor said, "he didn't die in vain."

In the living room of the suite, the other side of the closed bedroom door, Lee Allen Parke and some of his volunteers were pouring drinks and chatting up local celebrities. They were waiting, while the governor dressed, to have a private moment with him over a drink before escorting him and Mrs. Wheeler to the mayor's dinner.

For once the networks let the governor's speech run— heavily edited, of course, almost identically edited—but at least without the instant voice-over, a reporter's paraphrase of what the governor said. "Christianity has had two thousand years to tie this world together . . . and it has not done so. Islam has had six hundred years to tie this world together . . . and it has not done so. American democracy has had two hundred years to tie this world together . . . and it has not done so. Communism has had nearly one hundred years to tie this world together . . . and it has not done so. . . . Technology brings us closer together than any Biblical brothers! Technology makes us more interdependent than any scheme of capital and labor! Technology is integrating the people of this earth where love and legislation have failed! This is the new reality!" On all three channels The Man Who stood hatless, in his overcoat, on a platform, a corner of the forty-eight-starred flag and the facade of the First National Bank of Winslow behind him.

The governor had given much the same speech in Spiersville that afternoon. "You may not approve, Walsh," he had said, "but by repeating what I said I will prove I meant to say it."

"The President did not comment immediately on the governor's remarks," the network anchorpersons all reported.

Standing at the side of the bedroom, Walsh commented, "The old boy's waiting to see which way the wind blows."

"A White House spokesman did say the governor's remarks were of such a serious nature that the President wants time to consider them. However, Senator Graves, campaigning in the same primary election, had this to say:"

"Fools rush in," said Barry.

Senator Graves's wide face filled the screens, one after another, his strident voice cutting across America. "Did I hear Governor Caxton Wheeler say Christianity and democracy don't work? Well, I don't believe that. And I don't think most of the people in America believe that!"

The people in the bedroom of Governor Caxton Wheeler, including the governor himself, were absolutely silent. Walsh visibly swallowed hard.

The news anchorperson said, "Senator Upton could not be reached for comment since he was flying to Pennsylvania this afternoon, where his old friend and campaign aide died in an automobile accident this morning."

"See?" the governor said quietly. "Ol' Vic didn't die in vain. Kept Upton from having to make a statement before he was ready."

Studded with commercials, the news programs continued: Victor Robbins's car being lifted from the icy Susquehanna River by crane; eulogistic quotes on Victor Robbins from the President of the United States and most of the presidential candidates (the words differed slightly but the melodies were the same); the President in the Oval Office signing a bill obliging a tribe of Native Americans to exploit the natural resources of their reservation; more film of the hockey riot the night before, with interviews with players and fans. ("Someone punched me," each said. No one said, "I punched someone.") One network showed Governor Caxton Wheeler handing out coins to the children at Conroy School during the body of the telecast, with expert negative comments; a second used the item as a soft-news last feature; the third did not refer to it at all, but instead, for its last feature, used film of a monkey in Louisiana who had learned to write *hokku* on a computer.

None referred to the death of Alice Elizabeth Shields the night before.

"I don't know, Dad." Walsh shook his head. "I don't know."

"What don't you know?" The governor's voice was challenging.

"You did say something about Christianity and democracy not working."

"I did not!" the governor expostulated. "I said neither idea, no idea, has succeeded in integrating the world, the people of the world, as technology is doing. Dammit!"

"There's a difference between ideas and delivery systems for ideas," Walsh said sharply.

"There's a difference between ideas and facts," the governor said. "The people of the world will be better served with a few facts."

Barry Hines was walking along the floor on his knees, turning off the three television sets. Quietly, in the tone of a very young person, he said, "I think it was a good speech. What the governor said is true, when you think about it. Don't get thrown, Walsh, just because Graves took a cheap shot."

"Yeah," said Fletch. "You know how deep Graves is."

The door to the living room opened.

Doris Wheeler entered.

She wore an evening gown, with a taffeta wrap across her big shoulders. She closed the door behind her.

She took a step forward with all the presence of a Wagnerian soprano.

"Caxton," she said solemnly, "you've just lost the presidency."

The governor's face whitened. "Wait a damned minute!"

"Wait for what?" Doris Wheeler stepped nearer the center of the big bedroom. "For you to make an even bigger fool of yourself?"

Walsh faded into the shadows at the side of the room. Flash Grasselli retreated into the bathroom.

Doris addressed her husband as if they were in a room alone. "Everything you've done today has come as a complete surprise to me. Handing out money to schoolchildren. To *some* schoolchildren. Did Barry tell you what I had to say about that? Keeping Congresswoman Flaherty off the platform in Winslow. Don't tell me you didn't do that on purpose."

The governor looked at Barry, still kneeling on the floor, then back at his wife. It was clear Barry had not transmitted Mrs. Wheeler's criticism to Governor Wheeler.

"And what is this utter crap you uttered in Winslow?"

The governor narrowed his eyes. "Is it crap?"

Doris Wheeler's voice became that of a reasonable lecturer. "Caxton, you know damned well the farmers and merchants of Winslow, of the U.S.A., do not want to hear about the Third World. They want to hear about their taxes, their health programs, their Social Security, their defense, their crop subsidies. The voter is a totally selfish animal! Every time the voter hears the name of a foreign country, he thinks it's going to cost him money.''

"Doris, some things need to be said."

"And what," she asked in an exasperated tone, "is this utter crap about technology?"

Suddenly the governor, still in his chair, necktie still undone, was looking tired.

"You trying to be a statesman, Caxton?" she shouted.

"Mother," Walsh said hesitantly. "You don't want people in the living room hearing you."

"Why not?" she asked in the same loud tone. "They might as well hear! Governor Caxton Wheeler's campaign for the presidency of the United States is over! They might as well finish their drinks here, put their checkbooks in their pockets, go home, and offer their support to Simon Upton or Joe Graves!"

The governor's eyes flicked to Barry Hines as if for support. "Graves just took a cheap shot . . ."

Barry Hines had left a half-empty soft-drink cup on top of the television. With the back of her hand, Doris Wheeler slapped the cup off the television onto the rug.

Governor Wheeler looked at the brown fluid bubbling on the blue rug. Then, wearily, he stood up and went to the mirror and began to tie his tie.

Barry Hines was standing by the door to the living room.

"Caxton," Doris Wheeler said, taking only a step toward his back. "The American people don't trust technology. They don't understand technology. Technology is taking their jobs away from them."

"Come on," the governor said tiredly. "The American people are in love with their technology. Their computer games and toys, their cable televisions. They even have— what do you call 'em?—those things on their tractors, in their pickup trucks—"

"You scrape a layer of skin off your average American," Doris persisted, "and he'll still tell you all technology is the instrument of the devil."

"Oh, Doris."

"And you're up there like a big fool saying technology replaces religion?"

"I said nothing of the sort."

"Technology replaces democracy?"

As he turned from the mirror, he was buttoning the cuffs of his shirt. The muscles in his jaw were working hard.

"You've just quit, Caxton. You've just retired from politics! You retired me!" she shouted. "You self-destructed in one day!"

"It's all our fault," Walsh said. He bit his lower lip. "We were overimpressed by Victor Robbins's death this morning. With the primary in a couple of days, we were trying to make the nightly news."

"I don't need excuses made for me, son," the governor said with annoyance. "I said what I felt like saying, and saying it felt right."

"Well, it certainly cost enough for you to feel good." Her eyes were as hard as a rooster's.

"What real harm has it done?" the governor asked. He called on Fletch: "What's the reaction on the press bus?"

"I don't think they've digested it yet. Not really. I think most of them are just glad to hear something new."

"Sure," scoffed Doris Wheeler. "They'd be delighted to publish Caxton's suicide note."

"Actually—" Fletch hesitated. "Andrew Esty did head for the airport. Said he was leaving the campaign. Called you a godless person."

"Caxton!" exclaimed Doris. "Do you know the circulation of the *Daily Gospel*? Do you realize what that readership means to us? To this campaign?"

"Oh, Esty!" The governor snorted. "Jesus Christ wouldn't have pleased him. Jesus washed the feet of a whore."

Doris Wheeler's face was rising up the crimson scale. "How come you do these stupid things without even consulting me? How come you stood up on your hind legs in Winslow, and again in Spiersville, and spouted a pseudo-profound, pseudo-philosophical, pseudo-statesmanlike speech on the state of the whole world, without consulting me?"

"People are waiting," the governor said.

"Believe me," Doris Wheeler said, brushing Barry Hines aside and opening the door to the living room, "nothing more that is stupid and self-destructive is going to happen today. Not with me at his side. If you all can't stop him from making a fool of himself, I can."

Leaving the room, she left the door open.

The governor swung the door almost closed again. "Gentlemen," he said to Barry, Walsh, Fletch, "while greeting people in the living room, please drop casually into your conversations that we were just playing the television rather loudly in here. What's on television at this hour, Barry?"

Barry thought. "Most places, reruns of 'M*A*S*H,' Archie Bunker, and 'The Muppets.' "

"Right," said the governor. "We were watching a rerun of Archie Bunker while I dressed, with the volume on loud."

In the living room, meeting and greeting went on. Fletch found himself talking to the publisher and chief editorial writer of *The Farmingdale Views*. They wanted to be sure the governor believed absolutely in freedom of the press and had some ripe things to say about a certain federal judge; Fletch assured them the governor believed in freedom of the press without reservation and did not intend to appoint federal judges without thorough research into their local backgrounds.

The look of mild alarm and polite curiosity on everyone's face when the governor entered the living room dissipated slowly as more drinks were poured and Archie Bunker was mentioned.

Doris Wheeler was never still. She kept moving around the room, her eyes apparently in everyone's face simultaneously, appearing to hear, to agree with everything.

The governor stood with his hands in his pockets, chatting with a slowly changing group of people around him, making pleasantries, laughing easily.

Walsh was in earnest conversation near the bar table with five or six people in their twenties.

After a few moments, the governor came over to Fletch, gripped him by the elbow and, nodding at them kindly, faced him away from the publisher and the editorial writer. "Fletch.

Find Dr. Thom for me. Have him come up here. No black bag. He'll know what I need.''

The hand holding Fletch's elbow shook ever so slightly.

Fletch said, "Yes, sir.''

18

"Hello, Ms. Arbuthnot?" Fletch said into his bedroom telephone.

"Yes?"

"Glad I caught you in."

"In what?"

"The shower?"

"Just got out of it."

"And did you sing your 'Hoo boy, now I wash my left knee, Hoo boy, now I wash my right knee' song?"

"Oh, you know about that."

"Used to hear you through the wall in Virginia. Key of C in the morning, F at night."

"I take a cold shower in the morning."

"I was just about to order up a sandwich and a bottle of milk to my room. I could order up two sandwiches."

"Yes, you could, Fletch. If you want two sandwiches."

"I only want one sandwich."

"Then order only one."

"You're not getting the point."

"I'm trying not to be as presumptuous as some people I know."

"You see, I could order up one sandwich for me. And one for a friend. Who might come along and eat with me."

"Entirely reasonable. Do you have a friend?"

"I was thinking you might be that friend, seeing you've taken a shower and all."

"Nope. I wouldn't be."

"What makes you so certain?"

"I'm certain."

"We could eat and slurp milk and maybe even we could sit around and sing 'Great Green Globs of Greasy Grimy Gopher's Guts.' "

"Nope. We couldn't."

"Aw, Freddie—"

"Look, Fletch, would you mind if I hung up now? I'm expecting a phone call from Chicago. Then I have to call Washington."

"Okay," Fletch said. "I'll call you back after you change your mind."

He called room service and ordered up two club sandwiches and a quart of milk.

His shoes were already off. He took off his shirt and fell on his back on the bed.

His bedroom was virtually identical to the room he'd had the night before, to the same centimeter of space, to the autumnal, nondirtying color scheme, to the wall mirror tilted to reflect the bed, to the heating system that wouldn't cool off, to the number of too-small towels in the bathroom, to the television he had discovered produced only pink pictures. The painting on the wall was of mountaintops instead of a sailboat. For a moment Fletch thought of American standardization and the interchangeability of motel rooms, motels, airports, whole cities, national news telecasts, and presidential candidates.

The bedside phone rang. Fletch said into the phone: "Knew you'd change your mind. Ordered you a club sandwich."

A man's voice said: "Nice of you. Can you have it sent to Iowa?"

"I suppose so," agreed Fletch. "But who's in Iowa?"

"I am," the man's voice said. "Rondoll James."

Fletch sat up on the bed. "I. M. Fletcher, Mr. James."

"Call me James, please. My parents spotted me with a first name no one's ever spelled right—Rondoll, you know? like nothing else you can think of—so early on I gave it back to the Registry of Births."

"I know the problem."

"No one ever spelled your first name right either?"

"Everyone did. You want your job back?"

"Not right away. I'm in Iowa for the funeral of Vic Robbins."

"He died in Pennsylvania."

"His home is in Iowa. His body's being flown here tonight."

"You good friends?"

"The best. Vic taught me much over the years. Who wrote Caxton's remarks on Vic's death? Walsh?"

"Yeah. The governor was in a factory when we got the news."

"The statement would have been a hell of a lot warmer, if I had been there. Sometimes these guys forget who really runs American politics. So how do you like my job?"

"I'm not very good at it."

"Hey, you got the lead on all the network news shows tonight. Not bad, first day."

"Yeah, but didn't the story do more harm than good?"

"Get the space, baby. Get the network time and the newspaper space. Builds familiarity. Recognition of the candidate, you know? What the candidate is actually saying or doing is of secondary importance, you know?"

"Did anything like what he was saying come across to the people, James, do you think?"

"I'm not sure. He said technology is tying us together, integrating us, maybe making us more sensitive to each other, maybe even increasing the sense of responsibility for each other. That about it?"

"Yeah. I think so."

"Wonderful part of it was, I was sitting in an airport bar about a thousand miles away from where he was saying it, and I heard him and saw him say it. Sort of proves his point, don't you think?"

"What did other people in the bar think of it?"

"Not much. One guy said, 'There's ol' Caxton spouting off again. Why doesn't he tell me where my wife can get a job?' Gin drinker. The bartender? Typical. No good bartender ever takes sides. Costs him tips."

"Guess it'll be a day or two before anyone digests what the governor was trying to say."

"Longer than that, I. M., longer than that. Something ol' Vic taught me, and it's always proved to be true: statesmanship has no place on a political campaign. A campaign is punch and duck, punch and duck. Fast footwork, you know? Always smiling. The voters want to see fast action. Their attention won't hold for anything more. From day to day, give 'em happy film, and short, reassuring statements. If you really try to say anything, really ask them to stop and think, they'll hate you for it. They can't think, you know? Being asked makes us feel inferior. We don't like to feel inferior to our candidates. Against the democratic ideal, you know? The candidate's just got to keep giving the impression he's a man of the people—no better than they are, just doin' a different job. No one is ever elected in this country on the basis of what he really thinks. The candidate is elected on the basis of thousands of different, comfortable small impressions, not one of which really asks the voters to think."

"How about handing coins out to kids. Was that 'comfortable'? How did that come across?"

"Just fine."

"Yes?"

"You bet. Anytime you can get psychiatrists on television speaking against your candidate, immediately your boy is up three precentage points in the popularity polls. Psychiatrists shrink people, you know? People resent being shrunk."

"You're making me feel better."

"Don't intend to, particularly. And it's not why I'm calling. But as long as we're talking, take this advice: any time you see ol' Caxton looking like he's about to say something profound, stick a glove in his mouth.''

"Appreciate the advice. Why are you calling?"

"Why, sir, to tell you how much I love Caxton Wheeler. And explain to you what I've done for him lately.''

"What have you done for him lately?"

"Put myself out of a job, thank you. If not out of a whole career. Sacrificed myself on the altar of Athena. Wasn't she the goddess of war?''

"Oh, yeah: the broad standing in her backyard with a frying pan. Great statue. Seen it dozens of times, as a kid. The governor told me—''

"To hell with what Caxton told you. I'll tell you." Suddenly whatever James had imbibed in that airport bar became audible in his voice. "I've been with Caxton twenty-three years. I've been his eyes and his ears and his legs and his mouth for twenty-three years, night and day, weekends included.''

"I know."

"I want you to know I love that man. I admire him and love him above all others. I know more about him than his wife, his son, anybody. He's a good guy. I'd do anything for him, including sacrificing myself, which I just did.''

Fletch waited. Eulogies to a relationship never need encouragement from the listener.

James continued: "Caxton ought to be President of the United States. I believe that more than I believe I'm sitting here talking to you. But Doris Wheeler, in case you haven't discovered it, is his weak spot. She's horrible. There's no other way to say it. Horrible. She has no more regard for people than a crocodile. If anything around her moves, she lashes at it and bites it, bites deep. She's been lashin' at Caxton, bitin' him for thirty years now.''

"James, a husband and wife—not our business.''

"Not our business unless one of them is running for public office. Then it becomes our business. You ever hear her talk to a volunteer, or a chartered pilot?''

"Not yet."

"Or a junior reporter, or to her son, or to Caxton himself?''

Fletch didn't answer.

"The word is bitch. Doris Wheeler is an absolute bitch. Sometimes I've been convinced the woman is insane. She becomes violent. She's Caxton's biggest liability, and he won't admit it."

"He knows something—"

"He won't admit it. Always covering up for her. Over the years I've talked to him a thousand times, trying to get him to restrain the bitch. Even divorce her, get rid of her. He never listened to me. And she's getting worse, with all this pressure of the campaign on her. I couldn't keep covering up for her, I. M. I just couldn't. You understand that?"

"Yeah."

"I couldn't cover up for her anymore. Stories were beginning to get out about the way she bullies the governor, the staff, everybody. The way everything either has to go her way, or else she'll kick everybody in the crotch. *Her* campaign. *She'll* run it. And everybody better fall in behind her, or life won't be worth living for anybody."

"The visit to the children's burn center—"

"Was just one of a hundred things. She knew what she was doing. Walsh told her she had to go. Her own secretary, Sully, told her she had to go. Barry and Willy arranged another time for her to meet her friends for indoor tennis. She just walked off and played tennis."

"Why?"

"Because she always knows best."

"Yeah, but why? In this particular instance, so obviously stupid—"

"First, she's convinced she can get away with anything. Whatever happens, it's someone else's fault. Second: vanity. Wouldn't you love to appear among your old cronies, your peers, and play tennis with them as the wife of a presidential candidate?"

"The way I play tennis—"

"Listen—"

"Wait a minute. Wasn't she also raising money for the campaign playing tennis? Badly needed money?"

"I said: we had already arranged for her to play tennis two days later. She didn't even cancel the burn center. Just got in the car and went to play tennis. Look what happened. The nurses got all the kids into their wheelchairs, their roll-beds, into this special reception room. Photographers were there, reporters. The bitch never showed up. You realize the pain she caused? You don't move kids with burns, and then go play *tennis*!''

"So why does the governor blame you for it?"

"He can't blame his wife. He never blames his wife. Always before, I've covered up for her. Done a deal with the photographers, you know? Made some half-assed explanation, said, 'If you don't report this, I'll provide you with photo opportunities you never dreamed of—the governor in the shower stark naked smoking a cigar, you'll win the Pulitzer Prize,' you know? This time I couldn't do that, I. M. Wouldn't.''

" 'Wouldn't.' "

"I'd had enough of it. The governor wouldn't listen to me, all these years. The situation was getting more serious. She's getting worse. His chances of getting to the White House are getting better and better, and she's ruining them. So I let the situation get reported. I thought maybe if Caxton saw what all this looked like in the press, for once, he'd at least try to restrain the bitch.''

"What makes you think he can?"

"He has to. Somebody has to. Caxton Wheeler shouldn't be President of the United States because his wife's a nut?"

"They've come a long way together, James."

"That they have—a long way to fall over a cliff."

"If she's so impossible, why has he stuck with her? Divorce wasn't invented Sunday, you know."

"Want three good reasons why he hasn't divorced her?"

"Yeah. Gimme three."

"First, divorce still doesn't go over so big with the voters. Despite President Ronald Reagan. People can still be found to say, 'If a man can't run his own house, how do you expect him to run the White House?' "

"That's one."

"Two, she's got the money. She is a wealthy, wealthy lady in her own right. Her daddy horned in on the oil business and made a barrel of money. A politician's life is risky and expensive, you know. Nothing lubricates a politician's life better than oil."

"That's two."

"Three, I deeply suspect Caxton loves the bitch. Can you believe that? Don't ask me how or why. Sometimes people whom you'd think would know better actually do love the last person in the world they should love. I've known lots of jerks like that. Their wives are ruining them with every word and gesture and all these jerks say is, 'Where would I be without sweet ol' honey-pie?' Love, I. M., is as blind as justice. Maybe you've noticed."

"And just as elusive."

"Boy, am I glad my wife ran away with her psychiatrist fifteen years ago. There was a broad who needed shrinking. What an inflamation she was."

"I don't know, James. What am I supposed to do?"

"Carry on, brother. Carry on. I just want you to know what's between Caxton and me."

"His wife."

"I love him. I admire him. I want to see him President of the United States. I'd do anything to see that. Anything. What I'm saying is, feel free to call me anytime about anything."

"Thank you."

"They threw me over, but that doesn't matter. I'll still do anything I can for Caxton."

Fletch soon discovered that all he need do to make his phone ring was to put the receiver down into the cradle.

Immediately after he hung up from trying to make clear things that were not at all clear to himself for a rewrite editor at *Newsweek* magazine, he found himself answering the phone to his old Marine buddy, Alston Chambers.

"Nice to hear a friendly voice," Fletch said.

"What's happening, Fletch?"

"Damned if I know."

"Just heard on cable news you've been made acting press

representative for Governor Wheeler's campaign. I saw you on the tube.''

'' 'Acting press secretary'? I guess so.''

"Why are you doing that? You gone establishment?''

"Walsh called me late at night. Said he needed help desperately. I mean, he convinced me he was desperate.''

"Wow, a presidential campaign. What's it like, Fletch?''

"Unreal, man. Totally unreal.''

"I believe you. On television you were wearing a coat and tie.''

"Alston, there have been a couple of murders.''

"What do you mean, 'murders'? Real murders?''

"A couple of women beaten to death. One of them was strangled. They weren't really a part of the campaign, but I think somebody traveling with the campaign had something to do with it.''

"You're kidding.''

'' 'Fraid not.''

"Caxton Wheeler as Jack the Ripper. You're giving a whole new meaning to the phrase *presidential assassin,* Fletch.''

"Very funny.''

"Haven't seen anything about this in the news.''

"We're trying to keep it out of the news. At least, everybody's telling me to keep it out of the news.''

"Having had opportunity to observe you for a long time, Fletcher, I can say you're not good at keeping things out of the news. Especially concerning murder and other skullduggery.''

"You wouldn't believe this situation, Alston. It's like being on a fast train, and people keep falling off it, and no one will pull the emergency cord. Everytime someone falls off, everyone says, 'Well, that's behind us.' ''

"You're right. I don't get it.''

"It's just an unreal world. There's so much power. So much prestige. Everything's moving so fast. The cops are so much in awe of the candidate and his party.''

"Yeah, but murder's murder.''

"Listen, Alston, a lady gets thrown off the motel roof right above the candidate's room, right above where the press have their rooms. And in a half hour the mayor shows up and says to the highest-ranking member of the campaign he can get close to something like, 'Now, don't let my cops bother you.' And he says to the press, 'Please don't besmirch the image of my city by making a big national story of this purely local, unfortunate incident.' ''

"Yeah, but Wheeler. What does the candidate himself say?"

"He shrugs and says, 'There are sirens everywhere I go. I'm a walking police emergency.' ''

"And Walsh?"

"Walsh says, 'A local matter. We'll be gone by morning.' ''

"Taking the murderer with you. Is that what you think?"

"I'm trying to get the governor to permit an investigation. He's convinced the investigation would become the story of the campaign, and ruin his chances for the presidency."

"So ol' Fletch, boy investigative reporter who took an early retirement somehow, is investigating all by himself."

"My hands are tied. I can't go around asking the who-what-where-when-why questions. If I did that, I'd find myself with an airplane ticket home in about ten minutes."

"But you're in there trying, right?"

"Subtly, yes. I'm trying to get to know these people. Besides Walsh, I really only know a couple: Fredericka Arbuthnot, Roy Filby—"

"You'd better hurry up. Two murders in a pattern usually mean a third, a fourth . . .''

"I'm doin' my best, Mr. Persecutor. It's like trying to put out a fire in a circus tent, you know? I can't get anybody to admit there is a fire."

"When I started trying to get you on the phone, Fletch, my intention was to congratulate you on your new job. By the time you answered the phone, I was saying to myself, 'What's the barefoot boy with cheek doin' explaining the establishment to us peasants?' ''

"I like Caxton Wheeler. I want to solve this damned thing."

"What does he want to be President for anyway? If I had his wife's money, I'd buy a whole country for myself."

"A campaign sure looks different from the inside. On the outside it's all charm and smiles and positive statements. On the inside, it's all tension, arguments—"

"And murder?"

"In this case, yes."

"Sometime, when you're talking to Walsh, ask him why he left us so suddenly. I've always been curious about that."

"What do you mean?"

"Don't you remember? After we spent those three days tied to the tops of the trees like cuckoo birds, a few days after we got back to base camp, Lieutenant Wheeler suddenly went home."

"He got sent stateside."

"I know. But how and why? It wasn't time for him to get rowed home. We all knew that."

"How? Because his dad had political pull. Why? Because his dad had political pull. What's the mystery? Walsh didn't have to be in the front lines at all. His dad was a congressman."

"We never knew what happened to Lieutenant Wheeler."

"He had seen enough action."

"We all had."

"Alston, at that point any one of us would have pulled strings to get out of there. If we had strings. You know it. Our dads weren't politicians."

"With rich wives."

"So tell me about yourself. How do you like being chief persecutor?"

"In California, Fletch, we call ourselves prosecutors. And I'm not chief."

"Sent any woe-begones to jail lately?"

"Two yesterday. No outstanding warrants on you, though. I check first thing every morning."

"Haven't been in California lately."

"Well, if you ever really get to be a member of the establishment, Fletch, come on back. California can always use a few more people who wear suits."

The two-hundred-year-old man from room service apologized for being so slow, telling Fletch the hotel was full of reporters following the campaign of "that Caxton Wheeler. Sure wish he'd get elected. Got a cousin named Caxton. First name, too."

"Hello, Freddie?" Fletch had picked up the phone before the man from room service was fully through the door.

"Who's calling, please?"

"Dammit, Freddie."

"Oh, hello, dammit."

"I'm calling to tell you your sandwich is ready."

"Ready for what?"

"Ready to be eaten."

"So eat it."

"Dammit, Freddie, you used to be a nice, aggressive woman."

"Aggressive toward a sandwich?"

"Toward me! I'm not a sandwich! What happened?"

"Your job happened."

"You don't like my job? Neither do I."

"Fletcher, what would you think of a journalist who became too friendly with the press representative of a presidential candidate, upon whose campaign she's reporting?"

"Oh."

"What would you think?"

"Not much."

"You mean plenty, but not good."

"Gee, it's lonely here at the top."

"See? We agree on something."

"I'll quit! I'll quit right now! I've been looking for an excuse."

"What excuse have you got?"

"Wasting food, obviously. Can't waste this good sandwich. Think of all the starving children in Beverly Hills with nothing to eat but Sweet Wheat."

"Good night, Fletch. Sweet dreams."

"Aw. . . ."

Fletch first ate one sandwich, and then the other, and drank the whole bottle of milk.

His phone rang continuously. Members of the press from

around the world were calling him, asking for background to and interpretation of Caxton Wheeler's Winslow speech. Through mouthfuls of ham and chicken and bacon and lettuce and tomato and mayonnaise, Fletch said again and again that there was no background to the governor's speech; that the speech said exactly what it said, no more, no less.

The phone rang while he washed. It rang while he was putting on his shoes, his shirt, and his jacket.

It was ringing when he left the room.

19

"It's none of my business, but—"

"You're right," Bill Dieckmann snapped. Sitting at the bar, he didn't even look up from his beer.

"Just wondering if I can help." The bartender brought Fletch a beer. "Does whatever happened to you on the bus today happen often?"

"None of your business."

"Have you been to a doctor about it?"

"None of your business."

"Agreed," Fletch said. "Let me know if ever I can be of help." He looked around the bar. All motel bars are interchangeable, too. Even the people in them are interchangeable: the morose, lonely businessmen, the keyed-up, long-haul truck drivers, the few locals who are there solely for the booze. "Where is everyone?" Fletch asked. There were only a few campaign types in the bar.

"In their rooms, I guess," Bill answered. "Not getting anything to eat. At the mayor's dinner, not getting anything to eat. Betsy is at the 4-H Club dinner, trailing Walsh. She's probably getting something to eat. Solov's in his room, watching cable television.'' Bill grinned. ''He's not getting anything to eat, either.''

''Does that guy ever take off his overcoat?'' Fletch asked.

''No, no. He was born in it. You can tell he grew up inside it. Each time *Pravda* sends him out of the country his managing editor just moves the buttons for him.''

''Time they moved the buttons again.''

Dr. Thom entered. He put his black bag on the bar beside Fletch.

''Here's a doctor now,'' Fletch said brightly.

''Best bedside manner in the country,'' Bill said. ''If you don't have a temperature when Dr. Thom arrives, you will when he leaves. Good for business, right, Doc?''

''Journalists,'' Dr. Thom said. ''If any journalist ever spoke well of me, I'd instantly overdose on a purgative.''

''Looks like you already have,'' Bill said.

''It's a medical fact,'' Dr. Thom said to Fletch, ''that all journalists are born with congenital diarrhea. Double Scotch, no ice,'' he said to the bartender.

''I'm a journalist,'' Fletch said.

''I trust you vacated yourself before you entered the bar.''

''Mr. Fletcher?'' A woman was standing at Fletch's elbow.

''At least a journalist has to empty himself,'' Bill Dieckmann burped. ''Doctors are born vacuous, and vacuous they remain.''

''Yes?'' Fletch had turned to the woman.

''Are you Mr. Fletcher?''

''Yes. But you can call me Mr. Jones.''

''If only,'' Dr. Thom intoned ever so slowly, ''journalists would vacate themselves privately.''

''I'm Judy Nadich,'' the woman said. ''Feature writer for *Farmingdale Views*.''

''Great stuff you're writing,'' Fletch said. And then laughed. ''I'm sure.''

Judy grinned. ''You liked my last piece? On how to repair cracked teacups?''

''Thought it was great,'' Fletch laughed. ''Read it several times.''

''I knew that one would get national attention,'' Judy said.

''Sure,'' Fletch said. ''Everyone's got cracked teacups.''

"Hey," Judy said. "Seriously. I'm trying to get an interview with Doris Wheeler."

"I think you're supposed to see Ms Sullivan about that."

"I've asked and asked and she says no."

"Why?"

"She says there's no time on Mrs. Wheeler's schedule for a full, sit-down interview. What she means is that the readership of the *Farmingdale Views* isn't worth an hour of Mrs. Wheeler's time. She's right, of course. But it's important to me."

" 'Course it is." Despite her brown hair tied in a knot behind her head, her thick sweater, her thick skirt, her thick stockings and shoes, Judy Nadich was sort of cute. "What do you want me to do?"

"Get me an interview with Mrs. Wheeler," Judy said. "In return for my body."

"Simple enough deal," Fletch said. "Tit for tat."

"Tits for that," Judy said.

"I've never met Ms Sullivan. Never laid eyes on her."

"You could try."

"You want me to call her?"

"Yes, please. She's in Room 940."

"Would you be content with a follow-along?"

"What's that?"

"You just follow along with Mrs. Wheeler for an hour or two, you know? Up close. You don't really interview her. Report what she does and says to other people. 'An hour in the life of Doris Wheeler' sort of thing. Done right, makes damned good reading."

"Sure. Anything."

"Okay. I'll call Ms Sullivan. Watch my beer, will you?"

"Sure thing."

Dr. Thom was saying ". . . journalists are the only people on earth asked not to donate their remains to science. It's been discovered that journalists' hearts are so small, they can be transplanted only into their brethren mice."

"Keep these guys separated, will you?" Fletch asked Judy.

"Sure." She climbed onto Fletch's barstool. "Bet you guys don't know how to repair a cracked teacup..."

"Ms Sullivan? This is Fletcher."

The first few times Fletch had tried Room 940 he had gotten a busy signal.

"What do you want?" Her voice was surprisingly deep.

"Hello," said Fletch. "We haven't met."

"Let's keep it that way. As long as we can."

"What?" Fletch said. "No camaraderie? No *esprit de corps*? No we're-all-in-this-spaceship-together sort of attitude?"

"Get to it." Her voice was almost a growl.

"No simple cooperation?"

"Yeah, I'll cooperate with you," she said. "You stay on your side of the fence and I'll stay on my side. Okay?"

"Not okay. There's a young lady here, a reporter from the *Farmingdale Views*. She's spending tomorrow morning with Mrs. Wheeler. Just observing."

"Over my dead body."

"That can be arranged."

"She's a stupid, soft, little local bitch. Who are you to make arrangements for Doris?"

"I'm giving her a press pass to spend tomorrow morning with Doris Wheeler, close up, with photos. You don't like it, you can stuff it up your nose."

"Fuck you, Fletcher."

"Yeah, you say that," Fletch said, "but what are you going to do?"

Dr. Thom and Bill Dieckmann were gone from the bar. Judy Nadich sat over an empty glass.

"What happened to my beer?" Fletch asked.

"I drank it," Judy said.

"Was it good?"

"No."

He handed her the press pass he had written out and signed on a piece of note paper. "Here," he said. "You're spending tomorrow morning observing Mrs. Wheeler close up. Don't get too much in the way."

"Thanks." Judy looked dubiously at the handwritten note. "Sullivan was nice about it, huh?"

"Sure. Why not? Mrs. Wheeler will be very glad to have you with her."

Flash Grasselli had come over from a table at the back of the bar and was standing behind Fletch.

"Do I get to give you my body, now?" Judy asked.

"What town am I in?" Fletch asked.

"Farmingdale, dummy."

"Next time I come through Farmingdale," Fletch said.

"You rejecting me?"

"No," Fletch said. "Just don't believe in prepayment."

"Mr. Fletcher, may I buy you a beer?" Flash asked.

"Sure," Fletch said. "Hope it's better than the last one. Judy here says my last beer wasn't very good."

"Why are you called Flash?"

Flash Grasselli and Fletch had taken two fresh beers to Flash's small table at the back of the dark motel bar. Judy Nadich had left with her tote bag to prepare herself for her morning observing Doris Wheeler.

"From boxing."

"Were you fast?"

Flash seemed to be chewing his beer. "I'm not sure."

Flash had the eyebrow cuts of a boxer, but his eyes were steady and his nose had been born pug.

"They're always kidding me, the reporters," Flash said. "They come to me for real information about the Wheelers, and I never give them any. I just talk about the old days."

"What kind of things do they ask you?" Fletch asked.

"Oh, you know. The governor's life." Flash looked directly at Fletch. "His disappearances."

Fletch knew he was being handed a line of inquiry. "He disappears? What do you mean, he disappears?"

"His fishing trips. Sometimes they're called that. He doesn't know anything about fishing. So they call them hunting trips. The governor wouldn't shoot a rabbit if he was starving. You know." Flash smiled. "The trips the governor takes with those prostitutes he hires. His week-long sex orgies. You know about them. His drunken benders. He spends them in the mob's hideaways."

Fletch felt a sudden chill. "What the hell are you talking about?"

"Everybody knows." Flash grinned. "All the press. His drunken benders. He goes to consult with the mob. Sometimes they supply him all the women he wants. He disappears for days at a time. Everybody knows that. I go with him."

"The governor can't just disappear."

"He does as governor. He did as congressman. He's always done it. A few days at a time."

"Nuts. The governor just can't disappear. Be too easy to follow him."

"Impossible to follow him. He sees to that. I see to that. Trick is, there is no clue as to when it's going to happen. In the middle of the night, two or three in the morning, he rings my phone over the garage and says, 'Time to go, Flash.' I say, 'Yes, sir,' get the car out, and he's waiting by the back door. Once he even excused himself from a University Board of Governors meeting to go to the bathroom, see? And came out to me in the car and said, 'Time to go, Flash.' I always know what he means."

"And the press knows about this?"

"The great untold story. They don't dare report it, because they don't know what to report. Nobody can get any evidence. Am I saying that right? Nobody can get any evidence as to where he goes on these trips, or what he does. I'm the only one who knows." Flash sucked on his beer.

"Am I supposed to ask?"

"Governor had a girl friend, before he ever married. Barbara something-or-other. She was a designer of some kind—hats or clothes or something. I guess she had this cabin from her father. Inherited it from him. She and the governor used to spend time there, a long time ago, when they were kids, their early twenties, when he was in law school, I guess. She died. She left it to him. I guess it wasn't a sudden death. They knew she was going to die. No one has ever known he owns this cabin. Big secret of his life."

"So when he disappears he goes to this cabin? Alone?"

"I go with him. I know every route in and out of that place, east, north, south, and west. Every timber road. I could drive to that place blindfolded. And no one has ever succeeded in following me."

"You're talking about a cabin over thirty years old."

"Older than that. A lot older than that. It really rots. Rickety. Wet, cold. Falling apart. I try to do a few things when I'm there, keep it propped up. He never notices. Roof leaks. Fireplace smokes. Pipes are rotted. I bring water up in buckets from the lake. No real work has been done on it in over thirty years. I can't do much. What do I know? I'm a city kid."

Fletch watched the governor's driver–valet without saying anything.

Flash sat forward. "And you know what he does when he gets there? No broads, no booze. No mobsters. Just me. There's a picture of this girl, Barbara, on the bureau in the bedroom."

"Is she beautiful?"

Flash shrugged. "Not especially. She looks like a nice lady. Nice smile."

"So what does he do?"

"He goes to bed. He sleeps. He goes on a sleep orgy. We get there, immediately he goes to bed. It's a big, soft bed, usually a little damp. He never seems to mind the damp. I try to air out the little bed in the other room. He sleeps fifteen, sixteen hours. When he wakes up I bring food to him. Steak and eggs. Always steak and eggs. There's a phone, still listed in her name, I think, Barbara's name, after thirty years, if you'd believe it. What does the telephone company care? The bill gets paid. And he'll phone his secretary and maybe the lieutenant governor, and his wife, and maybe Walsh; do a little business, see that everything's all right. Then he'll go back to sleep. He doesn't even take a walk. Spends no energy at all. He's like a bear. Hibernates a few days. In all my years of doin' this with him, he's never gone down to the lake. He's never seen the outside of the cabin, except goin' in and comin' out, and that's usually in the dark. I don't think he even knows what a shambles it is."

"Flash, does he take pills to sleep so much?"

"No. Steak and eggs. Water from the lake. I've never even seen an aspirin bottle at the cabin. He just sleeps. Fifteen, sixteen hours at first. Then eight hours. Then like twelve hours. There are some old books in the cabin—Ellery Queen, S.S. van Dyne. He reads them sometimes, in bed. Never seems to finish them."

"You mean, his wife doesn't know about this?"

"Nobody does."

"When he calls them, where does he say he is?"

"He doesn't say. He's been doing this a long time. I know what they think. They think he's with some woman. In a way, maybe he is. The governor's out of town, they say. Private trip. Most of the press would give their left arms to know where the governor goes. I've been offered quite a lot."

"I bet you have."

"Until they know something, they can't report anything. Right?"

"Right. Did James know about this?"

"Nope. He used to get pretty mad about it sometimes. Yell at the governor. James saw some kind of danger in it. He'd say, 'Some day you're gonna get caught, Caxton, and then it will blow up in all of our faces.' "

"And what would the governor say?"

"Nothing. James was pretty smart. He played every trick in the book to get me to tell him where the governor goes, what he does. I don't know much, Mr. Fletcher, but what I know I shut up about."

"Flash, what's the big secret about this? If it's so innocent, if all the guy does is sleep—"

"I don't know. Maybe it shows he's human. What's the word? Vulnerable. He doesn't have all the energy in the world. He needs sleep. Maybe he's ashamed of it. Maybe it's because this woman was involved. Is involved."

"Maybe it's just because it's an eccentric thing to do."

"It's been goin' on a long time. As long as I've known him. That's how secrets begin, isn't it? At first you don't say nothin', and after a while you find you *can't* say nothin'. Maybe the ol' boy just enjoys puttin' one over on everybody. Here everybody thinks he's off boozin' with broads, and he's really asleep in a big soft bed up at the lake. Sleepin' like a baby. Readin' the same books over and over again, never finishin' them.''

"Then what happens?"

"After three, four days of this, sometimes five, he gets up, gets dressed, says, 'Time to go home, Flash,' we get in the car and go back to the mansion."

"He never says where he was."

"He says he was away. Only once there was some crisis, some vote that had to be taken. I guess he miscalculated, things moved faster than he expected, we had to come back earlier than he wanted to."

"How often does he do this?"

"Three, four times a year."

"Sounds pretty boring for you."

"Oh, no. I like looking at the lake. I keep sweaters up there, you know, and a big down jacket. It's quiet. I talk to the birds. I chirp back at them. You can get a real conversation going with the birds, if you really try. I like helping out the chipmunks."

Fletch gave this big, ex-boxer a long look. "How do you help out a chipmunk?"

"The place is so rotten. There's a stone wall under the cabin, a foundation, and then another between the cabin and the lake. The chipmunks live in the walls. They come in and out. The walls keep fallen down, blockin' up their doors. I move the big rocks for them. And I find nuts and leave them outside their doors for them. It's easier for me to find nuts than it is for them." The man said sincerely, "I can carry more nuts than a chipmunk can."

"Sure," said Fletch, "but do they thank you?"

"They take the nuts inside the walls. I think they do. They go somewhere." Fletch said nothing. "Why shouldn't I help them out?" Flash Grasselli asked reasonably. "I'm bigger than they are."

"Yeah."

"Sure. Haven't anything better to do."

"Don't see how he gets away with this. I don't see how he

gets away without making any kind of an explanation to Doris and Walsh.''

"Why? The guy's a success in every other way. Jeez, he's a presidential candidate. What more do you want? They put up with it. They mention it to me every once in a while. You know, thank me for takin' care of him when he disappears. They're fishin', too. I never say nothin'. God knows what they think. Sure it worries them, but so what? The guy lives in a glass suit. He has a right to some privacy.''

"He doesn't really trust them, does he?''

"He has a right to some privacy.''

"Flash, if the governor were off boozin' with broads, would you put up with it?''

"I dunno. Sure. I expect so. I like broads better'n I like chipmunks.''

"Would you tell the truth about it?''

Flash's eyes narrowed. "I'd shut up about it, if that's what you mean. The way I figure, everybody's gotta blow off steam in his own way. Everybody's gotta have a piece of hisself to hisself. Me, I go to my room over the garage at the mansion and I can do what I want. I never bring girls there, though. Not to the governor's mansion. I can do what I want. The governor, he wears a glass suit all the time. Except when he's at the lake. Just me and him. Then he zonks out. That's his thing.''

"And, Flash, drugs have nothing to do with it?''

"Nothin'. Absolutely nothin'. He doesn't even drink coffee there. If that shithead Dr. Thom and his little black bag ever showed up at the cabin, I'd drown 'em faster than he can insult me.''

"That's pretty fast.''

"Dr. Thom is an insult to the human race.''

"Has the governor done this lately? Disappeared?''

"No.'' Flash frowned. "Not since the campaign started. But we went up to the lake the day after Christmas. When no one was lookin'. A long rest. Back by New Year's Eve.''

"Okay. Flash, the question is obvious.''

The look on Flash's face indicated the question wasn't obvious.

"Why are you telling me this?" Fletch asked.

Simply, Flash answered, "The governor told me to."

"I guessed as much. The answer's obvious too. But why? Why did he tell you to tell me?"

Flash shrugged. "Dunno. I have a guess."

"What's your guess?"

"Maybe because he knows you don't like Dr. Thom and his little black bag any better'n I do. I heard Walsh tell him that."

Fletch shook his head. "So now I know something Walsh doesn't know? I don't get it."

"You see, Mr. Fletcher, the people around the governor don't care much about him, as long as he keeps movin', keeps walkin' and talkin', keeps bein' Caxton Wheeler, keeps winning. Including his wife and son. They remind me of a football team or somethin'. They work together beautifully, always slappin' each other on the ass and everything. But one of them breaks his back, like James, or like that guy who got killed today—what's his name? Victor Somethin'—no longer useful anymore, and they find they can play without him. They never really think of him again. There's that goal up the field there, and the point is to get that ball through that goal. That's the only point there is. The governor's the ball. They'll kick the shit out of him, throw him to the ground, land on him. He's just got to keep lookin' like a ball." Flash waggled his head. "You've been with the campaign what? Like twenty-four hours? And the governor wanted you to know this about him. I don't know what those friggin' pills are Dr. Thom feeds him. The governor wants you to know he's all right."

"I'm not sure you're right about Walsh."

"He cares?" Flash sat back. "Yeah, he cares. Too much. To him his dad is Mr. Magical Marvelous." Flash laughed. "I think the governor maybe almost wants his son to think he's up there somewhere burnin' up more energy with booze and broads. I think it would kill him if Walsh ever discovered the ol' man's just up at a rickety old cabin takin' a nap. You know what I mean?''

"Hell of a lot of pressure," Fletch said.

"Yeah, and this is the old man's way of beatin' it off. He's right. It's against his image. What could be worse for him than to have the *National Nose,* as he calls it, print that he's asleep? Jeez, it would ruin him. Better they think he's gettin' his rocks off—as long as they can't prove it."

"Well, well," Fletch said. "My daddy always said you can learn a lot in a bar, if you listen."

Walsh stuck his head in the bar, looked around, but did not come in.

Fletch said, "The governor wanted me to know he's not hooked on anything but sleep. Is that it?"

Flash shrugged. "The governor's a very intelligent man. I don't have any brains. Never did have. I'm just smart enough to know I should do what he tells me and everything will be fine."

"What did he tell you to say to me about Mrs. Wheeler?"

"Nothin'."

Fletch waited. He sipped his beer. He waited again. "What are you going to tell me about Mrs. Wheeler?"

"Nothin'. She's one tough, smart person. As strong as steel."

"Smarter and tougher than the governor?"

"Yeah."

"Tonight, when she yelled at the governor—"

"I didn't hear it. I was in the bathroom."

"You were in the bathroom on purpose. You knew she was going to do some such thing."

Flash said, "Yes."

"You call that smart and tough? You don't call that being out of control?"

"Mrs. Wheeler's kept things going all these years. She was probably right in everything she said tonight. I didn't hear her."

"You must have been trying pretty hard not to hear her."

"That's my business. She uses her tongue like a whip. She whips Walsh, yells at the governor, calls me a goon."

"Not just her tongue, Flash. She uses her hands."

"You know, you don't get to be a presidential candidate just by standin' out in the rain. Someone has to push you, and push you damned hard. You see, I know the governor's secret: he's a nice guy. If it weren't for her, the governor would have gone to sleep years ago. Read novels. Play with little kids. You know what I mean?"

"What's wrong with that?"

"Someone's got to be President of the United States," Flash said simply. "Why not a smart, honest, good man like Caxton Wheeler?"

20

"I completed, duplicated, and delivered tomorrow's final schedules," Fletch said. "I also issued the three special releases Nolting and Dobson have been working on. You saw them. On Central America, exploitation of Native American lands, on the Russian economic situation. I also made up some nice-guy stuff about your dad for the feature press—"

"Like what?" Walsh asked sharply.

They were in Walsh's bedroom on the twelfth floor of the hotel, sitting at the table under the shaded light.

"I told them how your dad used to give you your allowance. Make the coin disappear between his hands and then pretend to find it in your ear or something. Okay?"

"Okay." Walsh's eyes were darting around the areas of the room outside the light.

"Idea being to take the stink out of that scene this morning at Conroy School," Fletch said. "To imply he treats all kids as he would his own."

"I understand," Walsh said with a touch of impatience.

"Helped a local reporter get permission to spend some time with your mother in the morning."

"Did you go through Sully?" Walsh asked.

"I guess you could say that. I went through Sully."

"Your first run-in with Sully?"

"Yeah."

"What a bitch," Walsh said.

"Oh, you know that."

"Fletch, I think you'd better plan to spend some time with my mother tomorrow. Get to know her a little. See her as she really is."

"I would like that," Fletch said.

"I'll arrange it."

"My phone was ringing constantly, Walsh. All the world's pundits wanting to know the source of your dad's 'New Reality' speech."

"Did you tell them?"

"I said as far as I know it's the result of the governor's own thought."

"Is it?" Again, Walsh's question was quick and sharp.

"Walsh—"

"What was the source of the idea, Fletch?" And again Walsh's eyes were roaming restlessly around the room outside their circle of light.

"I said something. He asked. Maybe it was the germ of the idea. On the bus this morning. Your father was asking me what I thought. I'd never been asked what I thought by a presidential candidate before."

"You were flattered."

"Who wouldn't be? Of course, I didn't have time to think the idea out."

"You're not a speechwriter."

"What was I supposed to do?"

"The speechwriters are responsible for the consistency of what the candidate says."

"Anyway, Walsh, less than two hours later in Winslow your dad stands up and issues this perfectly eloquent speech, developing a couple of things I had said—"

"He was angry at the congressperson. He was angry at the

way the press handled the Conroy School incident. He was fighting back. We—I had put too much pressure on him over Victor Robbins's death to make the nightly news with something, anything.''

"I thought it was great."

"Of course you did. Piece of history. By your own hand. When history books pose the question, 'Why didn't Caxton Wheeler become President of the United States?' your grandchildren can read the answer. 'Because of an ill-considered speech in a snowstorm in a little town called Winslow where he criticized Christianity and the democratic process.' "

"Hey, Walsh. Maybe I just do that to authority. Any authority. Maybe I just get near authority and unconsciously start planting bombs. Your dad is one authority I like. I don't want to destroy him."

"Oedipus. Is that it?"

"Maybe. I'm a born-and-bred wise guy. I've never done well with authority. You should know that better than anyone. You remember Hill 1918. But I remember I got the platoon too stoned to go out on that earlier patrol. I knew it was suicidal.''

"You were right."

"You almost got court-martialed for it."

"The platoon that did go out got blown away."

"Hell, Walsh. I'm a reporter. I can't be a kept boy. Telling these reporters I love the stuff they're writing when most of them couldn't write their way out of a detention hall."

Walsh was looking into the dark of the room, clearly not hearing, not listening.

"What I'm trying to say is maybe I should pack my pistols and ride off into the sunset."

Walsh asked, "What was that thing you did between Betsy Ginsberg and me?"

"Got you to say hello to each other."

Walsh shook his head slowly.

"That too, Walsh." Still Fletch was not sure how much of Walsh's attention he had. "A lady I knew before this campaign ever started refused to have supper with me tonight because of my job. Because of the position I'm in. What do you do about the isolation, Walsh?"

"Fletch, I think your sex life can take a rest."

"I might get sick."

"So get sick."

"Another lady offered me her body for an interview with your mother in the morning."

"Did you accept?"

"Of course not."

"See? You're sick already."

"I think I ought to go back to bayin' at the moon, Walsh."

Walsh's eyes came back into the light, focused on the table surface. "You just gave Dad the coins. You didn't hand them out to the kids. To some of the kids. You just gave him the ideas. You didn't make the speech."

Fletch stretched his fingers. "Maybe that's what I like about your dad. He's a bit of a rebel, too. His mind's up there somewhere, kissin' the truth. At least he's not the complete phony I expected the front-runnin' politician to be'. Once in a while he actually says what occurs to him as the truth."

Abruptly Walsh sat up in his chair. "You're always making jokes. Is that how you escape?"

Slowly, carefully, Fletch said, "No. That's why the chicken crossed the road."

For the first time since Fletch had entered the room, Walsh looked him fully in the face. Then he grinned.

Fletch said, "Now that I have your attention . . ."

"Yeah, yeah, yeah," said Walsh. "You have my attention."

"James called me tonight. From Iowa. He's in Iowa to attend Victor Robbins's funeral."

"Bastard. He's there to get himself a job with the opposition."

"I wondered about that."

"You bet. As sure as God made anchovies."

"He talked a long time. Gave me some advice. Answered some questions."

"Said he loves Dad more than he loves himself. Will do anything he can to help out. Call him anytime. Am I right, or am I right?"

"You're right."

"He'd love a pipeline to this campaign. Don't talk to him."

"Except I think he was telling the truth. Twenty-three years—"

"Means nothing in history. A pimple on Tuchman's tuchis."

"Okay, but—"

Walsh shook his head *no* rapidly. "He was out to get my mother. Can't have that. No such thing as being loyal to my father, to the campaign, while you're sluggin' away at my mother."

"He doesn't see it that way."

"You trying to get James his job back? Your job?"

"Maybe it's impossible."

"It's impossible. The jerk self-destructed. People make mistakes in this business. But to go after the candidate's wife with bare knuckles, that's the way you get a one-way ticket home."

"Walsh, listen to me."

"I'm listening."

"He says your mother's temper is getting worse, that people, the press are beginning to know about it . . ."

Again Walsh was shaking his head *no*. "When you've got dozens of people talking at once, somebody's got to yell."

"That scene tonight in your father's room—"

"Aw, that's just Ma's way of blowin' off steam. Everyone's gotta blow off steam." Fletch was watching Walsh's eyes. "What harm did it do?" Walsh asked. "So people now think the candidate watches Archie Bunker on television. So what? Makes him seem human."

Fletch said, "Your father isn't human, Walsh?"

Walsh said: "He's human."

"But only Flash Grasselli knows how human, is that right?"

Walsh glanced at Fletch. "I see the press has been pumping you on Dad's sojourns away from home. I should have warned you."

"Do you know where he goes, Walsh?"

"Sure. There's a place he goes. Belongs to a friend. He

goes there, fishes, relaxes, reads history. Works on political strategy.''

''How do you know that?''

''He's told me. Just doesn't want anyone to have his phone number. He calls us. We don't call him. He calls regularly. Doesn't want the press to know. Can't blame him.''

''Who's this friend?''

''Someone he knew in school. In law school. One of his lawyer friends, I think.''

The phone rang. Walsh jumped to answer it. ''Be right up,'' he said into the phone. He hung up and said to Fletch: ''Mother.''

Remaining seated, Fletch asked, ''When do you get to sleep, Walsh?''

Walsh said, ''Plenty of time for that in the White House.''

21

Fletch got off the elevator on the fifth floor to go to his own room.

Down the corridor a man was leaning against the wall. His back was to the elevators. His right hand was against the wall, his arm fairly straight. His left hand was raised to his head.

Fletch went to him. "Bill?"

Bill Dieckmann's eyes were frosted over. They were not focusing at all. Clearly he did not recognize Fletch. Maybe he knew someone was there.

"Bill . . ."

Bill's knees jerked forward. Fletch did not catch him. He was too surprised. He put his own hands around Bill's head and went to the floor with him. Together they landed softly.

Fletch disentangled himself and sat up. Bill Dieckmann was unconscious. Some, but not all, of the pain was gone from his face.

The room key in Bill's jacket pocket read 916.

Dieckmann was heavy. Fletch raised him in the fireman's lift.

With Dieckmann over his shoulders, Fletch waited for the elevator.

Andrew Esty was on the elevator when it arrived. He was wearing his overcoat, *Daily Gospel* button in the lapel. In one hand he had a suitcase; in the other a typewriter case.

"I thought you left the campaign, Mr. Esty." Fletch pushed the button for the ninth floor.

"I was ordered back."

Esty did not seem to notice that Fletch had a large man over his shoulders. He had barely made room for them in the elevator.

"Nice to have you back," Fletch said from behind the folds of Bill's suit jacket.

"It's not nice to be back."

"But," said Fletch, "you have a job to do."

"Do you really think," Esty asked, "we should allow this anti-American, anti-Christian campaign to go unreported?"

"Are we on the ninth floor?"

There was a moment before Esty admitted they were on the ninth floor.

Fletch said, "Gotta call 'em as you see 'em." He staggered with his load of Bill Dieckmann through the elevator door.

Fletch lowered Bill Dieckmann onto the bed in Room 916. Then he picked up the telephone.

"What are you doing?" On the bed, Bill's eyes were open, wary.

"Calling Dr. Thom," Fletch said.

"What are you doing in my room?"

"You collapsed, Bill. On the fifth floor. You've been unconscious."

"Put the phone down."

The hotel's operator had not yet answered. "Are you sure?" Fletch asked.

"Put it down."

Fletch hung up.

"Now get out."

"You might say thanks for the ride, Bill. I carried you up here."

"Thanks for nothing."

"Bill, I'm not your wife, boss, brother, friend . . . you know the rest of the speech?"

"No," Bill said. "You're not."

"Something's wrong with your head, man. Twice I've seen you trying to twist it off. Tomorrow you might succeed."

"None of your damned business." Bill sat up, put his feet on the floor, his head in his hands.

"You've said that before. It's no secret you're having trouble, Bill. Dr. Thom may be a strange man, but he's not going to call your managing editor first thing with a complete medical report. Doctors still have to keep their mouths shut, even Dr. Thom."

Dieckmann appeared to be listening.

"Anyway," Fletch continued, "suppose you succeed at twisting your head off one of these times? Think of the disgusting sight. You walking around with your head in your hands, down around your pockets. Blood bubbling up from your neck and dribbling all over your suit. I know you'd still get the story, Bill. But think of the ladies. You want Fenella Baker to see a thing like that? Might make her face powder fall off. That would be really sickening."

Head in hands, Bill said, "Get out of here, Fletch. Please. Go bother somebody else. Go bother Ira Lapin. He's got bigger problems than I have."

"What are his problems?"

"Housemother you're not."

"Agreed. But, Bill, you just collapsed. You weren't even on the right floor. You had no idea what you were doing. Before you went unconscious, you didn't even recognize me."

"Okay, okay. What am I supposed to do about it?"

"Get medical attention. This primary campaign isn't worth your life, Bill. You know what I mean? At least to you, it isn't."

"I'm all right."

"You're about as all right as a snowman on the Fourth of July."

"Leave me alone."

"Okay. If you say so." At the door, Fletch said, "You sure there's nothing I can do?"

"Yeah. There's something you can do."

"What?"

"Tell me if I'm on the right campaign. Who's going to win this damned primary?"

"Gee, I dunno, Bill."

"Then you're no good to me."

"But I can tell you that after this primary election, there's another one. And then another. And another . . . Good night, Bill."

22

"' 'Mornin'. Thank you," Fletch said into the bedside phone. It had rung and he assumed it was the hotel operator calling to tell him it was six-thirty.

"You're welcome," said the strong voice of The Man Who. Fletch looked at his watch. It was only six-twenty.

"' 'Morning," Fletch said in a voice that wasn't too strong. He sat up in the bed. His shoulders and chest and stomach were wet with sweat. Steam was clanging in the radiators. The room had been cold when he went to bed. He had put on an extra blanket from the closet. Now he threw the blankets off.

"You're up early," said Governor Caxton Wheeler.

"Am I?"

"Apparently."

"Oh, yes," Fletch said intelligently. "I must be."

"Are you awake now?"

"Sure. Ask me a riddle. Never mind, you know the answer."

"Look, Fletch, I've just called Lansing Sayer. Asked him to join me in the car on the ride out to the hospital."

"Hospital?"

"I'm visiting the Farmingdale Hospital this morning."

"Oh, yeah. I mean, oh, yes. Sir."

"He can interview me in the car on the way out. I want you to come along. To keep me honest."

"Okay. I mean, yes, sir."

"We'll leave about eight-thirty. Flash will drive us out."

"Yes, sir."

"See you out front at eight-thirty. Are you awake?"

"Like a snowman on . . ."

"What were you doing when I called?" There was laughter in the governor's voice.

Fletch ran his thumb down his chest and stomach. "Sweating."

"Great," said The Man Who. "Nothing like exercise first thing in the morning. Do a push-up for me. I'll feel the better for it."

Fletch padded to the door, opened it, and saw the stack of newspapers a volunteer had left for him in the hotel corridor.

Newsbill was on top. The front page of the tabloid had nothing but the headline on it:

DEATH STALKS WHEELER CAMPAIGN

Fletch knelt on one knee and scanned the story, with many photographs, which began on page three:

Farmingdale—Presidential Candidate Caxton Wheeler and his staff have refused to answer questions about the murders of two young women which have happened on their campaign trail within the last week.

The second young woman, Alice Elizabeth Shields, 28, was found naked and beaten on the sidewalk just below Wheeler's seventh floor hotel suite.

Campaign officials even refuse to state they have no knowledge of the women or of their murders. . . .

The by-line read Michael J. Hanrahan.

"Well, well," Fletch muttered into the empty hotel corridor. "The dam has broken. Somebody better get a mop."

23

"No, no eggs for me," Ira Lapin said. He and Fletch were in a booth in the hotel's coffee shop. "My doctor gave me a big warning against cholesterol. No bacon, either. I forget what's wrong with bacon. I'm sure something is. No coffee, of course." He ordered oatmeal, unbuttered toast, and tea. "What is cholesterol, anyway? Little boomies that gang up trying to get through the doorways to your heart?"

"I think it gives you hardening of the head or something."

"I'd never notice," Ira said. "If my head were any harder I could never sneeze."

Fletch ordered steak and eggs, orange juice, and coffee.

"What is it with you young people?" Ira asked. "Can't afford to go to a doctor and never enjoy breakfast again?"

"My worry is the population explosion," Fletch said.

"And that's your answer to the population explosion? Commit suicide at breakfast?"

"Not suicide," Fletch answered. "I just don't hope to take up space beyond my allotted time."

Ira nodded sagely. "An original point of view."

"Everybody has to worry about something."

"These doctors kill you," Ira said. "Everything's bad for you. Booze is bad for you. Tobacco. Coffee. Red meat. The egg is bad for you. What can be more innocent than the egg? It isn't even born yet."

"Milk, cheese, chocolate. Water. Air."

"They want us to go straight from our incubators to our coffins. No outside influences, please; I'm living."

"Tough life." The waitress brought them their tea and coffee. "Doubt we'll ever adapt to it."

"I take from the unhealthiest doctor I could find. He's a wreck. Fat as the federal budget. He smokes like a public utility; drinks as if he has as many different mouths as a White House source. When he breathes, you'd think someone is running a caucus in his chest. Thought he'd be easy on me. Tolerant. Relaxed. Not a bit of it. Still he gives me that old saw, 'Don't do as I do; do as I say.' I guess I should. Already he's invested in a burial plot, he tells me. And he's only thirty-two."

Breakfast came.

"How do you like the campaign so far?" Ira Lapin asked the candidate's press representative.

"Getting some surprises," Fletch said.

"Like . . .?"

"Caxton Wheeler's brighter than I thought. More honest. More sane."

"You didn't know him before?"

"No."

"You knew his son."

"Yes."

"What do you think of the press, now that you're seeing us from a different angle?"

"Cute."

"What do you mean, cute? Or are you referring only to La Arbuthnot?"

"That incident yesterday with the governor and the kids and the coins. The magic show he put on. I would never see that as a national issue."

Ira nodded. "I reported it. I didn't report it as an issue. I just reported it. Let people make of it what they will."

"You mean, the editors, news directors . . ."

"It's the little things that count," Ira Lapin said. He had spooned cream and sugar onto his oatmeal, cream and sugar into his tea. He had put a quarter of a pot of jam on his toast. Blissfully, he was eating everything. "You know you've been thrown in here as a sacrificial lamb. Yes. You have. You've been thrown to the wolves. To me. To us. You're surprised? Eat your steak. Steak for breakfast. You'd drive my doctor to drink. Never mind. For him it's not a long ride. We're at the point in the campaign where they need someone young in your job. A throwaway. Nothing wrong with James except he was tired. His tricks were tired. He was boring us. You're young, and people say you have a crazy mind. You do. Ignore the doctor because you worry about the population explosion. You'll keep us entertained, all right. There's a story you gave Solov a bottle of eyedrops. You do that?"

"No."

"They can make up stories about you. Deflect from the candidate. After these stupid, high-energy primaries are over, you'll be used as the scapegoat. You'll be what's wrong with the campaign. You'll be gotten rid of as a concession to the press, an answer for everything that's wrong. Then they'll march the professionals in. You think I don't know what I'm talking about?" Fletch was eating and listening, not registering surprise to the degree Ira Lapin wanted. "They have one ready. You ever hear of Graham Kidwell? He's already on the campaign as media consultant. I'll bet you this piece of toast, what's left of it, Wheeler's already talked with him this morning, maybe twice. Kidwell is sitting in a big Washington office, partner in a rich public relations firm, primed for the job of press secretary to the President of the United States. You think you're going to the White House? Think again. I've seen it before. 'A presidential campaign is a crusade of amateurs.' Where did he get that? Some amateur. Caxton Wheeler's an amateur like a Georgetown madame. And his wife, the dragon lady. She could make the finals in any contest you happened to run. Including mud wrestling. During the primary campaigns, in all these rinky little towns, a good campaigner wants to give the impression of amateurism. Makes the campaign seem more real. More like a people's movement. Gets the volunteers out, the bucks up. The people see the fumbling around, say, 'Gee, I can help,' throw down their shovels and golf clubs, and go to work for the candidate. Later, only professionalism sells. Then the image of competence is needed. So right now, in this road show, you're the lead amateur.'' Ira drained his teacup. ''Thought I'd let you know.''

''Thanks,'' Fletch said cheerily enough. ''I expect you're right.''

''No probably about it. I know I'm right. Campaigns at first need idealism and youth. Once the primaries are won, cynicism takes over and idealism gets a bus ticket home. You don't mind being used?''

''Everybody gets used,'' Fletch said. ''Depends on what you get used for.''

''Idealism,'' scoffed Ira Lapin. ''Idealism goes home on a bus.'' Ira poured the last drops from his teapot into his coffee cup. ''I feel sick.''

''You don't look well.''

''What I need is some coffee.'' He signaled the waitress. ''I should contribute to the population explosion?'' The waitress came over and he ordered a pot of coffee. Then he said to Fletch: ''You know my wife was murdered.''

''No. My God. When?''

''Two years, five months ago. A block from our apartment in Washington. Stabbed by a mugger.''

''Stabbed to death?''

''She was stabbed. Would you believe it was hitting her head on a stone step when she fell down that killed her? Stone steps leading to a house.''

Fletch shook his head. ''How do you accept a thing like that?''

''You don't. You don't accept it. You don't think about it. You just leave it out there somewhere, like a part of town you never visit. You put the anger, the rage, the fury in another part of town, and you never visit it.'' The waitress brought the pot of coffee and a fresh cup and saucer for Ira. "Thank you," he said to her. "You're killing me." He poured the coffee slowly into his cup. "I was in Vienna with the President when I got the cable. Did you ever see a piece of paper you couldn't believe at all? I mean, no matter how many times you read it, it just sits there like an impossible lie? I don't even remember the trip home. I remember Marty Nolan of the *Boston Globe* packing my bags for me."

"Any kids?"

"Grown. They were devastated. Who was their mother to get stabbed? A nice little person."

"Did they ever catch the guy who did it?"

"A man was seen running away carrying a purse. Maybe she had fifty dollars in the purse. I doubt that much. He didn't steal the new tablecloth she had just bought. The whole thing was unnecessary. We already had a tablecloth."

"I dunno," Fletch said. "I'm real sorry for you, man."

"It's not that." Ira waved his hand in front of his face. "It's just that every time I hear of one of these murders— women getting killed—just stirs the whole thing up again."

"Sure."

"Jeez. You can't come down to breakfast without hearing about some woman getting killed down the corridor."

"What do you mean?" Fletch asked.

"You didn't hear? Some reporter you must have been. A chambermaid got killed last night. Strangled."

"In this hotel?"

"Yeah. The kitchen help found her when they came in this morning. At four o'clock. In a service elevator. Two nights ago was it?—a woman gets pushed off the roof of the motel we were in. I don't know. We go through this whole election process as if we were civilized human beings. What good does it do? It's just a big pretense that we're civilized."

Fletch wanted to say, *Wait a minute....*

"What's the matter with you?" Ira asked. "Now *you* look sick. What happened to your tan? Didn't know it was the kind you could rub off. Better take some of my coffee."

"No. Thanks."

"Take it. You look like your heart just sat down and took off its shoes."

"Thanks."

"Sure. Have some coffee. No good for me anyway. My doctor says it makes me nervous."

24

"You all right, Fletch?" Betsy Ginsberg asked. She was standing in the hotel lobby outside the coffee shop.

"Sure."

"You look white."

"Just saw Paul Szep's editorial cartoon." In fact, he had. Roy Filby had showed it to him at the coffee shop's cash register. "So how do you like Walsh," Fletch tried to ask easily, "now that you know him?"

Michael J. Hanrahan went by into the coffee shop. He grinned/grimaced at Fletch and held up three fingers.

Fletch ignored him.

Betsy returned the question. "What do you really think of Walsh?"

"He's a cool guy," Fletch answered. "Forgiving, reassuring, absolutely competent. Totally in control."

"I don't know," Betsy said.

"So he didn't fall all over you," Fletch said. "Think of the position he's in."

The Man Who was getting off the elevator. The eyes of everyone in the lobby were attracted to him. He was smiling.

People intercepted him as he crossed the lobby. Several had children by the hands. A few snapped pictures of The Man Who, as if the world were not being nearly saturated with pictures of him. The Man Who was shaking hands, listening briefly, speaking briefly, as he came across the lobby. He patted some of the children on their heads. He did not take coins from their ears.

Fletch walked close beside him. Quietly he said, "We've got to talk. Privately. Soon."

"Sure," the governor said. "What's up?"

Into the governor's ear, Fletch said, "Ira Lapin tells me another young woman has been murdered."

The governor reached through the mob, went out of his way to shake a bellman's hand.

With his public grin on his face, the governor spoke almost through his teeth. "Two people in the United States are murdered every hour, Fletch. Didn't you know that?"

"Talk," Fletch said.

"Sure, sure."

25

"I'm glad you asked me that question." Sitting behind Flash in the rented black sedan, Governor Wheeler's eyes twinkled at Fletch sitting in the front passenger seat. Sitting behind Fletch, Lansing Sayer had just asked some general question about the "New Reality" speech The Man Who had delivered in Winslow the day before. Sayer had a tape recorder going and also was working a pen and notebook. "I guess I made a rather sweeping statement."

It was a raw, bone-chilling day with a heavy sky. Flash had the car heater on high.

"Senator Upton says you're proposing a technocracy," Lansing said.

"I'm not proposing anything," the governor said. "I'm simply making an observation."

Fletch remembered James's advice that when he thought the candidate was about to say something profound and statesmanlike he ought to stick a glove in his mouth.

"Just observe," the governor said slowly, thoughtfully, "what technology is getting the major share of the governments' attention. Advanced weaponry. Machines of death and destruction. Do you realize what a single tank costs these days? A fighter aircraft? An aircraft carrier? I don't just mean our government. I mean all governments. Some governments are exporting weaponry at a high rate; others are importing at a high rate; some do both. The technology upon which almost all governments concentrate is the technology of weaponry. Advanced bows and arrows.''

It was true: Flash drove slowly. He hugged the right lane of the city's main street and proceeded at only slightly better than a pedestrian's pace. Fletch had been in funeral processions that went faster.

"At the same time," the governor continued, at about the same pace as the car, "over the earth has been spreading a communications system that does or can reach into every hovel, capable of collecting and dispersing information instantaneously. An amazing technology, for the most part developed by free enterprise, private business—particularly the entertainment business.

"Through this technology, the people of this earth are beginning to recognize each other, know each other, and realize their commonality of interest.

"This technology is far more powerful, and far more positive I might add, than the thermonuclear bomb.''

It was hardly noticeable when the car came to a full stop, but, indeed, they were stopped at a red light. The people crossing the street in front of the car had no idea they were so close to a leading presidential candidate. They were all hurrying someplace, to work, to shop. None looked in the car. And none knew what was being discussed in that black sedan.

"Governments lie now, and all the people know it. A government runs a phony election, and all the people of the world witness it. Governments put on brushfire wars now for some diplomatic or ideologic reason, and all the world see themselves being maimed and killed.''

Lansing Sayer dropped his hands, his pen and notebook in his lap, and said, "I don't know what all this is about.''

Flash had taken off his gloves and dropped them on the seat beside Fletch.

The car oozed forward again.

"I'm talking about the gathering and dissemination of information," the governor said, "instead of weapons."

Lansing said, "Graves stated that in your speech yesterday, you seemed to be disparaging—among other ideologies—Christianity, Judaism, and democracy."

"I don't disparage ideas at all," the governor said. "I'm having one, am I not?"

"You said technology is tying this world together, integrating the people of this world, in a way no ideology ever has or ever could."

"Isn't that true? We're all brothers in the Bible. We're all comrades under Marxism. But it is through our increased factual awareness of each other that we're discovering our common humanity as a reality."

Lansing Sayer wasn't getting much into his notebook.

"Am I wrong to think that most of the bad things that happen on this earth happen because people don't have the right facts at the right time? It's all very well to believe something. You can go cheering to war over what you believe. You can starve to death happily over what you believe. But would wars ever happen if everybody had the same facts? There is no factual basis for starvation on this earth," Governor Caxton Wheeler said softly. "Not yet, there isn't."

"It's the interpretation of facts that counts," Lansing Sayer said.

"Facts are facts," said The Man Who. "I'm not talking about faith, belief, opinions. I'm talking about facts. How come most children in this world know Pele's every move playing soccer, know every line of Muhammad Ali's face, and yet this same technology has not been used to teach them the history of their own people, or how to read and write their own language? How come a bank in London can know, up to the minute, how much money a bank in New York has, to the penny, but a kid in Liverpool who just had his teeth bashed out doesn't know three thousand years ago a Greek analyzed gang warfare accurately? How come the governments of this world know where every thermonuclear missile is, on land, under land, on sea, under sea, and yet this technology has never been used for the proper allocation of food? Is that a dumb question?''

"You're saying, regarding technology, governments are looking in the wrong direction.''

"I'm saying governments are out of date in their thinking. They've been developing negative technology, rather than positive technology. You have to believe something, only if you don't know. We now have the capability to know everything.''

Lansing Sayer looked at the governor. "What has this to do with the presidential campaign? Are these ideas of yours going to be implemented in some kind of a political program?''

And the governor looked through the car window. "Well . . . we're having international meetings on arms control. We have had for decades now, while arms have proliferated through this world like the plague. Translating this observation into policy . . .'' In the front seat Fletch again was amazed at how simply issues were raised and answered on a political campaign, how naturally problems were stated and policy formulated. ". . . I think it's time we started working toward international understandings regarding the use and control of this technology,'' The Man Who said. "Obviously no one—no political, religious, financial group—should have control of too large a section of this technology. Consider this.'' The governor smiled at Lansing Sayer. "Electronically, a complete polling of a nation's people, a complete plebiscite, can take place within seconds. Where is the time needed for the people to reflect? Maybe there should be an international understanding, agreement, that such a plebiscite is to be used only as an advisory to a government, but does not give a government authority to act.''

The car was going up the hill to the hospital.

"Great,'' the governor said. "Easily accessible hospital. Good roads leading to it. That's good.''

Lansing Sayer took off his glasses and rubbed his forehead.

"Flash will take you back to the hotel,'' the governor said

to Lansing Sayer, "then come back and pick us up. I have to make a television tape after this."

Lansing Sayer asked, "Is this what your campaign is about, Governor? Shifting governmental interest from bombs to communication?"

"Bombs are a damned bad way to communicate," The Man Who said. "Deafen people."

The car stopped. The governor was leaving the car through the back door.

Lansing Sayer leaned over. "Governor! May I report this is what your campaign is about? Coming to international understandings regarding the new technology?"

Governor Caxton Wheeler looked back inside the car at Lansing Sayer. He grinned. He said: "Presidential campaigns ought to be about *something*."

Walking from the car to the hospital entrance, where administrators were waiting to greet him, Governor Caxton Wheeler chuckled and said to Fletch, "You know, sir, I'm beginning to *want* to be President of the United States!"

26

"Ah!" The concerned, consoling expression fell off the governor's face when he saw the only one present in the private hospital room was I. M. Fletcher. The door behind the governor swung shut. "And what are you in hospital for?"

"Anxiety," Fletch answered. "Acute."

"I'm sure they'll have you fixed up and home in no time."

While the governor had toured the happier wards of the hospital—maternity, general surgery, pediatrics (he was kept away from intensive care and the terminal section)—Fletch had arranged with a hospital administrator to have the governor shown into an unoccupied private room. His excuse had been the governor's need to use the phone.

More seriously, the governor asked, "What are you so anxious about? What's up?"

"Hanrahan wrote his usual muscular piece for this morning's *Newsbill*." Fletch took the tabloid's front page and two of its inside pages from his jacket pocket and handed them to the governor. "I want you to see what all this looks like in print."

Standing near the window, the governor glanced through the pages. "So? Who cares about *Newsbill*? They once reported I had been married before. As a law student."

"I'm afraid Hanrahan has a point. In the third paragraph."

The Governor read aloud: "Campaign officials even refuse to state they have no knowledge of the women or of their murders. . . ."

He handed the pages from *Newsbill* back to Fletch. "How are we supposed to comment on something we don't know about?"

"Plus there was a woman murdered at the hotel last night. A chambermaid. Strangled. So Ira Lapin tells me. By the way, did you know Lapin's own wife was murdered?"

"So he's off murdering other women?"

"Maybe. Somebody is."

The governor paced off as far as the hospital room would permit, and then back to the window. "Do you think someone's out to get me?"

"I never thought of that."

"Think about it. It is, or could be, the net effect of these murders. To bring this campaign to its knees."

"It certainly increases the pressures . . ."

"Getting rid of me, casting a pall, a question mark over my campaign, is the only motive I can think of." The governor shrugged. "Or maybe paranoia is an occupational hazard for a political campaigner. You think the murderer is someone traveling with the campaign?"

"Good grief, don't you think so? It's why Fredericka Arbuthnot, crime writer for *Newsworld,* is traveling with us. She's not as careless and sensational as Hanrahan, but now that Hanrahan has blown the story, she'll have to write something."

"I'd better get Nolting to whip up some statements, figures on the high incidence of crime. I can say things like, 'Everywhere I go, it seems like someone is getting murdered.'"

"Governor . . ." Fletch hesitated.

"Yes?"

"I understand. You have to protect yourself. You have to

protect the campaign. But making statements won't make the matter go away."

"What else can we do? The primary is in a couple of days."

"The best way to make the matter go away is to find out who is murdering these women."

"How are we supposed to do that? We're at full gear here, traveling at high speed. How many people are traveling with us—fifty or sixty? Is someone trying to sabotage my campaign? Just when I'm beginning to say something that is at least of interest to me? Who? Upton? Unthinkable. Graves? This goes a bit beyond dirty tricks. Some foreign agent? That guy from *Pravda*—"

"Solov."

"That his name? Looks like a complete basket case to me. You know he's never approached me with a single question? What's he here for? The press. You said Andrew Esty left yesterday, and there was a murder last night. So that lets him off."

"He came back. He was ordered back. Saw him in the elevator last night. Why do you mention him in particular?"

"That guy's a nut. Did you ever see him smile? He's as tight as a tournament tennis racquet. One of those guys who thinks he's absolutely right. Anyone who thinks he's absolutely right is capable of anything, including murder. Some kook among the volunteers. Lee Allen can't do very thorough checks on their backgrounds. We're traveling too fast, don't have the resources. I trust everyone on the staff implicitly. Believe me, they've all been vetted. You're the only one I don't know well personally, and you weren't with us at the time of the murder in the Hotel Harris. What the hell am I supposed to do? Go before the electorate, and say, 'Hey, guys and gals, I'm not a murderer.' Has an unfortunate ring to it. 'I'm not a froggy-woggy; I'm a toaddy-woaddy.' "

"Yes, it's time to say something," Fletch said. "It's also time to do something. I love what you're saying about the 'New Reality,' but the true reality is that the people are going to be concerned about unsolved murders touching your campaign."

The governor waved his hand at the pages from *Newsbill* still in Fletch's hand. "Did you show that filth to Walsh?"

"He had already left his room when I called this morning."

The governor looked at his watch. "I'm due at a television studio for a taping in twenty minutes. I will refer to these women's deaths, and say I am appalled. We have got to do something about violent crime in this country. It's affecting all of us. There's the big rally in Melville tonight. I have to fly to New York to be on that network program, 'Q. & A.,' live tomorrow morning. Everybody tells me I've got to attend a church service somehow in the morning, seeing I'm accused of slurring Christianity in Winslow."

For a moment the two men were silent. Recitation of schedule did not make the problem go away, either. "Damn," the governor said. "It's snowing again."

Fletch said, "Now will you get some federal investigators to travel with us?"

"No." The governor thought a moment, and then said: "Your job, Fletcher, is to make sure this doesn't touch me. Doesn't touch the campaign. That's your only job." The Man Who had fallen into the cadence of a public speech. "No matter who is doing this string of murders, for whatever reason, it is to have no bearing on my candidacy. The primary in this state is in a couple of days. No one can solve a string of far-flung murders in a couple of days. I cannot go into that primary election day with people thinking of murder, associating this campaign with the murder of women. Do what you have to do, but keep this away from me. Is that clear?"

"Yes, sir."

"We'd better go."

Fletch opened the swing door of the hospital room for the governor. "Do you know the President has announced a press conference for two o'clock this afternoon?"

"Yes."

"Saturday afternoon press conference. Most unusual."

Going through the door the governor said, "I expect he's going to speak well of Christianity and democracy and drop a bomb on me."

27

"Here I am." Freddie Arbuthnot announced her presence at Fletch's elbow.

Actually, using one of the hotel's house telephones, Fletch had been trying to find Walsh Wheeler. His room didn't answer. Barry Hines wasn't sure where Walsh was. He thought Walsh was meeting with Farmingdale's Young Professionals Association. Lee Allen Parke thought Walsh was visiting an agronomy exhibit about fifty miles from Farmingdale. (Fletch was to discover Walsh breakfasted with the Young Professionals Association, then visited the agronomy exhibit.)

"You are looking for me, aren't you?" Freddie asked.

"Always." Fletch gave up on the phone. "Have you packed yet?"

"I never really unpack."

"Neither do I. But I ought to go up and throw things together. Come with me?"

"Sir! To your hotel room?"

"Yeah."

"Sure."

Judy Nadich burst off the elevator.

"Hey!" Fletch said to her.

She turned around, her tote bag swinging against her leg. She was crying.

"What's the matter?" Fletch asked.

"That bitch!" Judy said.

"Who?"

"Your Ms Sullivan." She stepped closer to Fletch. "And your Doris Wheeler!"

"What did they do?"

"Nothing. Threw me out. Called me a squirrel."

Fletch couldn't help smiling.

"Told me to go cover the flower show!" Fresh tears poured from her eyes. "That's not for a month yet!"

"So screw 'em," Fletch said.

Judy tried to collect herself in front of Freddie. "How?"

"Screw 'em in what you write." Fletch realized James had been right: Mrs. Presidential Candidate Doris Wheeler badly needed a lesson in manners. The realization made him hot.

"I don't have anything to write!" Judy almost wailed. "I didn't even see what the inside of her suite looked like!"

"Oh," he said lamely.

"This story was important to me." Judy Nadich walked away, head down, her tote bag banging against her knees, back to do stories about flower shows and cracked teacups and the funds needed to clean the statues in the park.

"Poor local press," Freddie sighed. "I was one once."

Fletch pressed the elevator button. "Where?"

"New York City."

"New York City is not local. Even in New York City, New York City is not local."

"On a national campaign like this," Freddie said, stepping into the elevator, "local press is seduced with a weak drink, and granted a kiss on the cheek."

"So this is how you live." Freddie looked around his hotel room. "Your suitcase is dark brown. Mine is light blue."

"Yeah," Fletch said. "That's the difference between boys and girls." He went into the bathroom to collect his shaving gear. "You know anything in particular about the woman who was murdered this morning?"

"Mary Cantor, age thirty-four, widowed, mother of three. Her husband was a Navy navigator killed in an accident over Lake Erie three years ago."

Fletch tried to visualize the three children, then decided not to. "Has the woman in Chicago been identified yet? The one found in a closet off the press room?"

"Wife of an obstetrician. Member of the League of Women Voters. Highly respectable. Just not carrying identification that night. Maybe she left her purse somewhere and someone walked off with it."

Fletch came back into the bedroom. Freddie was stretched out on the unmade bed. "I don't see what the women have in common," he said. "A society woman in Chicago—"

"A socially useful woman, you mean."

"Alice Elizabeth Shields, a bookish woman with her own mind, two nights ago. And last night, a mother, Air Force widow, a night chambermaid."

"They all have something in common."

"What?"

"They're all women."

"Was the woman found last night raped?"

"Haven't talked with the coroner himself yet. A lab assistant says she believes the woman was not raped. There's something very rapelike about these murders, though."

Fletch was rolling up his dirty shirts. He hadn't been in any hotel long enough to get his laundry done. "What do you mean?"

"Rape isn't a sexual thing," Freddie said. "Not really. The main element in rape is to dominate a woman, subject her, mortify her. Degrade her. Sexually victimizing her is secondary to victimizing her."

"I understand that. But without the element of actual rape, Freddie, there is no absolute proof that the murderer is a male. The murderer could be a strong woman."

"Yeah," Freddie said from the bed. "Fenella Baker. She tears off her blouse and turns into a muscle-bulging Amazon."

"How was the woman last night murdered?"

"Strangled with some kind of a soft cord, the police say. Like a drapery tie, or a bathrobe sash. They haven't found whatever it was."

"The lack of sexual rape bothers me." Fletch took a jacket from the closet, folded it quickly, and put it in the suitcase. "A strong woman . . ."

"Terrible." Freddie got up, took the jacket out of the suitcase, and folded it properly. "Got to make clothes last on a trip like this."

"I never wear that jacket."

"Then why do you carry it?"

"That's the jacket I carry." He pointed to one on the unmade bed. "That's the jacket I wear."

Freddie tossed the clothes in his suitcase like someone tossing a salad with her fingers. "Fletcher, this suitcase is full of nothing but laundry."

"I know."

"You've got to do something about that."

"Where? When?"

"Or we'll put you off the press bus. There are enough stinkers on the press bus as it is. You notice no one will sit next to Hanrahan?"

"I notice he's always stretched out over two seats."

"He smells bad." She resettled his shaving kit so the suitcase could close.

"Will you leave my damned laundry alone?"

She dropped the suitcase lid and stared at it. "Relationships between men and women can be nice. I guess."

He watched her from the chair where he was sitting. "Can't say you never had one, Freddie."

"I live out of a suitcase, Fletcher. All the time. Anything that doesn't fit in the suitcase can't come with me."

"Why? Why do you live this way?"

She was running the tips of her fingers along the top edge of Fletch's suitcase. "Why am I Fredericka Arbuthnot? Because I have the chance to be. I'd be a fool to pass it up. Enough women get the chance to be girl friends, wives, and mothers." She sat in the hotel room's other chair. "Where would the world be without my sterling reporting?"

"Want me to order up coffee?"

"We'd never get it."

Not giving any neighborhood snail a good race, Flash driving, Fletch had gone to the television studio and sat through the governor's taped interview. Deftly, The Man Who had turned the interview to the high incidence of crime in this country. He even referred to having heard about the chambermaid murdered in his hotel that morning. The interview with the candidate was to be shown on the noon news.

"You saw Hanrahan's shit this morning?" Fletch asked.

"Sure."

"So now you'll have to write something."

"Already have," Freddie answered. "I was fair. Reported that the murders have happened on the fringe of the campaign, no connection with the campaign has been made, the police so far don't even think the murders are connected."

"You indicated it could all be coincidence."

"Yes."

"Do you believe that?"

Freddie shrugged. "If I did, I wouldn't be here. Also I had to say, as did Hanrahan, that the candidate has not made himself available for questioning on this matter."

"Truly, he hasn't anything to say."

"Truly . . ." Freddie was stretched out in her chair, her head against the chair back. "Fletch, what does Wheeler really say about these murders?"

"He treats them like flies on his porridge. He keeps trying to brush them away. To him, this story is the story of the campaign itself. He doesn't want it turned into a murder story."

"It would ruin the campaign."

"He's talking about organizing the new technology to gather and disperse information, goods, and service for the betterment of people worldwide, and someone keeps dropping corpses on him."

"Who?"

"Tell me."

"Would he have any other reason for avoiding our questions? Inquiry? Investigation?"

"Isn't the ruination of his campaign enough of a reason?"

"I suppose so."

"You mean, like his own guilt?"

"Sally Shields was found on the sidewalk beneath his windows. As Hanrahan reported, and I didn't, Doris and Caxton Wheeler have separate suites. Doris is a rich bitch. People tell me she can be real nasty. Who says he has to love her?"

"You think the candidate is using disposable women?"

"Who knows?"

"I don't think he'd throw one out his own window."

"Things get out of hand," she mused. "Things can get out of hand."

"There is an idea . . ." Fletch hesitated.

"Lay it on me. I can take it, whatever it is."

". . . that whoever, or whatever is doing this, is doing so to torpedo the campaign of Caxton Wheeler. To destroy him as a presidential candidate."

"Whose idea is that?"

Again Fletch hesitated. "Caxton Wheeler's."

"I thought so. Even to you he tries to steer inquiry away from himself. Was he in his suite at the time Alice Elizabeth Shields landed on the sidewalk, or wasn't he?"

Fletch shifted in his chair. "The timing doesn't work out. He says he got out of a car, didn't see anything like a crowd on the sidewalk, didn't see the people leaving the bar, and yet when he got to his hotel room, he says he saw the lights from the police cars and ambulance."

"All that can't be so," Freddie said.

Fletch didn't say anything.

"Is Wheeler pointing his finger at anyone else?"

"He's mentioned Andrew Esty."

"Esty?" Freddie laughed. "I don't think his religion condones murder."

"He's been with the campaign three weeks. He left yesterday, came back, there was another murder. I saw him in the elevator last night. He was frustrated, angry—"

"Esty wouldn't want to be caught as a murderer." Freddie smiled. "The Supreme Court might prohibit prisoners from praying."

"Bill Dieckmann," Fletch said.

"Bill's pretty sick, I guess."

"Last night I found him in the corridor of the fifth floor of this hotel. He was having one of his seizures. When I came across him, he was leaning against the wall. He didn't recognize me. He didn't know where he was or what he was doing. He collapsed. I carried him to his own room on the ninth floor. When he came to, he didn't know how he got there."

"What was he doing on the fifth floor?"

"Who knows? But this morning I realized he was standing between the main elevators and the service elevators. The chambermaid was found in a service elevator, right?"

Freddie's face was sad. "Poor old Bill. He's got five kids." Then she laughed. "Did you see Filby's face yesterday when he realized he had missed the whole 'New Reality' speech? You'd think the doctor had just told him he'd have to have his whole stomach amputated."

"That would be hard to swallow."

"Joe Hall has an uncontrollable temper," Freddie said. "I saw him lose it once. At a trial in Nashville. A courtroom marshal wouldn't let him in. Said his press credentials were no good. Joe went berserk. He began swinging at people."

"And you can't tell me," Fletch said, "that Solov is your normal Russian boy-next-door. If what you all say is true, he sits there watching pornography all night. He must build up a hell of a head of steam. Goin' out and beatin' women to death might be his way of finishing off a night of such entertainment."

"Poor Russians," Freddie sighed. "They have so little experience handling smut."

"Are you listening to me?"

"He bears watching."

"I think he's a very good candidate. Might even oblige Wheeler's theory of someone wanting to sabotage the campaign."

"So where does Wheeler go when he disappears?" Freddie asked.

"You keep bringing the conversation back to Wheeler."

"You keep steering me away from Wheeler. And his staff. You keep pushing it on the press. Have you forgotten yourself so easily? Really, how quickly one becomes a member of the establishment."

"I'm trying to be honest with you. I trust you."

"Now that you know I really am Freddie Arbuthnot."

"Yes. Now that we both agree you're Fredericka Arbuthnot."

"There are plenty of kooks on staff. Dr. Thom, who clearly got his medical degree from Bother U."

"He has his hatreds."

"That Lee Allen Parke is a manipulator of women, if I ever saw one. And I've seen plenty. The governor's driver—"

"Flash Grasselli."

"—has the body of a brute, and the brain of a newt. Barry Hines is twitching so fast you can't even see him."

"I guess we've got kooks on this campaign."

"Fletcher, dear, you're almost beginning to seem normal to me."

"You mean, next to Solov?"

"Next to Solov, Maxim Gorky would seem a fun date."

Fletch glanced at his watch. It was twenty to twelve. "We've got a press bus to catch." He went to the bed and closed his suitcase. "The rally at the shopping mall is at one o'clock. Tonight in Melville is the last big rally of this campaign."

She hadn't moved from her chair. "So where does the governor go when he disappears?"

"Oh, Flash gave me some cock-and-bull story about his going to some unnamed mountain cabin on some unnamed lake and going on a sleep orgy."

"A sleep orgy?"

"He reads and sleeps for a few days."

"I'll bet."

"I'm not sure I believe it."

Freddie stood up. "Fletch, let's keep talking about this to each other, okay?"

"Absolutely."

She crossed the room to the door. "There must be things we're not noticing, not hearing, not seeing. You know—like that Ms. Sullivan, the way she just treated that woman reporter from a local newspaper. She's a tough, vicious broad."

Fletch had put his suitcase on the floor. He had not opened the door. "Promise me something else, Freddie?"

"No."

"Keep your eyes and ears open for your own sake. Someone traveling with us likes to maul women. You're a woman."

"I've never proven that to you."

"I watched you fold my jacket."

"Oh."

"Going to kiss me on the nose again?"

"You're exploiting me," she said.

She kissed him warmly on the mouth.

Fletch let Freddie out and went back to answer his phone.

"More of the same tomorrow," a whiskey voice grated in Fletch's ear.

"Am I supposed to know who this is?"

"This is *Newsbill*'s star writer, you jackass."

"Gee, Hanrahan. I thought you'd dashed to New York to catch your Pulitzer Prize."

"More tomorrow," Hanrahan said, "of specifically who refuses to talk to me about the murdered broads. I'm going to publish a list of questions I'm not getting answered. Like where was Caxton Wheeler when Alice Elizabeth Shields got exited through his bedroom window? In whose bedroom had she spent the previous four nights? Why was Barry Hines thrown out of the University of Idaho? While Walsh Wheeler was in the Marines, did he machine-gun a bunch of kids?"

"No."

"Questions don't matter, sonny. Just the answers or lack thereof."

"Barry Hines flunked out of the University of Idaho. Chemistry. Many do."

"Who cares? You got my point?"

"You're doin' fine, Hanrahan. If I actually let you talk to someone, will you really write down what he says and print it, like a reporter? Or just use the opportunity to write fiction?"

"Guess you got to take that chance, jackass. If I can't print something that looks like answers, I'm going to print something that looks like questions."

"Oh, I see," Fletch said brilliantly. "That's why people refer to what you write as questionable. 'Bye, Mike."

Using his hotel room phone, Fletch then communicated with Barry Hines and told him to find Walsh and tell Walsh he must plan to see Michael J. Hanrahan and Fredericka Arbuthnot.

28

Fletch opened the back door of the rented black sedan. "Walsh said I should drive with you to the shopping plaza."

Doris Wheeler gave him a friendly nod. "Fine."

He had found Walsh, without topcoat or tie, standing on the sidewalk outside the hotel. Coldly, Walsh said he had agreed to meet with Fredericka Arbuthnot and Michael J. Hanrahan, if Fletch thought it so necessary.

"Shall I sit in front?" The two women, Doris Wheeler and Ms Sullivan, pretty well filled up the backseat. Fletch did not recognize the car's rented driver.

"No, no," Doris Wheeler said. "Plenty of room back here. Go around and get in the other side."

Fletch went around the back of the car and got in the other side. Which pushed the tall, short-haired, big-nosed Ms Sullivan onto the middle of the seat, her feet onto the high gasline bump. Which made her look like a large dog in a small box.

"We haven't met," Fletch said to her. "I. M. Fletcher."

Ms Sullivan raised her upper lip in greeting. "Sully."

189

The campaign bus was pulling away from the curb in front of the hotel, followed by the press bus. Around the area, other cars—those of volunteers and station wagons filled with television equipment—were rolling forward to form a caravan.

"Get behind the second bus," Doris Wheeler ordered the driver.

In the road was slow confusion. The hotel's doorman was trying to stop traffic so the caravan could assemble itself, but Farmingdale drivers were not impressed by his green-and-gold suit, or his brown derby hat. They honked their horns at him and insisted upon going directly about their own business.

A volunteer's green van and a blue pickup truck ended up between the press bus and Doris Wheeler's sedan. The bumper sticker on the pickup truck read: HONK FOR UP-TON.

The rented driver honked his horn.

"Stop that," Doris Wheeler said.

"I hear you had some difficulty with a local reporter this morning," Fletch ventured.

"Cow," said Sully.

"Was she rude or something?"

"Stupid."

Doris said to the driver, "I told you to get directly behind the second bus."

All the vehicles were jammed together at a red light. The driver looked at Doris through the rearview mirror and did nothing. There was nothing he could do.

"How did she offend you?" Fletch asked.

"I make appointments for Mrs. Wheeler," Sully said.

"She didn't need a real appointment. All she wanted to do was hang around and watch, listen."

"We didn't have time for any such person this morning," Sully said. "Furthermore, you are not to force people upon us, Fletcher. All this is none of your affair."

"My 'affair,' as you call it," Fletch said, "is the whole campaign. We're supposed to be working together."

"Now, now." Doris Wheeler patted Sully's knee. "Mr. Fletcher is working for this campaign. We're looking forward to his help. You're going to start being a great help to us, aren't you, Mr. Fletcher?''

Doris Wheeler's voice was abrasive even in dulcet tones in the back of the car.

At the appearance of a green light the caravan had sprung forward.

"Pass those two vehicles," Doris Wheeler said.

"We won't lose the buses, ma'am," the driver said.

"Pass them, I said!"

Again the driver glanced through the rearview mirror. On the main street of Farmingdale he swung the car out into oncoming traffic. An approaching yellow Cadillac screeched on its brakes. A Honda smashed into its rear end. The rented driver got back into the right lane ahead of the pickup truck, but still behind the volunteer's car.

"Imbecile," Doris Wheeler said. She pronounced it *imbeseal*. "Get ahead of this car."

"When I have room," the driver muttered.

"Don't you speak to me that way," Doris Wheeler said. "Do as you're told!"

They were far enough away from the center of Farmingdale so that the traffic had lightened. The driver swung out, waved the volunteer's car back, and pulled up snug behind the press bus.

"Ought to be nice to the local press," Fletch said. "Judy Nadich may be a feature writer for the *Farmingdale Views* this year. But three years from now she may be a columnist for the *Washington Post*."

"Three years from now," Sully said, "she'll be up to her nose in diapers and burning meatloaf for a beery husband."

"I don't know what you two are talking about," Doris Wheeler said.

"That stupid cow who appeared at the door this morning."

"Which one?"

"The smiling one. She thought she had permission from this Fletcher here. She showed me some scribble on a piece of notepaper." Sully sniffed. "She thought it meant something."

"Did you send her up, Fletcher?"

"You could have made a friend for life. She's a young woman reporter and this story would have set her up."

"Have you been on a political campaign before, Fletcher?" Doris Wheeler asked.

"No, ma'am."

"I have no idea why Caxton took you on."

"To make mistakes, ma'am," Fletch answered evenly. "To create an aura of youth and amateurism about the campaign." There was a surprised hard gleam in Doris's eyes as she stared sideways at him. "To be blamed for everything and get fired, probably just before the Pennsylvania and California primaries. To warm the seat for Graham Kidwell." Even Sully was looking at him as if he were a kitten messing with her dinner bowl. "To get sent home on a bus."

They were entering the highway. There was another snow squall.

Doris said, "I don't know why Walsh happened to think of you."

"I know how to run a copying machine."

"What you did for my son while you were in the service together was nice." Doris Wheeler settled her coat more comfortably around her shoulder. "But really, I don't think he needs that kind of help now."

The driver was keeping the car so close behind the press bus that the car was being sprayed by slush and sand from the highway. He had the windshield wipers going full speed. The whole car, even the rear windows, was being covered with mud.

"Imbecile!" Doris shouted at him. "Slow down! Let the bus get ahead of us!"

"Don't want anybody to pass us, ma'am," the driver drawled.

"Imbecile! Where did Barry find this man?" Doris asked Fletch loudly. "The local games arcade?"

"In my spare time—when I'm not driving idiots—I'm a fireman."

Doris's eyes bulged. "Well, my man. You just lost both jobs."

Sully took pad and pen from her purse and made a note.

Through the rearview mirror the driver looked at Fletch.

"Now," said Doris Wheeler, again settling her coat over her big shoulders, "let's talk about what you can do to be helpful."

Fletch put on his listening expression. He had learned to do that in junior high school.

"My husband, Fletcher, is a dependent man. Very bright, very energetic—all that is true. But he's always going around asking people what they think. You see, he's not really confident in what he himself thinks."

"He listens to advisors?" Fletch speculated.

"He listens to everybody. Caxton," Doris Wheeler confided, "is very impressed by the last idea he hears."

"Whatever it is," Sully added.

"He's impressionable?" Fletch conjectured.

"I've known the man thirty-odd years."

"Ever since Barbara died?"

She stared at him as if he had burped resoundingly in public. "Who's Barbara?"

"Oh," he said.

"I dare say," she continued, "he flattered you by asking you what you thought."

"He did."

"And you came up with that whole 'New Reality' nonsense."

"Not really."

"Young people always think it's clever to disparage our institutions."

"It's not?"

"Politically, it's suicide. As I said last night. You can knock the institutions on their goddamned asses," her voice grated, "as long as you always give them lip service. That's the *only* reality."

"The governor gave an interview on all this to Lansing Sayer this morning," Fletch said. "It was pretty good. It sounded to me like he's actually coming up with a program."

The driver had slowed down so much that the buses were way ahead of them. Clearly the volunteers did not dare pass Doris Wheeler's car.

"The trouble with Caxton," Doris Wheeler said, "is that he doesn't always think. Even if he really were saying

something here, he doesn't always stop to think of the effect
of his saying it. I spent a long time with Andrew Esty this
morning.''

"You did?''

Sully vigorously nodded yes.

"Told him all about my grandfather, who was a fundamentalist
preacher in Nebraska. . . .'' Doris Wheeler then proceeded to
tell Fletch all about her grandfather who was a fundamentalist
preacher in Nebraska. It was his son, Doris's father, who had
discovered oil.

Fletch put on his not-listening expression. He had learned
that in junior high school, too.

The NBC Television News station wagon pulled out of the
caravan and began to pass Doris Wheeler's car.

"Speed up!'' she shouted at the driver. "You're losing
them.''

The driver began racing with the news wagon.

"Ah, good,'' said Fletch. "I always wanted to be in *Ben
Hur*.''

"Imbecile,'' said Doris Wheeler.

Close behind the NBC wagon was the CBS wagon. The
ABC news wagon appeared on the right side of the car. Doris
Wheeler's car was getting pelted with slush from both sides.

"You must be careful what you say around Caxton,'' Doris
Wheeler concluded. "It's your job to protect him—from
himself, when necessary. Not to walk him down the garden
path.''

Up ahead, the buses had disappeared altogether.

"What do you ladies think of these murders?'' Fletch
asked.

"You mean, the women?'' Doris Wheeler asked.

"You're aware of them.''

"Of course.''

"Any theories?'' asked Fletch.

The turnoff to the shopping mall was at the top of a small
rise. By then all the vehicles in the caravan were going so fast
that slowing down properly and turning was problematical.
There was some skidding. The volunteer's green van missed

the turn altogether and had to go miles west and then east and then west again to get back to the right turnoff.

"No. No theories," Doris Wheeler said. "Why should we have theories? It's a police matter."

The campaign bus and the press bus were in the middle of the shopping plaza's parking lot. A crowd of two or three thousand people was standing around in the cold slush, waiting for the candidate.

"We don't have any police traveling with us," Fletch commented.

"What this campaign doesn't need," Sully said, "is a police investigation."

"Don't believe in law and order, huh?" Fletch asked.

Sully's look told him she thought him something not to be stepped in.

The driver parked far away from the buses. He parked in the middle of the biggest puddle in the parking lot. Then he sat there. He did not get out to open doors.

"This car is filthy," Doris Wheeler told him as she opened her own door.

"Don't worry," the driver muttered. "You'll never see it again."

"I told you I'm going to report you," Doris Wheeler said, lifting herself off the seat.

"You may be Mrs. President of the United States!" the driver shouted at her through the open door. "But in Farmingdale, you're just a big old bag!"

Sully had followed Doris Wheeler out of the car. Fletch got out his own side.

"I wouldn't vote for your husband for dogcatcher!" the driver shouted. "He doesn't know a bitch when he sees one!"

The driver accelerated, splashing all of them.

"My God." Doris Wheeler looked at her splattered skirt. At the size of the puddle they were all standing in. At the back of the rapidly disappearing car. "That car was hired for all day. He can't just leave me here."

Fletch watched the filthy rented car climb back onto the highway. "Actually, he can," Fletch said. "He just did."

29

"Good afternoon. I have just a brief announcement," said the President of the United States.

"I guess you do," Phil Nolting said to the television set. "When did you ever give a Saturday afternoon press conference? Sports fans won't love you."

Barry Hines said to Fletch, "You're to call someone named Alston Chambers. He says you have his number. Also Rondoll James has called you twice. Here's his number."

"You can forget James," Walsh muttered.

The campaign bus had pulled into a rest area and stopped. Even the bus driver was watching the President's press conference.

The press bus had stopped a mile down the road at a tavern to watch the press conference.

"He wants to inspire a million Sunday sermons, I bet," Paul Dobson said. "Up with God and country."

His head resting against a pillow, a cut on his cheek, The Man Who sat on the bench at the side of the bus, watching the television, saying nothing.

The rally at the shopping plaza had not been a success.

The governor climbed to the roof of a volunteer's Ford, microphone in hand. Every time he said something the sound system screeched horribly. Again and again the governor tried to speak while Barry Hines and the bus driver scurried around trying to discover what was causing the screeching. Then he tried speaking without the microphone. The wind, the sound of traffic in the parking lot, the noise of jet airplanes passing overhead made the governor look like a frantic, laryngytic opera singer.

Doris Wheeler completely ignored the crowd. She went directly to the campaign bus, spluttering about her wet shoes and splattered skirt. Sully followed her as if she were on a short leash.

Fletch said to Walsh, "Don't ask me to drive in the car with your mother again. Please."

"Yeah," Walsh said. "That Sully." Through his open shirt collar his Adam's apple rose and fell. "Tough broad."

"The driver went off and left them here. In the middle of a puddle."

Walsh looked around the parking lot. "That's okay. A volunteer will drive her to the senior citizens' home. That always looks better anyway. No problem."

The governor climbed down from the wet car roof. He handed the microphone to Lee Allen Parke, who handed it to a volunteer, who handed it back to Barry Hines.

Then The Man Who walked into the crowd, both hands out to the people, allowing himself to be grabbed, pulled, pushed, jostled nearly off his feet. A little girl sitting on her father's shoulders vomited on his head. Somehow an older woman, trying to kiss the governor, gashed his cheek with her fingernail. The Man Who kept reaching over people's heads to shake hands with people behind them so the crowd kept pressing closer and closer to him. Shortly a fistfight broke out near the back of the crowd. From where Fletch was standing, he could see that three men had gotten a man in a black leather jacket down on the ground and were beating him pretty well. Two short, older men were trying to get them to stop. Walsh went into the crowd, turned his father around, and literally pushed him back onto the campaign bus.

Doris Wheeler and Sully got into the backseat of the volunteer's Ford and were driven away.

The campaign bus left ahead of schedule.

As the bus was leaving, the man in the black leather jacket was staggering through the thinning crowd, yelling at them incomprehensibly through broken teeth and blood.

Aboard the bus, Flash cleaned the scratch on the governor's face. He put antiseptic on it. The governor grinned at his staff. "Winning the hearts and minds of the people...There must be an easier job than this."

"Sorry," Barry Hines said.

Walsh said, "It's this damned weather."

So the caravan went on until nearly two o'clock and then parked at the tavern and in the rest area to watch the President's news conference.

Aboard the campaign bus everyone was silent while the President read his statement: "The technology we have available today, especially the technology of communications, is not being used for the betterment of the people of the world. Clearly, the people of all nations would benefit from a fuller, more responsible use of this technology, to bring basic education to all people, to exchange scientific data, programs of cultural merit, health information, and the facts that can provide for a more equitable and waste-free worldwide allocation of food. Proper use of this technology should be encouraged by responsible governments. Therefore, today I am naming a special White House panel of distinguished citizens, and charging them with reporting to me how the technology of communications can be better used, worldwide, to encourage the peace and increase the prosperity of all nations." The President blinked through the television lights at the White House press corps. "Now I'll take questions."

"The son of a bitch stole your issue," Walsh said quietly.

The Man Who sat with his head back against the pillow. He continued to watch the press conference silently.

Most of the questions were about Central America, the economy, the Middle East, the Russian economic situation, and whether the President would agree to debate any or all of the other people running for the presidency and, if so, when. "It's much too early to discuss that."

At the end of the press conference, Barry Hines clicked off the television set.

Loudly, more firmly, directly at his father, Walsh said again, "The son of a bitch stole your issue."

"That's all right." The governor looked around at his staff and chuckled. "At least the son of a bitch got me out of trouble with my wife."

30

"How do, Mr. Persecutor." Fletch had taken the moment to lie down on his bed at the Melville First Hotel and return Alston Chambers's call. "Only got a minute. Got to meet Walsh and a couple of members of the press in a bar about a matter of death and death. And death."

"How's it going, Fletch?"

"Feel like I'm dancin' to the 'Three Page Sonata,'" answered Fletch. "Have to do more listenin' than dancin'."

It was five o'clock. The rally at Melville's public auditorium was to begin at eight o'clock.

From three to four that afternoon, Fletch had sat through a call-in radio talk show with The Man Who in the town of McKensie. Many of the people who called in had intelligent, pertinent questions regarding Social Security, farm subsidies, federal highway funds. A significant percentage called The Man Who with personal problems. *"My wife is working now, we need the extra income, you know, to eat? This means my kids come home from school to an empty house, we ask a neighbor to watch over them, but she has arthritis, she can't*

*move none too fast, we never know what they're doin', you
know? Why can't things be like they were? When I was a kid,
my mother was home . . .''* The high incidence of crime came
up more than once, naturally, and the governor made the most
of the opportunity, referring to the chambermaid found murdered
in his hotel that morning. For an hour The Man Who made a
sincere effort to answer all questions, public and private.

And then the slow crawl by car over dark roads from
McKensie to Melville. Flash drove. In the backseat, the
governor read. In the front seat, Fletch watched the fifty-five-
mile-per-hour signs approach at thirty miles per hour.

At the Melville First Hotel, messages were waiting for
Fletch. Asking him to contact journalists traveling with the
campaign (Lansing Sayer, Fenella Baker, Stella Kirchner).
Asking him to contact other journalists calling in from around
the country (plus one from Mexico City and one from the
Times of London). There were three messages asking him to
return the calls of Rondoll James in Iowa.

He had returned Alston Chambers's call.

Alston said, "Thought I'd tell you I followed up on that
question I asked you last night."

"What question?"

"About Walsh's sudden departure from the field. After our
three days hanging in the trees."

"Sure. He was tired. He'd had enough of it. His poppa had
the political pull to bring him home. I would have gotten out
of there at that point, too, if I could have. Any of us would
have."

"Yes, but not quite. Walsh sassed a superior officer."

Fletch blinked. "Who didn't?"

"I talked to Captain Walters. He runs a book distribution
center in Denver now, by the way."

"Nice man. Used to get reading books for all of us. Never
lost his cool."

"Yeah, well he says that at one point, Walsh did."

"You're kidding."

"Laced into Major Leslie Hunt."

"First time I ever heard her name pronounced with an *H*."

"That she was. You remember her."

"Awful bitch. Resented soldiers being men."

"Remember the thing she was always going on about?"

"Yeah. Mess tent had to be in the middle. Regulations. Forget the snipers. Mess tent in the middle to impress the enemy. As they shot at us. Impress them with our stupidity."

"Two guys from K Company got shot on their way to breakfast. One in the leg, not bad; one in the back, pretty bad."

"I don't remember that."

"Walters says that's what started it off. Walsh yelled at Major Hunt in staff meeting."

"He got sent home for that? Should have gotten a free night at the Officers' Club."

"No. Later he threatened her."

"Good."

"With a rifle butt. That's where his dad's pull came in. There were two or three witnesses. Captain Walters said that charges might have been brought against Walsh, probably would have been, if his dad weren't in Congress on some military appropriations committee."

"Hell, Walsh had been through three of the worst days in any man's life. The major was a stupid bitch. Never been to the front herself, so she wanted to make heroes in the chow line."

"All true. Thought I'd tell you."

"So Walsh lost his temper at her. Good for him."

"Walters remembers you. Asked for stories about you. I said there weren't any."

"Walsh isn't so stupid," Fletch said. "Scared the shit out of a bitch, and got a quick ride home. His momma didn't have no fools."

31

"I agreed to meet with you two against my better judgment," Walsh said.

They sat at a small round table in a dark corner of a bar a block from Melville's First Hotel. Peanuts glistened in a bowl in the center of the table. A glass of beer had been placed in front of each of them: Walsh, Fletch, Michael J. Hanrahan, and Fredericka Arbuthnot. Hanrahan had been served a shot of rye as well.

The juke box was playing "Limpin' Home to Jesus."

Hanrahan downed his rye.

"Fletch, here, insisted upon it, apparently because of the shit you published in *Newsbill* this morning, Hanrahan," Walsh continued in a low tone. "A few hours after you join the campaign, apparently you can make headlines in your rag by writing no one would talk to you about some murders or something that happened sometime, somewhere." Walsh rolled his eyes upward and shook his head. "I expect there are a few examples of breaking and entering that have happened around us you also might ask us about. And don't forget sodomy. A lot of sodomy goes on in these motels." His voice was almost a tired drone. "What we're really meeting about is very simple. You're not political writers, either of you. Fletcher tells me you're crime writers. There's no reason I can think of why we should make room for you on the press bus. You've asked for this meeting, and I'm going to give it to you. But at the moment, I can't think of any reason why I shouldn't ask Fletch to deny press credentials to you both."

"Speech over?" Hanrahan asked.

Freddie had glanced at Fletch. "Denying us press credentials wouldn't do you much good. Riding the press bus isn't the most pleasurable experience of my life."

"Yeah," Hanrahan said. "*Newsworld* would supply Arbuthnot with a limousine and driver. Me, I'd get a helicopter. In other words, stuff it, Wheeler."

Walsh popped some peanuts into his mouth. "Fletch and I have to be at a staff meeting in a few minutes." Chewing, Walsh's neck muscles were visibly tight through his opened shirt collar. "If you've got any questions, you'd better roll 'em out."

Hanrahan had downed his beer. For a moment, his eyes sparkled. "How long had you known Alice Elizabeth Shields?"

"I never knew her," Walsh answered.

"You met her in Chicago?"

"I did not know her."

"Who did—your dad?"

"My father did not know her."

"Then, how come she ended up dead outside his motel room window?"

Walsh snorted. He didn't answer.

"Walsh," Freddie said. "It might help matters if we had a list of the people who were in your father's suite the night Alice Elizabeth Shields was murdered."

"A specific list would be impossible, Ms. Arbuthnot. There were some of the local press. I do not know their names. A couple of local political coordinators. One was named William Burke, the other something-or-other Blackstone. There was national press: Fenella Baker, Lansing Sayer, your own Mary Rice"—he nodded to Hanrahan—"Dieckmann, O'Brien, a few others."

"Were you there?" Hanrahan asked.

"I was there. In and out."

"Was Solov there?" Fletch asked.

"I don't remember."

"Was Dr. Thom there?" Freddie asked.

"I don't remember. I doubt it. He avoids the press, for the most part."

"Back home," Hanrahan announced, "your Dr. Robert Thom is known as a Dr. Feelgood. Writes more prescriptions than anyone in the county. How come he's your dad's private physician?"

"Dr. Thom is the physician traveling with the campaign, available to all."

"How much of a drug addict is your dad?" Hanrahan asked. He reached over and took Freddie's beer.

"My father is not addicted to anything," Walsh answered. "Never has been."

"Then how come they have to cart him away three or four times a year to clean out his head?"

Walsh said, "I'm not going to dignify that with an answer."

"Where does your father go?" Freddie asked. "You know, when he suddenly disappears."

"He doesn't 'suddenly disappear.' He takes advantage of breaks in his schedule, when they occur. He goes fishing. He reads history. Even Caxton Wheeler gets to take a few days off, now and again. During last calendar year, my father took exactly fifteen days away from his desk. Make a scandal of that, if you can."

"Specifically, where does he go?" Hanrahan asked.

"None of your business."

"He always goes alone," Freddie said.

"No," Walsh answered. "A staff member always goes with him."

"Flash Grasselli," Hanrahan scoffed. "A packing case on wheels."

"A packing case with a computer inside," Fletch said.

"Again, it might help put questions to rest," Freddie said,

"if we could work out your father's timetable the night Alice Elizabeth Shields died. When, precisely, he got back to the hotel . . . that sort of thing."

"I doubt he knows," Walsh said. "There are four time zones in this country. On a campaign, we're back and forth across time zones all the time. Living this way, one loses a sense of time, you know. Precise time."

"I doubt you do, Walsh," Freddie said.

"Oh, stuff it, stocking-mouth." Hanrahan finished the rest of her beer. "Just 'cause *Newsworld* let you have their telephone number, don't think you're a real journalist."

Freddie smiled at Fletch.

"This broad in Chicago," Hanrahan said. "This Mrs. Gynecologist—"

"Elaine Ramsey," Freddie giggled. "Wife of an obstetrician. Want to make a note of that, Michael? Or should I phone *Newsbill* for you?"

"You and your dad both knew her."

"I don't think either of us knew her," Walsh answered.

"You were seen talking to her at that press reception at the Hotel Harris." Hanrahan picked up Fletch's beer. "So was your dad."

"Hanrahan, we talk to a lot of people. A lot of people talk to us. That's what a political campaign is all about."

"And some of them end up dead." Beer sprayed through Hanrahan's teeth.

Now the jukebox was playing "I'm Rushin' to Coke High."

"Okay," Freddie said. "You state neither you nor your father knew Mrs. Ramsey."

"I can't speak for my father. I certainly don't believe he knew her. I don't see how he could have. I did not know her."

"You can't speak for your old man," Hanrahan said. "Why don't you wheel the old boy out here, give me a shot at him? Dr. Thom can pop him up for the occasion."

Pointedly, Walsh looked at his watch.

"Maybe you can answer some questions about last night," Hanrahan said. "Does your memory go back that far?"

"What questions?" Walsh asked patiently.

"Coroner places the death of Mary Cantor, the hotel maid, at between eleven P.M. and two-thirty A.M. You weren't in your room at twelve midnight."

"Were you there?" Walsh asked easily. With a tighter jaw, Walsh said, "You'd better not violate the privacy of myself or my family ever again, Hanrahan. Or staff members."

"Where were you?" Hanrahan asked.

"After I came in, Fletch and I had a brief meeting in my room. That was about eleven-thirty, wasn't it, Fletch? Then I went to my mother's suite. We had a few things to discuss. Then I went back to my room to clear up a few papers."

"That doesn't account for three and a half hours," Hanrahan said.

Walsh shrugged. "What can I say?"

"Can you tell me where you were at the time Alice Elizabeth Shields tried to dent the sidewalk?"

"I don't remember. I was in the bar. Before that I had been in my room."

"Using the telephone?" Hanrahan asked.

"I suppose so."

"The hotel operator says your room's telephone didn't answer from eight o'clock on that night."

"Sometimes I don't answer the phone when I've got work to do. I had a meeting with Barry Hines. Phil Nolting and I were trying to work out the South Africa thing. I was in the bar, waiting for Fletch to arrive. People were calling about Rondoll James, friends of his on the press, so I wasn't answering the phone. Sorry I can't give you a perfect alibi."

"Wheeler, when you were in the Marines overseas, you were almost court-martialed."

The muscles in Walsh's jaw tightened.

The jukebox was playing "Give Me the Land of the Free."

"What do you mean?" Walsh asked.

"You refused to lead a patrol one night. The patrol that did go out got slaughtered."

"He didn't refuse," put in Fletch. "We were all too stoned to go. Everyone was too stoned. Everyone except the lieutenant."

"You're fishing for minnows, Hanrahan," Walsh said. "I wasn't court-martialed."

"No. Your dad prevented it."

"My dad had nothing to do with my service record."

"And he arranged to get you home ahead of schedule."

"I was ordered to Washington," Walsh admitted. "And my father did have something to do with that. I studied statistics in college. I was assigned to a bureau of statistics at the Department of Defense to serve out the remainder of my time. Make of that what you will."

"You were assigned for just two months?" Hanrahan exclaimed.

"There was a statistical mess," Walsh answered. "My father wanted to see if the statistics being published by the Pentagon had any particular reality to a young officer who had been in the field."

Hanrahan said: "Bullshit."

"While we're speaking of statistics, let me say this." Walsh leaned forward in his chair and crossed his forearms on the table. "Over twenty thousand Americans get murdered a year. Over thirty percent of American families get touched by crime one way or another every year. In this interview, I'm not going to spout a lot of sociological reasons for these figures, or how Caxton Wheeler's administration might bring these figures down. I wouldn't so insult Ms Arbuthnot. It's an epidemic. But I will point out to you, statistically, that right now, none of us—presidential candidate or not—can go anywhere, be anywhere, without a violent crime happening somewhere up the block, down the street, in the park across from the hotel. That's all the news I have for you crime writers. I have no personal knowledge of these crimes. Neither has my father. If you think they're connected with this campaign somehow, then I suggest you take a close look at your colleagues on the press bus. Frankly, I think it's just a fact of contemporary American life."

"Broads aren't gettin' knocked off on the Upton campaign," Hanrahan said. "We haven't been assigned to travel with the Graves campaign."

"So be it," Walsh said. "Be careful what you write. This

is a political campaign you're covering, not a Halloween parade.''

Fletch followed Walsh's lead in getting up to go. Only Walsh's beer had not been consumed by Hanrahan.

"Hey, Wheeler," Hanrahan asked. "How come you never married?"

Looking back from the door, Fletch saw Hanrahan alone at the table. Walsh's beer was now in front of him. On Hanrahan's face was the grin/grimace.

Freddie followed them back to the hotel at a discreet distance.

"Filthy, foul-smelling, crude bastard." Walsh grinned. "Do you think I did much good with him?"

"Sure," said Fletch. "You prevented him from printing a lot."

32

"A slight change of plans," The Man Who announced to his staff. "I've decided that Mrs. Wheeler, who is to be on the platform with me tonight at the big rally anyway, will say a few words." Everyone in the room remained expressionless. "She'll speak just ahead of me. In fact, after she says what she wants to say, she'll be the one to introduce me. Walsh, make sure that the local dignitary, whoever it is, understands he is to introduce your mother, not me."

"Congressman Jack Snive."

"Ah!" The governor grinned. "We finally made it into his district."

Walsh hitched forward in his chair. "The congressman wants to introduce you, Dad. Not introduce Mother. It's important to him."

"Well, he's going to introduce your mother," the governor said coldly. "Who else is to be on the platform?"

"The mayor of Melville, a judge—"

"Have I got briefing papers on all of them?"

Walsh handed his father a sheaf of papers.

The staff was meeting in the living room of the candidate's suite at Melville's First Hotel. The standardization of hotel rooms in middle America was beginning to give Fletch a homey feeling.

"Barry?" The governor glanced through the papers. "Anything to report?"

"Yes, sir," Barry Hines said briskly. "You're down four points in the Harris poll, three points in the Gallup."

The governor looked up, mildly surprised. "I thought we were doing well."

"The current statewide polls," Barry continued, "put Upton eight percentage points ahead of you, Graves four points behind you."

The governor's index finger went over the scar on his cheek.

"Upton," Lee Allen Parke said. "He hasn't even been here. He's been in Pennsylvania and Iowa."

"Absence must make the heart grow fonder," Phil Nolting said.

"That's not so good," the governor said. "I guess some of the things I said in Winslow . . ."

". . . hurt." Paul Dobson finished the sentence for him.

"Doris was right," the governor admitted.

"We were all right," Dobson said.

"Maybe it's that green suit Walsh is wearing," Lee Allen Parke said. "Makes the voters see us as 'a crusade of amateurs.' "

"More to the point," Walsh said, "the President seems to have taken the best part of your issue and run away with it."

"Not exactly," said the governor. "He's done what he can do—trivialized it, named a White House panel. Paul and Phil, I want you to work up a first-class speech for me. I'll deliver it Monday night. Is television guaranteed Monday night?"

"Yeah," said Barry. "We bought it."

"This is to be a major speech," the governor said. "The theme is to be that I want to promote international meetings, most definitely including all the nations of the Third World, to reach international agreements for further, universal development and control of the new technology of communications.'' The governor was speaking extremely slowly. Nolting was writing down his instructions word for word. ''My point being not to control the new technology, but to draw up a sort of international constitution guaranteeing that no one—no nation, no political party, no group—gets to control too large a share of the new technology.''

''Isn't that all rather statesmanlike?'' Dobson asked.

The governor glowered at him. ''Do your best, Paul.''

In a lighter tone, Nolting asked, ''Shall we use such phrases as 'to encourage the peace, and increase the prosperity of all nations'?''

''Has a nice ring to it,'' the governor said wryly. ''I'm afraid you'll have to try coming up with a phrase or two of my own.''

''Dad,'' Walsh said, ''you're on 'Q. & A.' from New York in the morning. That's national television exposure. Plus an intelligent, more than usually thoughtful Sunday morning audience. If you want to hit a big idea like this, wouldn't you be better off hitting it on 'Q. & A.' than at a noisy rally at the state capital the night before election?''

''Maybe.'' The governor thought. ''Always a good idea to save the big guns until last. The 'Q. & A.' audience is a good audience.''

''For statesmanlike statements,'' Dobson said.

''So telegraph your punch,'' Fletch said.

''Yeah,'' the governor said. ''On 'Q. & A.' I'll indicate I'm not through with that topic, that Upton, Graves, the President didn't respond fully or accurately, and that I'll have something more to say on it Monday night.''

Barry Hines nodded. ''People should listen.''

''Speaking of full and accurate response to the Winslow speech,'' Walsh said, '' 'Q. & A.' goes on the air at eleven o'clock. We have you scheduled to attend service at the Thirty-sixth Street Church at nine o'clock. While you and Fletch were doing that talk show this afternoon, Barry and I rigged up press coverage for your appearance at the church. By the way, Fletch,'' Walsh said, ''do not go to church with Dad.''

''You're telling me not to go to church?''

"Don't want anything like a press representative escorting Dad into church. You get the idea."

"I'm being told not to go to church."

"When do I sleep?" the governor asked.

"The pilot's been told to expect to take off for New York from Melville Airport at about twelve-thirty tonight," Walsh answered. "You'll be asleep by two-thirty."

"Who's going with me?" the governor asked.

"Fletch and Barry will be with you. And Flash."

"And Bob," the governor said.

"And Dr. Thom," Walsh confirmed.

"You don't have to worry about drinking New York water," Paul Dobson said.

Walsh turned his head to look at Dobson. The muscles in Walsh's neck were visibly tight through his unbuttoned collar.

The governor said to Nolting and Dobson, "Have the Monday speech pretty well roughed out for me by the time I get back tomorrow."

"We expect you in the state capital tomorrow around four, four-thirty," Walsh said. "We'll try to have a hoopla at the airport for you, but it won't be easy on Sunday afternoon. The N.F.L. game will be on."

"Who gets to run the nation," the governor commented, "takes second place to who gets to run with a football." He looked up at his staff. "Anything else?"

Walsh said, "Fletch, come to my room with me while I change. I've got a stack of recent press clippings for you. Particularly from Wisconsin. Got to start learning the Wisconsin journalists."

"Yeah," Fletch said to the room at large. "There is something else we've got to discuss."

Everyone resettled in his chair.

"A chambermaid named Mary Cantor, widow of a Navy navigator, was murdered in the hotel we were in last night. A woman named Alice Elizabeth Shields, a store clerk, was murdered in the motel we were in two nights ago."

"Jeez," said Walsh.

"And a woman named Elaine Ramsey, wife of an obstetrician, was found murdered in a closet next to the press reception room at the Hotel Harris in Chicago while you were staying there.''

''Do you think the New York Cosmos will win the cup this year?'' Barry Hines asked.

''I saw *Newsbill*,'' Phil Nolting said. ''I think you should have done whatever you had to do to contain this story through the election Tuesday.''

''Okay,'' said Fletch. ''I never said I'm very good at this job.''

''Your sympathies are still with the press,'' Dobson said simply. ''You don't care what a story is. Instinctively, you want it reported. The sleazier, the better.''

''Hang on,'' the governor said. ''There is a worrisome point here. There have been these murders. There is the possibility someone is doing this to sabotage the campaign.''

''Like who?'' asked Lee Allen Parke.

''Bushwa,'' said Walsh. ''Simon Upton may have a fifth column in this campaign, but he isn't murdering women to get himself to the White House.''

''Of course not,'' said the governor. ''But given the axiom that someone is doing this, the first question is why?''

''Someone's a nut,'' Lee Allen Parke said simply.

''Any suspects, Fletch?'' Barry asked.

''Too many of them.''

''Solov,'' nodded Barry Hines. ''You should see his phone bill.''

''Why?'' asked Fletch.

''He almost doesn't have one. He hardly ever calls anywhere. He must file with *Pravda* by carrier pigeon.''

''Actually, that is significant,'' Nolting said.

''Floats his reports across the North Atlantic in vodka bottles,'' Parke said.

''What's your point, Fletch?'' Walsh asked.

Fletch waited until all eyes were on him. ''I think it would be helpful if every member of the staff sat down with me— *soon*—and established a perfect alibi for at least one of each of these murders.''

''Hell,'' said Walsh.

''I won't do it,'' said Dobson.

''It would give me some quiet ammunition,'' Fletch said.

The governor stood up. "I've got to get ready. It's seven-twenty. Is my watch right?"

"Yeah," said Walsh.

Phil Nolting said, "Fletch, in trying to develop defensive evidence for us, you're going to give the impression we have some reason to defend ourselves."

"I think we do," Fletch said.

Everyone else was standing up.

"Looks like you lost your audience, Fletch," Walsh said.

Then Fletch stood up. "What the hell else do you expect me to do?" he asked. "This is a time bomb, ticking away—"

"So throw yourself on it," Dobson said, leaving the room.

"Wait a minute," Fletch said.

"Fletcher," the governor said, "why don't you stop playing boy detective?"

"Come with me, Fletch." Walsh stood at the door. "On the way to my room, I'll buy you a copy of *True Crime Tales*."

"Guess I'd better drop that topic," Fletch said.

"Guess so." In his own room, Walsh took off his shirt and grabbed a fresh one from his suitcase.

"This is like trying to put out a fire at a three-ring circus."

"No," said Walsh, "it's more like trying to unclog a pipe in one of the bathrooms at a three-ring circus."

"Local police everywhere are too in awe of the candidate, too busy trying to protect him, to run any kind of an investigation as to what's going on. The national political writers are too sophisticated to count the number of murders on their fingers, and say, 'Hey, maybe there's a story here.'"

"It's perfectly irrelevant." Walsh took a suit from the suitcase, frowned at it, slapped it with the flat of his hand, and proceeded to change into it. "The clippings you should go through are over there." He nodded at the table where his briefcases were.

"So you're changing from a reasonably pressed suit into a wrinkled suit?"

"Only have one tie that goes with that suit. Must have left it in a car. There are a couple of articles in that stack by

Fenella Baker you're not going to like. One hits us on defense spending; the other on our lack of clarity regarding Social Security. She's right, of course.''

Standing by the table, Fletch was scanning an article by Andrew Esty: *Governor Caxton Wheeler terms abortion ''essentially a moral issue.'' Does he imply politics is amoral?*

"By the way," Walsh said, knotting his tie. "Lansing Sayer. Don't trust Lansing Sayer. Brightest, most sophisticated member of the press we have traveling with us. And I'm glad he's with us. But as far as I'm concerned, he's a straight pipeline to Senator Simon Upton. Capable of anything."

"He just knows how to play both sides of the street," Fletch said.

"Got to get going." Walsh pulled on his dark suit coat. "Barry and I are going to check out the sound system at Public Auditorium ourselves. Don't want a repeat of what happened this afternoon at the shopping plaza."

"That was a disaster," Fletch said.

"No need for you to come now." Walsh opened the door. "Get some supper. Dad won't be speaking until at least nine-thirty, quarter to ten."

33

"I. M.? This is James."

Arriving back at his room, Fletch found a vase with twelve red carnations in it. The note accompanying the flowers read: *Fletcher—Glad to have you with us—Doris Wheeler.*

Waiting for his sandwich from room service, he had returned phone calls, except those from Rondoll James.

After his supper arrived, he took a shower and then sat naked on his bed, cross-legged, munching and going through the stack of newspaper articles Walsh had given him.

He tried ignoring the phone while he ate, but it rang incessantly.

"Sorry," Fletch said. "My mouth is full."

"You've got to do something. Fast."

"I've got to fast?"

"A reporter traveling with you called me this afternoon. Told me about the murders. Why didn't you tell me about them? The three women who were murdered."

"Who called you?"

"A woman named Arbuthnot."

"Figures. Are you still in Iowa?"

"Yes."

"What did you say to her?"

"Told her it was all news to me."

"Is it?"

"I. M., I know who the murderer is. So, incidentally, does Caxton."

Fletch pushed his sandwich plate aside with his shin.

"Have you talked with Caxton about this at all?" James asked.

"Extensively."

"What has he said?"

"Suppose you tell me what you know, James."

"I can't understand the guy. Why hasn't he done something?"

"James—"

"Edward Grasselli."

"Ol' Flash?"

"No question about it."

"Why Flash?"

"You don't know who he is? Everybody forgets."

In Flash's personnel folder had been just a photo and identification sheet. "So who's Flash Grasselli?"

"He's a murderer. A convicted murderer, for God's sake. He beat a guy to death. With his fists. A professional boxer. His hands are lethal weapons. He served time for it—almost fifteen years."

"What are you talking about?"

"Late one night, this guy happened to be walking his dog. Big dog. Flash Grasselli was coming down the street. As the dog passed Flash, the dog nipped Flash in the leg. Bit him. Flash yelled at the guy, told him he was going to report the dog, demanded the guy give him his name. So the guy sicced the dog on Grasselli. Grasselli knocked the dog out somehow, I don't know how, kicked the dog's head against a wall or something. And then went after the man. He beat the guy to death. In front of a half dozen screaming witnesses."

"My God, James."

"The dog was out cold. No longer a threat. You don't beat

someone to death after an incident is over. It was not self-defense.''

"Ol' Flash did that?''

"Deliberate murder.''

"Why did the governor pardon him?''

"Big Italian family that kept up the campaign to let their man go. A boxing association kept up the campaign, got the state boxing commissioner into it. Grasselli served good time. He was never any problem in prison. Once maybe he saved the life of an old guy in prison who was choking to death on some food, but that sort of thing can always be arranged.''

"Had the governor known him before?''

"No. After he was pardoned, Grasselli and his mother went to the mansion to thank the governor. Caxton offered him the job.''

"It's a different kind of murder, James. Beatin' up a guy in the street in bad temper is different from beating women to death.''

"Beating a human being to death is beating a human being to death. Very few people are capable of it. Are you?'' James continued in a rush: "Let me ask you something. When you have forty, fifty people together and people keep gettin' beaten to death, and we know one member of the group has already done this extraordinary, vicious thing before, has found it possible in himself to beat a human being to death— what are the chances of his being the guilty party?''

"Pretty good.''

"It's Flash, all right.''

"I believe the governor has talked to me frankly enough about other matters. Why wouldn't he have mentioned this to me?''

"Because he knows Flash is guilty. Tell me this: has Caxton vigorously been trying to find the murderer?''

"That doesn't make sense. Covering up for Flash would make the governor a party to the crime. I can't believe he'd do that.''

"Think again, my boy. Think of all that Flash has on Caxton.''

"Like what?''

"God! Everything! Flash is Caxton's driver, valet, body-guard. He's always with him. Flash accompanies Caxton on all those damned secret vacations, disappearances, that Caxton's been taking all these years. The booze. The broads. God knows what else."

"You believe about the booze, the broads?"

"Listen, I've known Caxton more than twenty years. And I've never known a plaster saint. Caxton's a man. All that energy. Think about it. Screwing Doris must be like screwing a Buick."

"Flash told me about those trips."

"Sure he did. I suppose he said they go to the mountains to pray."

"Almost."

"If the trips are innocent, why the secret? Why are they a mystery, hanging out there tantalizing every journalist in the state, now the country?"

"Okay. So the governor knows it's Flash, and he's afraid if he blows the whistle on Flash, Flash will spill beans about the governor."

"Yes."

"Maybe Flash wouldn't talk."

"All right. Even if that were so, which I doubt, think what it means about the governor's judgment. He picks as a bodyguard–valet a guy who beats women to death every night after dessert. What would the public think of that? Who would he pick for secretary of state? they'd ask. Himmler?"

"James, I don't know what to do. Everyone's over at the Public Auditorium."

"Pin Grasselli. However you can. I don't know. Do something."

"James, I don't see myself going ten rounds with Flash Grasselli. He's old and he's slow but he's practiced."

"Find him. Don't take your eyes off him. Buy him a one-way ticket to Tashkent. Get him committed. Quietly. Do something. Jeez, I wish I were there. If I were there, all this would have been settled yesterday, if not sooner. That bitch, Doris Wheeler. If it weren't for her—"

"Okay, James."

"Yeah. Get movin'."

• • •

It was while Fletch hurriedly was getting dressed that he noticed some of the articles in the stack Walsh had given him were separate from the loose pile. Five had been pinned together. They were at the foot of the bed.

He leaned over and looked closely at the one on top.

The first was from the *Chicago Sun-Times*.

Chicago—The body of a woman was found by hotel employees this morning in a service closet off a reception room at the Hotel Harris. Police say the woman apparently had been strangled.

The night before, the reception room had been used by the press covering the presidential campaign of Governor Caxton Wheeler.

Chicago police report the woman, about thirty, wearing a green cocktail dress and high-heeled shoes, was carrying no identification.

The second was from the *Cleveland Plain-Dealer*.

Cleveland—A woman known on the street as Helen Troy, with a Cleveland police record of more than forty arrests for open solicitation over a ten-year period, was found beaten to death early this morning in a doorway on Cassel Street.

Police speculate Troy was drawn to the area by the crowds who had gathered the previous night to see presidential candidate Caxton Wheeler, who was staying at the nearby Hotel Stearn.

"Oh, God," Fletch said aloud.

The third was from the *Wichita Eagle* and *Beacon*.

Wichita—A resident of California, Susan Stratford, 26, was found beaten to death in a room at Cason's Hotel early yesterday afternoon. The medical examiner reports she had been dead some hours.

The hotel employee, Jane Poltrow, who discovered the

body, said she was later than usual cleaning that room because of the extra work caused by the campaign staff and press traveling with presidential candidate Caxton Wheeler, who had stayed in the hotel the night before.

Ms Stratford, a computer engineer, was in Wichita on business. Police say apparently she was traveling alone.

"God, God." Fletch looked at the remains of his sandwich on the bed and felt nauseous.

The fourth article reported the death of Alice Elizabeth Shields, "believed to have been pushed or thrown from the hotel's roof, a few floors above the suite of presidential candidate Caxton Wheeler."

The fifth article was from the *Farmingdale Views*.

Farmingdale—Mary Cantor, 34, who has worked as a chambermaid since shortly after the death of her husband, a Navy navigator, three years ago, was found strangled in a service elevator of the Farmingdale Hotel early yesterday morning. . .

Turning, Fletch steadied himself with his fingertips on the bureau. "God." He saw himself start to sway in the mirror and closed his eyes. "And there are five. . . ."

Numbly, Fletch answered the phone.

"Fletcher . . . ?"

"Can't talk now," Fletch said. "Sorry. I shouldn't have answered."

"Fletcher . . ." The voice was horrible. Low. Slow. It almost didn't sound human. "This is Bill Dieckmann."

Fletch shook his head to clear it. "Yes, Bill?"

"Help me."

"What's the matter, Bill?"

"You said . . . you'd help me."

"What's wrong?"

"Fletch, my head. My head. It's happening again. Worse. I'm scared. I don't know what . . ."

"Bill, where are you?"

"Public . . ."

"Where in the auditorium, Bill?"

"Phones. At the back. By the phones."

"Bill, look around you. Do you see anyone you know? Bill, is there a cop there?"

"Can't see. It's awful. What . . . ?"

"Bill, stay there. I'll be right there."

"I'm about to . . . I don't know . . ."

"I'll be right there, Bill. Don't do anything. Just stand there. I'll be there as quick as I can."

34

Fletch revolved through the hotel's front door, saw the street in front of the hotel was empty, and revolved back into the lobby. He hurried across to the desk clerk.

"How do I get a taxi around here?"

"Just have to wait for one, I guess," was the solution of the young man behind the desk. "They come by."

"I'm in a big hurry," Fletch said.

The young man shrugged. "There's no one to call. This is a regular big city. Have to take your chances."

"Where's Public Auditorium?"

"Up eight blocks." The young man waved north. "Over three blocks." He waved east. "You need a taxi."

"Thanks."

Fletch hit the revolving door so hard it spun him into the street. The area was as devoid of taxis as a cemetery at midnight. He looked at his watch. With the side of his hand he chopped himself in the stomach. His muscles were tight. "I'll race you," he said to himself.

He began running north on the sidewalk. *Jacob, make the*

horse go faster and faster. If it ever stops, we won't be able to sell it. Within three blocks of this "regular big city," accumulations of snow caused him to run in the street. The surface of the street was wet and there were icy patches. It was a raw night. He was sweating. He was glad he didn't have an overcoat. *Five murders, not three . . .* There were no taxis anywhere in the streets. An old car clanking tire chains came down the street behind him. Waving as he ran backward, Fletch tried to get the car to stop, pick him up. The driver swung wide of Fletch.

At the end of the eighth block, Fletch turned east. Ahead of him he could see a block brightly lit. *"There is the possibility someone is doing this to sabotage the campaign,"* the governor had said. At the corner, Fletch jumped over a mound of snow. His left foot slipped landing on the ice. His ankle twinged with pain. *"Someone's a nut,"* Lee Allen Parke had said.

The brightly lit Public Auditorium entrance was bedecked with bunting.

Caxton Wheeler for President.

Many, many people were standing on the sidewalk and street outside the auditorium.

Those standing nearest the door wore fire department and police department uniforms.

Fletch squeezed through the crowds on the steps to the main door.

As Fletch was reaching for the door handle, a man in a fire department suit grabbed his elbow. "You can't go in there."

"Got to," Fletch panted.

"Fire marshal's orders. The hall is beyond capacity now."

"Matter of life and death," Fletch said.

"That's right," said the fireman.

Taking a deep breath, Fletch reached for his wallet. "Name's Fletcher. I'm Governor Wheeler's press secretary. I've got to get in."

The fireman did not look at Fletch's identification. "Right now we wouldn't let Wheeler himself in there."

"Someone's sick in there," Fletch said. "A reporter.

Dangerously sick. Let me go get him out. That way you'd be ahead in numbers by one."

"Let someone else bring him out." The fireman began to restrain an old lady with yellow berries on her black hat. "That way we'll be ahead in numbers by two."

There wasn't much light in the alley beside the auditorium. Mounds of dirty snow and ice ran along the base of both walls. Through the old brick walls and the auditorium leaked the sounds of a brass band. People were cheering and stomping.

The humidity made Fletch's breath cloud the air in front of his face.

Halfway down the alley was a fire escape. The bottom ladder of the fire escape was balanced with weights to keep its bottom step four meters off the ground. Stepped on from above, the bottom of the ladder would lower to the ground.

Fletch knew he couldn't jump that high, but he knew he could try.

He ran on the uneven, slippery pavement as well as he could. He jumped not very high at all. He slipped. He lowered his hands toward the pavement. He skidded. His head smashed into an orange crate filled with garbage.

An empty tomato sauce can fell from the crate onto the alley. Fletch kicked the can away. It bounced off the opposite wall and landed noiselessly in the snow.

He picked up the crate and turned it over. Grapefruit skins, eggshells, bones poured over his shoes. He placed the crate upside down under the fire escape. He climbed onto the crate, jumped straight up from it, reaching his hand for the bottom rung. Coming down, his feet crashed through the orange crate. He found himself standing on the pavement again, his left ankle twinging again. He was wearing wood around the calves of his legs.

"Ummm," Fletch said. "Man can't fly."

The alley at the side of the auditorium was broad enough for a truck to go through. It was clear that rubbish trucks sometimes, but not frequently, did go through.

"Matters not," Fletch said. "Man has brain."

Running back and forth, Fletch collected enough barrels, crates, boxes to stack into a stairway to the fire escape.

He climbed his stairway rapidly, as each stair gave way as he stepped on it.

He finally knelt on the bottom rung of the fire escape. Creaking, it lowered him back into the mess he had made in the alley.

It swayed as he ran up it.

Halfway up the fire escape was a metal fire door. There was no handle on the outside, of course. Not even a keyhole. Metal strips along the edges of the door covered the jamb.

"Man has brain," Fletch said.

The fire escape rose from this central landing. Fletch ran up it.

At the top was a smaller landing and one window. Thick, frosted glass, veined with the wires of an alarm system. Locked, of course.

He kicked in the window with his heel. Eggshell went onto the broken window; glass onto his shoe.

The alarm bell went off. It sounded like a school bell, more angry than loud. Inside the building the brass band was playing "The Battle Hymn of the Republic." The crowd was chanting "Wheel along with Wheeler! Wheel along with Wheeler! Wheel along with Wheeler!" Under the circumstances, Fletch expected the alarm bell to attract as much attention as the usual school bell.

He kicked a big hole in the little window and pushed the wires aside with the sleeve of his jacket. Pointing one shoulder toward the sky, he stepped through the window onto its inside ledge.

When he had both feet inside the building, he jumped into the dark. The floor on which he landed was higher than he had calculated. His left ankle hurt him right up to the small of his back. He punched the pain in his back with his thumb.

More the sense of light than actual light itself emanated from his left. The band and the chanting had quieted now. A man's amplified voice strided.

Sliding his feet along the floor so he wouldn't fall down any steps that might be there, Fletch went to his left. After several steps he felt himself against a wall. He turned right, following the sound of the man's voice—"Protect this great republic"—toward greater light, against another wall, right again, around a corner. He found himself at the top of a dimly lit, old, wooden staircase.

He could no longer hear the alarm bell.

His ankle and back not complaining too much, he ran down the stairs.

He pushed through the wide door to the corridor of the balcony. On the corridor's side, the door was concealed as a mirror.

To orient himself, Fletch went onto the balcony.

Every seat in the balcony was taken. People were standing.

Onstage, Doris Wheeler and Governor Caxton Wheeler were sitting in the center of a half-moon of local dignitaries. Their plastic chairs were the sort designed to be uncomfortable in fast-food restaurants, to make people tip forward, eat fast, and get out. The speaker at the podium could have been Congressman Jack Snive.

In front of the stage, facing the audience, smirked a large band in high school marching uniforms. The uniforms might have been the right sizes for the band marching, but they were too big for them sitting down. All the drummers' hands were in their sleeves.

The floor of the auditorium was filled. People clogging the aisles were urging other people to move. There was some movement, but it was more circular than directed.

Across the hall, nearer the stage than the balcony, was a separate box. In the box sat Freddie Arbuthnot, Roy Filby, Fenella Baker, Tony Rice, others. He could not see who was in the matching box, to his right.

Fletch left the balcony and ran down the stairs to the lobby of the auditorium.

To the left of the main door was a bank of three wall telephones. Bill Dieckmann was not there.

Fletch looked around what corners there were. No Bill Dieckmann.

There were no other phones along the back of the auditorium. Even the foyer was crowded.

The fireman who had stopped Fletch outside the auditorium was now inside. He spotted Fletch. "Hey!" he shouted. He started toward Fletch.

Moving sideways very fast, Fletch kept the crowd between himself and the fireman.

Fletch ran back up the stairs to the balcony.

"Freddie?" Fletch sat down beside her. There was more room in the press box than there was anywhere else in the auditorium. "Have you seen Flash Grasselli?"

She shook her head no. "Something occurred to me," she said.

"I need to find Flash."

"Don't you think it odd," she asked, "that a few days after I join the campaign, Walsh hires you?"

Fletch said, "Help me find Bill Dieckmann."

"I mean, you're an investigative reporter. Like me."

"Bill called me at the hotel. From here. Asked me to help him. Apparently his head was going again."

Her brown eyes were fully on Fletch's face.

Fletch said, "It sounded like he was afraid of what he might do, or something."

"How long ago was that?"

"God." Fletch looked at his watch. "More than a half hour ago. Man can't fly."

"I haven't seen Flash." She started to get up. "I haven't seen either of them."

Fletch stood up. "I told him to stay by the phones at the back of the auditorium. He's not there."

Fletch's eyes were running over the audience below him. The aisles had been pretty well cleared, except for firemen and policemen.

Freddie leaned to her left and spoke with Roy Filby and Tony Rice.

Below Fletch, Betsy Ginsberg was sitting in about the middle of the audience.

Roy and Tony were standing, too.

"They'll help," Freddie said. "I told them about Bill."

Fletch stood aside to let the three of them out the row of

seats. "Just fan out and look for him anywhere," he said. "Check the rest rooms, I guess. He sounded real bad."

"Could the police have taken him out?" Roy asked.

"I don't think they had by the time I came in."

As they were leaving the box, Fletch took one more fast look at the audience seated on the floor of the auditorium.

Betsy had risen from her seat and was working her way along the row to the aisle.

Shit! Fletch said to himself. *Betsy!*

Fletch ran out of the press box so fast he tripped against Tony Rice.

"Fletch!" Freddie called after him. "Did you see him?"

"No!"

He ran down the corridor behind the balcony and down the stairs to the auditorium lobby.

There was a bigger crowd of people in the lobby, grumbling about having been removed from the aisles. Some were angrily refusing to leave the building.

Fletch pushed through them. Some shoved back.

"Wheel along with Wheeler," Fletch said.

Fletch glowered at the big stomach of a policeman standing in the main doorway to the auditorium.

"Get out of my way, please," Fletch said. He pushed past the policeman.

"Trying to start a riot?"

"Sorry," Fletch said over his shoulder.

The fireman who had stopped him outside the auditorium and yelled at him inside the auditorium saw Fletch push past the policeman from the lobby. "Stop him!" he yelled. "Hey! Get that guy!"

He pushed past the policeman, too.

Over the heads of the people seated in the auditorium, Fletch saw Betsy at the right of the auditorium, near the stage, going through a door marked Exit.

Moving as fast as he could, dodging people standing at the back of the auditorium, Fletch went to his right along the wall at the rear of the audience. He was passing behind Hanrahan.

Hands grabbed both of Fletch's shoulders and turned him around.

"Wait one minute," the fireman said. He was crouched a little, as if to swing. "You're causin' one hell of a lot of trouble."

"Sorry," Fletch said, taking a step backward.

Michael J. Hanrahan had turned around.

The fireman grabbed Fletch's arm.

Fletch did not resist.

"You're comin' with me," the fireman said.

With his grin/grimace, Hanrahan said, "Trouble, Fletcher?"

"I'm in an awful hurry, Michael."

"That's fine." Hanrahan lurched forward onto his right foot, and sent his left fist into the fireman's coat.

The fireman dropped his grip on Fletch.

In a second, he had twisted Hanrahan into a half-Nelson wrestling hold.

Fletch said, "Thank you, Michael."

Hanrahan's face quickly turned crimson. "That's all right, Fletcher. Always glad to slug a cop."

"Michael!" Fletch said, backing away. More uniforms were appearing in the dark at the back of the auditorium. "You slugged a fireman!"

"Listen," Hanrahan was saying in a choke to the gathering uniforms. "Don't you guys read *Newsbill*? I'm Hanrahan, for Chrissake!"

Fletch walked fast down the aisle under the balcony. He pressed his weight against the metal bar-release of the door marked Exit and found himself in a bright, empty corridor.

To his left was a door that obviously led to the stage area.

To his right the corridor had to run back to the lobby of the auditorium.

Down a short corridor straight ahead was a sign: EXHIBITION HALL, TUESDAY-SATURDAY, 10-4.

In the auditorium, the speaker roared at the audience, "The man who will be the next President of the United States," and the audience was roaring its approval.

Fletch went down the short corridor and turned right into the entrance to the Exhibition Hall. Massive, double, polished wooden doors. Locked, of course.

He turned around.

Across the corridor, in the reciprocal alcove, was a small service door. The sign on it said: STAFF ONLY. Over it a sign said: NOT A FIRE EXIT.

He crossed to the door and tried the ordinary doorknob. Not locked. He pushed the door open.

Overamplified, the voice of Doris Wheeler was bursting from the auditorium. "My husband, son, and I are glad to be in Melville. Years ago, when we were first married . . ."

On the other side of the door were stairs falling to a basement. The small landing was lit by an overhead light. The stairs themselves were lit by occasional, dim, baseboard safety lights. The basement itself was dark.

". . . and the friends we made around here then . . ."

From the basement came a woman's shout: "No!"

The sound sent a pain searing from Fletch's left ankle through his back to his neck.

As he started down the stairs he heard what sounded like a slap of skin against skin, a hard slap. A scuffling of feet on cement.

Near the bottom of the stairs, he stopped to detect where the sounds were coming from.

There was the sound of a light piece of wood falling on the cement floor.

There was then the sound of a woman's outraged, frightened scream. "Stop!"

"Betsy!" Fletch shouted toward his right.

A few safety lights were on here and there throughout the vast space of the basement. Everywhere in the basement were large, bulky objects, crates and counters and stands from the Exhibition Hall, he guessed, and scenery flats from amateur productions in Public Auditorium. Facing him was the tranquil scene of an English garden.

". . . my husband and I listen to you, have known your problems . . ."

Fletch moved forward toward the center of the basement, around the English garden scene.

"Betsy . . . ?"

Doris Wheeler's amplified voice was coming through the ceiling like so many nails. "We know what you have paid into your schools, your farms, your stores, your families, your lives.'' Each phrase came through the ceiling hard, bright, penetrating, scratchy.

In the basement there was a flubbery cry.

"Betsy!" Fletch bellowed.

Again there was the sound of feet scuffling on cement.

Fletch's eyes finally were adjusting to the dim light.

And then there was what sounded like a hard punch.

There was an explosion of air from lungs, a gasp, a shrill, hysterical scream.

"Walsh!" Fletch yelled.

He threw his weight against a huge packing crate, which must have been empty. Lightly it skidded across the floor.

Fletch fell. He rolled over on the floor and looked up.

His back to Fletch, a man had a woman pinned into a corner of the basement.

Sitting on the floor, quietly Fletch said, "Walsh."

Walsh twisted his neck around to look at Fletch. Walsh's face was wild.

He had one hand behind Betsy's head. The other was over her mouth.

Her fingers were against his biceps. She was trying to push him away. Her eyes were bulging.

"Hey, Walsh," Fletch said. "You're out of your mind. You don't know what you're doing."

"... you will have a friend in the White House, a man who..."

Walsh looked up at the ceiling of the basement. The low safety lights lit the whites of his eyes.

Fletch stood up. "I'm here, Walsh. There's nothing more you can do."

After a moment of applause, Doris Wheeler's voice again penetrated the ceiling. "Someone in the White House..."

Walsh's left hand pushed Betsy's head forward from the wall. He looked her in the face. He raised his left hand from behind her head.

Walsh's right fist slammed into Betsy's face.

Her head banged into the corner of the walls and bounced out. Her eyes became entirely white.

"Walsh! Let go!"

Standing behind Walsh, Fletch raised his own arms as high as they would go, and brought the sides of his hands down full strength onto the muscles between Walsh's neck and shoulders.

Walsh dropped his arms.

Betsy's knees jerked forward. Bleeding from her nose, chin on her chest, Betsy slumped forward.

Fletch tried to catch her.

Walsh staggered into him.

Betsy fell into the corner on the floor.

Walsh backed along the wall. His head was lowered. He was trying to raise his hands.

"Take it easy, Walsh. Just stay still."

Walsh turned. He stumbled along the wall.

Fletch grabbed him by a shoulder. Spun him around. Hit him hard, once, in the face. Once in the stomach.

Walsh fell. He could not raise his arms to protect himself as he fell. He landed flat.

He gasped for air. He brought one hand, slowly, to his bleeding face.

"Stay there, Walsh," Fletch said.

Betsy was unconscious. Her nose was broken and pouring blood. Her left cheekbone was bruised blue. There was a bleeding gash at the back of her head.

Gently, Fletch pulled her out of the corner. He put her on her side on the floor, against the wall. He put his suit jacket under her head. Some blood ran out of her mouth.

Walsh had rolled over and was lying on his back.

Fletch stood over him. "It's over now, Walsh."

Walsh was breathing hard. His face was bloody, too.

"...Caxton Wheeler, 1600 Pennsylvania Avenue..."

"Can you walk, Walsh? Betsy's hurt. We've got to get an ambulance for her."

Walsh's glazed eyes were staring at the ceiling.

Through the ceiling Doris Wheeler's voice came, insistent, demanding: "...the White House...the White House...the White House..."

Walsh said: "God, damn Mother."

35

"It's open," said Governor Caxton Wheeler. "Come in."
Fletch had knocked softly on the ajar door to the governor's suite. He had not known if the governor might be asleep. He doubted it. On the other hand he did not know the full magic in Dr. Thom's little black bag. He had not even known if the governor was still in town.

" 'Mornin'," Fletch mumbled.

The electric lamps in the living room of the suite were still on. Their lights were fading fast in the dawn light coming through the windows.

Dressed as they had been onstage at Public Auditorium the night before, Doris and Caxton Wheeler were sitting on a divan. On the cushion between them they were holding hands. Two out-sized people, ridiculously dressed for that hour of the morning; two world-famous faces now wearing new expressions of utter dejection; two human beings devastated by tragedy.

"Is Walsh all right?" Caxton asked.

"Broken collarbone. Cut on his face," Fletch answered. "Dazed. Deep in shock, I guess."

"And the woman? Ms Ginsberg?"

"Severe concussion. No skull fracture. Cut on the back of her head. Broken nose. Some loss of blood. She's in shock, too, of course."

"I'm in shock," said Doris Wheeler. Numbly, she was staring at the floor. "Do you believe Walsh killed all those women?"

"Yes," Fletch said. "I believe he did."

Fletch had to sit down. His legs ached with exhaustion.

"What in God's name did we do wrong?" Doris Wheeler asked. "How could he do these things?"

Silently, Fletch waited for the governor's reaction. Caxton Wheeler looked sympathetically at his wife.

Doubtlessly the two of them had been asking themselves those questions all night.

Finally, Fletch said: "We all thought Walsh was seamless. There is no such thing as a seamless human being. All the pressures of the campaign were coming down on him. Too much. Too long. He had to play Mister Competent, Mister Cool, take all the punches, roll with them, understand and forgive everybody else, but never forgive himself. He had no outlets himself, no way of blowing off steam. He was the one guy who couldn't yell at anybody," he said, looking at Doris Wheeler. Then he looked at the governor. "He wasn't even getting any sleep. Everybody kept packing it into him. He had to blow off. Everybody has to, sooner or later, one way or another."

"How did you know Walsh was doing these things?" the governor asked. "How did you know enough to find him last night in the basement, stop him?"

"I didn't know, until just before. He had given me a stack of newspaper clippings to go through, to acquaint myself with the Wisconsin reporters. Out of the stack fell five articles, pinned together, reporting the deaths, the murders, of the five women."

"Five . . ." Doris Wheeler said.

"Five. There was a woman in Cleveland, apparently, and a woman in Wichita, we didn't know about."

The governor said, "My God."

"Up to that point, Walsh had been pretending to know nothing about these murders, the three he was questioned about. He said he didn't know anything about them, didn't care. He was aloof from all that. When I found his private collection of clippings, I realized he knew more than he was saying, more than we did. That he had a very real anxiety about them."

"He knew he was committing these murders?" the governor asked.

"I'm not really sure," Fletch said. "I think he had sort of a nightmare knowledge of them. I don't think he really knew what he was doing. But the mornings after, he had enough knowledge, or nightmare sense of them, to tear these articles from the newspapers."

The governor leaned forward, elbows on his knees, hands over his face. "My God."

"When I saw his collection of articles," Fletch said, "it suddenly dawned on me he hadn't been wearing a necktie all day. He told me he had left it in a car somewhere. The woman the night before, Mary Cantor, had been strangled with some kind of a soft cord, such as a necktie. When I thought it might be Walsh doing this, doing these things, I felt perfectly sick." Sitting in the chair, Fletch felt sick again. He waited for the moment to pass. "And there had been that incident overseas, I understand, of threatening a superior officer. A female superior officer."

"Hit her," the governor said, head still in hands.

"What?"

The governor stood up and walked slowly to the windows. "He hit her. Several times."

Fletch said, "I see."

"I had friends in the Pentagon. Well, I had pull. Enough pull to get him out of there quick, get him home, get him assigned to some statistical job in Washington. To keep the incident off his record. I guess I shouldn't have."

"There was so much at stake, Caxton," Doris Wheeler said.

"Yes," the governor said. "There was a lot at stake."

Cautiously Fletch asked: "Did you suspect Walsh? Were you protecting him by refusing to permit an investigation?"

There was a long moment before the governor answered. "It was a dreadful thought. I didn't really let myself think about it. It was inconceivable."

"But you did conceive of it," Fletch said.

Another long moment before the governor said, barely audibly: "Yes." He turned around. Even with the light behind him from the windows, tears were visible on the governor's cheeks. "He really went berserk when he beat up that major overseas," he said. "So the witnesses said."

"He had been under pressure then, too," Fletch commented. "More pressure than a man should bear."

"There is no such thing," Doris Wheeler said, "as 'more pressure than a man can bear.'"

Fletch ignored her.

He said to the governor: "I thought you might have been protecting Flash."

"Flash?" The governor shrugged. "Never thought of him, to tell the truth. Oh, I guess the idea did cross my mind. You know, I've watched that man harvest nuts for squirrels and chipmunks." The governor smiled. He wiped the tears off his big face.

"The primary election system," Fletch said. "It's too much pressure for everybody. It's too long. It goes on for six, eight months. It's crazy. Even one of the reporters, Bill Dieckmann, is in the hospital this morning with some kind of a nervous disorder. What's it all supposed to prove?"

"Just that," the governor said easily. "That one can take the pressure. It seems strange for me to say it this morning, but the system is good. If the candidate, and his family, and his team, can't take the pressure, it's better that it show up on the campaign trail than on Pennsylvania Avenue." He had gone to a sideboard. He picked up some papers beside an open briefcase. He dropped them into a wastebasket. "I must say, though: I think I was beginning to say some interesting things. Even if I didn't win, I was beginning to voice some interesting questions.''

On the divan, Doris Wheeler shifted uncomfortably. She held a wet handkerchief to her face. "Oh, Caxton, can't we go on? Isn't there some way . . . ?''

"I will resign the governorship. I plan to be with Walsh through this. Try to see he gets whatever treatment he needs to make him whole again, in hospital, in prison, whatever, now and forever, I guess." The governor's voice was low, but strong. "I'll do anything I can to try to make restitution to the families and loved ones of those women. . . .''

On the divan, Doris Wheeler sobbed into her handkerchief.

There was a kind of an animal noise from the governor's throat, or his chest.

Fletch said: "There isn't much of anything you can do for Walsh right now. The judge who was on the platform with you last night did the unusual thing of opening his court at three o'clock this morning. To avoid a three-ring circus, he said. He sent Walsh away for thirty days psychiatric observation. Walsh has already gone.''

"Psychiatric observation," the governor repeated from across the room. "Walsh . . .'' When he turned around, fresh tears glistened on his cheeks.

There was a tap on the door.

Flash entered the little hall. In one hand he carried his own suitcases and his black topcoat.

In the other hand he carried a sheaf of yellow telegram sheets.

"I still can't figure out precisely what I'm doing here," Fletch said. "I can't figure out whether Walsh asked me to join the campaign to protect him—you know, when the first crime writer, Freddie Arbuthnot, showed up? Or whether, way deep in his mind somewhere, he had the idea I might rescue him again.''

Doris Wheeler stood up. "Either way," she said, "you didn't do a very good job, did you?''

Flash said to the governor, "I've got a car. A comfortable car. I rented it myself. I figured we wouldn't want to go through any airports.''

"That's right, Flash," the governor said.

Flash held out the telegrams. "These are from the President, the other candidates . . ."

The governor pointed at the wastebasket. "Put them in there, Flash."

Flash dropped the telegrams in the wastebasket.

Caxton Wheeler took his wife's arm.

"Come on, Mother," he said. "It's time we went home."

36

"Going my way?" Fletch asked the girl with the honey-colored hair and the brown eyes, standing next to her blue suitcase in the airport terminal.

"No," she answered. "I'm on my way up."

"I'm glad to see you," he said.

He set down his own luggage.

After seeing Doris and Caxton Wheeler off in the dark, rented sedan, Flash driving away at a funereal pace, Fletch had returned to his room at Melville's First Hotel and slept well beyond checkout time. His sleep was troubled. The hard edges of Walsh's eyes when he first turned and saw Fletch in the auditorium basement penetrated every corner of his sleep. The pained crawl of the dark sedan carrying the Wheelers back across midland America weighted Fletch's sleep with sadness.

Awaking, he ordered steak and eggs and orange juice and milk and coffee, made his travel arrangements by phone, then settled his hotel bill with the cashier, paying for his extra few hours use of the room himself.

"Yeah," Fletch said to Freddie Arbuthnot in the airport terminal. "I lost my job again."

"You're good at that."

"I think it's what I do best."

"Fletch," she said, "I'm sorry about your friend. I'm sorry about Walsh."

"I'm sorry about everything," he said. "The women. Caxton Wheeler."

A large group of people were waiting just outside one of the arrival gates. Some of them wore UPTON FOR PRESIDENT badges.

On the fringes of the welcoming group were Roy Filby, Tony Rice, Stella Kirchner. Andrew Esty stood separate from the others, his nose pointed at the arrival gate, wearing more the expression of a judge than a reporter. His heavy overcoat buttoned tightly around him, Boris Solov leaned against a car rental counter. His eyes were closed.

"Did you get your story?" Fletch asked Freddie.

"Yeah. Thanks for tipping me off to be at the courts at three A.M. There are some stories I'd rather not write." She smiled at him. "But if a story has to be written, I don't mind scooping the world with it."

"I appreciate this story's being written fairly and accurately," Fletch said.

"Poor Michael J. Hanrahan." Freddie did not succeed in restraining a laugh. "He didn't get to file any story at all, did he?"

"Michael J. Hanrahan," Fletch said, "is in jail. For striking a fireman. For interfering with an official performing his duty. For being drunk and disorderly in a public place."

"Poor Michael J. Hanrahan," Freddie giggled.

"I'm very grateful to him. I tried to arrange bail for him while I was at the police station, but the local police seemed to think he needed a few days' rest. He was shouting from the cell, 'Doesn't anyone around here read *Newsbill*?' He was in no condition to be put back on the street."

"Mr. Bad News missed his biggest bad news story."

"At least Mary Rice wrote the story for *Newsbill* as the tragedy it is."

Across the terminal, the welcoming committee was beginning to stir, bunch up at the arrival gates. Television lights were switching on.

Wordlessly, Fletch and Freddie Arbuthnot watched the arrival of Senator Simon Upton in Melville, just a day before that state's primary election.

The tall, tanned, graying man stopped in the center of the television lights. Hands behind his back, he said a few words into the microphones held out to him. Fletch and Freddie could not hear what he was saying. Either of them could have written the words: "... this great, personal tragedy that has befallen Caxton Wheeler, his wife, family, staff, friends, the murdered women, everyone involved. A great human tragedy ..."

Then the candidate, a man who, reached for hands to shake. Gracefully he moved across the terminal, smiling and waving. His staff and welcoming committee streamed after him. The members of the press traveling with him straggled along at the rear of the procession, carrying their own luggage, looking bedraggled.

The other side of the terminal's big windows, a campaign bus, a press bus, a couple of television vans, the odd cars of volunteers awaited the candidate and his party.

"I'll have to come back here," Freddie said. "To cover the trial."

"Of course."

"And you'll have to be here for the trial, Fletch. I was just thinking that."

"Yes."

"We'll just keep bumping into each other, I guess."

"I guess."

After a moment, she said, "I'm on the flight to Chicago. It's all booked up."

"Oh."

"Then on to Springfield," she sighed. "To interview a woman just being released from prison after forty years."

"Me too," Fletch said. "I'm going to Springfield."

"You are not."

"I'm not?"

"No."

"How do you know?"

"Because you think I'm going to Springfield, Illinois, don't you?"

"I do?"

"I'm going to Springfield, Massachusetts. The flight to Chicago is booked, and there are only fifteen minutes in Chicago between flights." She laughed. "Oh, Fletch! Caught you this time. Thought you were clever, did you? Now you know where I'm going, but it's too late for you to sneak around and get tickets for yourself."

"I just happen to be going to Springfield, Massachusetts," Fletch said. "It's pretty there, this time of year."

She stopped laughing at him. She searched his face to see if he was serious. Then she blinked. "Are you on my flight to Chicago?"

Fletch took his tickets out of his jacket pocket and showed them to her. "Melville to Chicago to Boston to Springfield," he said. "Massachusetts."

She studied the tickets. "These are my flights."

"Mine, actually. You mean to tell me, you are going my way?"

She looked up from the tickets at him. "How did you do that?"

"Do what?"

"Know where I'm going and arrange identical tickets for yourself?"

Outside, Senator Simon Upton's campaign bus was pulling away from the curb.

"Gee, Freddie." He took the tickets away from her and shoved them into his own pocket. "Why do you want to make a mystery out of everything?"

Mystery...Intrigue...Suspense

__FLETCH AND THE WIDOW BRADLEY
by Gregory Mcdonald   *(B90-922, $2.95)*
Fletch has got *some* trouble! Body trouble: with an executive dead in Switzerland. His ashes shipped home prove it. Or do they? Job trouble: When Fletch's career is ruined for the mistake no reporter should make. Woman trouble: with a wily widow and her suspect sister-in-law. From Alaska to Mexico, Fletch the laid-back muckraker covers it all!

__FLETCH'S MOXIE
by Gregory Mcdonald   *(B90-923, $2.95)*
Fletch has got plenty of Moxie. And she's just beautiful. Moxie's a hot movie star. She's got a dad who's one of the roaring legends of Hollywood. She's dead center in a case that begins with a sensational on-camera murder and explodes in race riots and police raids. Most of all, she's got problems. Because she's the number one suspect!

__DUPE
by Liza Cody   *(B30-367, $2.50)*
Anna Lee is the private investigator called in to placate the parents of Dierdre Jackson. Dierdre could not have died as the result of an accident on an icy road. She had driven race cars; the stretch of road was too easy. In search of simple corroborating evidence, Anna finds motives and murder as she probes the unsavory world of the London film industry where Dierdre sought glamour and found duplicity...and death.

Don't Miss These
Other Great Books By
P. D. JAMES!

MYSTERY...SUSPENSE... ESPIONAGE

___THE GOLD CREW
by Thomas N. Scortia
& Frank M. Robinson   *(B83-522, $2.95)*
The most dangerous test the world has ever known is now taking place aboard the mammoth nuclear sub *Alaska*. Human beings, unpredictable in moments of crisis, are being put under the ultimate stress. On patrol, out of contact with the outside world, the crew is deliberately being led to believe that the U.S.S.R. has attacked the U.S.A. Will the crew follow standing orders and fire the *Alaska's* missiles in retaliation? Now the fate of the world depends on what's going on in the minds of the men of THE GOLD CREW.

___THE PARK IS MINE
by Stephen Peters   *(B30-035, $2.95)*
At night, New York's Central Park is a jungle of terrors, both imagined and real. Now, in an act of incredible daring, a lone, angry shadow—his formidable skills of war honed in another jungle thousands of miles away—has transformed the Park into a bloody free-fire zone.

___THE HAMLET ULTIMATUM
by Leonard Sanders   *(B83-461, $2.95)*
World takeover is HAMLET's goal! The mysterious terrorist group has already sabotaged all the computer networks it requires, even that of the C.I.A. Now the group is ready for its ultimatum to the U.S. government: Surrender or watch the entire Northeast burn in a nuclear disaster. Only ex-agent Loomis can stop them. And only Loomis and his team has the courage to oppose the President and fight the world they want to save.

WARNER BOOKS PROUDLY PRESENTS

___**A BAD MAN**
by Stanley Elkin   (95-539, $2.75)
"A very funny book... The prose, dialogue and imagery are brilliant... The laughs alternate with the philosophy and sometimes merge with it."   —*The Saturday Review*

___**BOSWELL**
by Stanley Elkin   (95-538, $2.75)
Boswell wrestled with the Angel of Death and suddenly realized that everybody dies. With that realization he begins an odyssey of the ego, searching out VIP's and prostrating himself before them. BOSWELL "crackles with gusto and imaginative fertility."   —*Book Week*

___**THE DICK GIBSON SHOW**
by Stanley Elkin   (95-540, $2.75)
Like *The Great Gatsby*, he wants life to live up to myth. He is the perpetual apprentice, whetting his skills and adopting names and accents to suit geography. Elkin's "prose is alive with its wealth of detail and specifically American metaphors... compulsively readable and exhilarating."
                                      —*The Library Journal*

___**CRIERS AND KIBITZERS, KIBITZERS AND CRIERS**
by Stanley Elkin   (91-543, $2.50)
"An air of mysterious joy hangs over these stories," says *Life* magazine. Yet the *New York Times Review of Books* reports that "Bedeviling with his witchcraft the poor souls he has conjured and set into action, Stanley Elkin involves his spirits sometimes in the dread machineries of allegory and fantasy."

5 EXCITING ADVENTURE SERIES
MEN OF ACTION BOOKS

__THE HOOK
by Brad Latham
Gentleman detective, boxing legend, man-about-town, The Hook crosses 1930's American and Europe in pursuit of perpetrators of insurance fraud.

__#1 THE GILDED CANARY	(C90-882, $1.95)
__#2 SIGHT UNSEEN	(C90-841, $1.95)
__#5 CORPSES IN THE CELLAR	(C90-985, $1.95)

__S-COM
by Steve White
High adventure with the most effective and notorious band of military mercenaries the world has known—four men and one woman with a perfect track record.

__#3 THE BATTLE IN BOTSWANA	(C90-134, $1.95)
__#4 THE FIGHTING IRISH	(C30-141, $1.95)

__BEN SLAYTON: T-MAN
by Buck Sanders
Based on actual experiences, America's most secret law-enforcement agent—the troubleshooter of the Treasury Department—combats the enemies of national security.

__#1 A CLEAR AND PRESENT DANGER	(C30-020, $1.95)
__#2 STAR OF EGYPT	(C30-017, $1.95)
__#3 THE TRAIL OF THE TWISTED CROSS	(C30-131, $1.95)

__NINJA MASTER
by Wade Barker
Committed to avenging injustice, Brett Wallace uses the ancient Japanese art of killing as he stalks the evildoers of the world in his mission.

__#3 BORDERLAND OF HELL	(C30-127, $1.95)
__#4 MILLION-DOLLAR MASSACRE	(C90-177, $1.95)

__BOXER UNIT—OSS
by Ned Cort
The elite 4-man commando unit of the Office of Strategic Studies whose dare-devil missions during World War II place them in the vanguard of the action.

__#2 ALPINE GAMBIT	(C30-019, $1.95)
__#3 OPERATION COUNTER-SCORCH	(C30-128, $1.95)
__#4 TARGET NORWAY	(C30-121, $1.95)

The Best of Suspense from WARNER BOOKS

___PSYCHO II
by Robert Bloch   (B90-804, $3.50)
...You remember Norman Bates, the shy young motel manager with the fatal mother fixation. Now, years after his bout of butchery that horrified the world, Norman is at large again, cutting a shocking swath of blood all the way from the psycho ward to the lots of the Hollywood movie makers.

To order, use the coupon below. If you prefer to use your own stationery, please include complete title as well as book number and price. Allow 4 weeks for delivery.